TWICE UPON AN APOCALYPSE

EDITED BY SCOTT T. GOUDSWARD AND RACHEL KENLEY

Let the world know:
#IGotMyCLPBook!

Crystal Lake Publishing
www.CrystalLakePub.com

OTHER ANTHOLOGIES BY CRYSTAL LAKE PUBLISHING

Gutted: Beautiful Horror Stories

Tales from The Lake Vol.1, Vol.2, and Vol.3

Children of the Grave

The Outsiders

Fear the Reaper

For the Night is Dark

Or check out other Crystal Lake Publishing books for your Dark Fiction, Horror, Suspense, and Thriller needs, and join our newsletter while you're there.

CONTENTS

INTRODUCTION

ONCE UPON A CONCEPT

AS I WRITE this, the new television season has dropped on us like a curse from Heaven, bringing with it a cornucopia of new and returning series that cannibalize—um, er, uh . . . make that draw their inspiration from—fairy tales of old. We have, for instance, *Grimm*; *Once upon a Time*; and *Sleepy Hollow*. These past couple of years have also seen "re-imagined" fairy tales hit the big screen with all the power of an instant tax write-off: *Oz the Great and Powerful*; *Hansel and Gretel: Witch Hunters*; *Jack the Giant Killer*; *Snow White and the Huntsman*; *Maleficent*; *Cinderella* . . . I'm sure I've overlooked a few, but you get the idea.

All of the above have sprinklings of admirable qualities—stunning visuals, some sharp performances, moments of genuine cleverness, scenes so beautifully choreographed they look almost like a ballet (in the case of something like *Hansel and Gretel*, an absolutely ludicrous ballet)—but for each successful element, there remains at the core of each this sense that its creators seem to harbor an obstinate belief that they are re-inventing the wheel; the creators of the two *Once Upon a Time* series seem to me particularly guilty of this because even though both nicely maintain the less-than-whimsical tone of the tales from which they draw their inspiration, the concept of the real world being invaded by the fantasy world (and vice-versa) is presented as something that has never been applied to fairy tales before, and as a result, many of the twists and turns of the plots cause me to respond with a "Yeah, *and* . . . ?" rather than a gasp of surprise.

Another inherent difficulty that most of them have yet to overcome (I subtract *Sleepy Hollow* from this simply because it had the good sense to throw canon out the window from the start) is the grafting of modern-day sensibilities into the fairy-tale worlds—not as the result of reality and fantasy infecting one another (which would make sense) but rather presented as if these sensibilities and moral codes had always been this way, even before the two worlds began to interfere with one another. If the idea of Sleeping Beauty being an independent human being who doesn't need to be rescued by a prince's kiss or Rumpelstiltskin suffering from onion layers of deeply-rooted emotional trauma had been the result of quantum intrusion—that is to say, of their modern-day counterpart affecting the contemporary social awareness gleaned from present-day experience when the two of them "crossed beams," so to speak—I'd have no problems with it. But when such elements are presented as already being present in the fairy-tale world, it doesn't amount to re-imagining as far as I'm concerned; it amounts to lazy storytelling whose creators don't see any problem grafting anachronistic pop-psychology into a time and place where it would not have naturally evolved.

I keep hammering this point because the well-defined, almost vindictive morality at the heart of traditional fairy tales is, to my mind, the single most important element they possess—how could one otherwise attribute such terms as "timeless" to them? This timelessness doesn't stem from the cleverness of their telling but is a result of central universal themes that remain unchanging; subtract the " . . . and the moral is . . . " element from any fairy tale, and it ceases to be a fairy tale, merely the echo, a wisp, a what-became-of-it. The Brothers Grimm, Charles Perrault, Hans Christian Anderson, may very well have been critics of the social upheavals of their times, but they were also, first and foremost, hard-core moralists when it came to the stories they told; even Oscar Wilde's stories written for children were very much grounded in deceptively simplistic but nonetheless resonating truths depicted in unapologetic black and white terms (read Wilde's "The Star Child" or the devastating "The Happy Prince" if you don't believe me—and make sure you have a few tissues nearby when you read the last lines).

File all of this away for a few moments; we'll come back to it soon enough.

Let's briefly address the current (and, hopefully, *fading*) trend of "mash-ups"—the type of fiction characterized by taking a pre-existing text of literature and combining it with a different genre—behold *Pride and Prejudice and Zombies*, the novel that is credited with starting this trend. Don't get me wrong; I am not necessarily against mash-ups in *theory*: it's the vast majority of their at-best misguided results that drive me to despair. The idea of a mash-up can work well if the one doing the mashing begins with two dictums in mind: 1) I am not reinventing the wheel; the best I can hope for is a clever variation that pays homage to the original work while casting an amusing parallax view to the proceedings; and, 2) I am not, repeat *not*, going to mine the original's prose to fill in the gaps of my narrative; I am instead going to employ its central conceit and combine it with something else in order to not re-invent the wheel.

I almost added a third dictum: Mash-ups never work at novel length; novella and short stories only, please. So let us imagine how the thought process behind *Twice Upon an Apocalypse* must have worked:

1) End of the world stories are always popular
2) Fairy tales are always source material
3) Can this be done to something other than zombies?
4) Maybe. So we want to do an anthology of apocalyptic stories based on traditional fairy tales but don't want zombies
5) Sounds like horror/dark fantasy to me
6) Okay, yes, horror/dark fiction it is then
7) But what kind? Quiet? Extreme? Psychological? Cosmological?
8) I say all of the above
9) Say what?
10) Three words: Howard Philips Lovecraft

And there was much rejoicing—and why shouldn't there have been?

INTRODUCTION

The idea of taking a traditional fairy tale and setting it in Lovecraft's universe seems so inspired that it has to already have been done, right?

Not that I've been able to find, and I'm pretty well-read. I mean, good grief, Charlie Brown—how could one want to retell "The Fisherman and His Wife" and *not* have it set in Innsmouth? You'll find that story in here, and it plays that concept to the hilt. Ichabod (though not Crane) shows up on the campus of Miskatonic University. A brilliant *10* re-imagining of "Donkeyskin" shows up here in a most disturbingly Lovecraftian form. Charles Perrault's "Cinderella" gets one hell of a macabre makeover for her . . . let's call it her "date" with Yog-Sothoth.

You'll find re-imaginings of "The Snow Queen," "Jack the Giant Slayer," "The Little Mermaid," and several other well-known tales herein, all of them dropped without warning or apology into Lovecraft's cold and merciless universe.

It wasn't until I was halfway through Winifred Burniston's unnerving "Curiosity" (based on Perrault's "Bluebeard") that I realized what a stroke of genius it was to combine these heavily moralistic fables with Lovecraft. In Lovecraft's universe, there is no room for morality; it, like love, like prayer, like individual purpose, like everything else that we associate with a fulfilling life that goes beyond just breathing and taking up space, *all of it* is meaningless because this particular universe *doesn't give a damn*. It is a cold, uncaring place with no concept of mercy or compassion and even less use for these things if they *did* exist. Placing these stories with their black-and-white morality into a world where virtue, ethics, courage, decency, and goodness are at best cruel jokes freed the writers from having to worry about the moral core of their chosen fairy tale being compromised because here, *here* that moral code is D.O.A., the characters just don't know it yet, so the core remains unaltered.

I will be honest; when first approached to write this introduction, I was a bit skeptical of everyone's ability to pull this off: I now gratefully bake that skepticism into a pie full of crow and heartily dine on it. *Twice Upon an Apocalypse* is one of the most refreshingly inventive, entertaining, thoughtful (and thought-provoking), not to mention *unnerving* anthologies I've read in years; that each writer manages to seamlessly blend their chosen fairy tale with Lovecraft's world of shambling subterranean eldritch horrors is in and of itself quite an accomplishment and would by itself be reason enough to savor this collection from cover to cover; that they also manage to merge these with distinctly individual narrative voices *and* pack their narratives with impressive (and sometimes jaw-dropping) variations (I won't use the tired term "twists") only strengthens this collection's success; but when you realize, as I did, that by taking two well-known and -respected genres and "mashing" them together, each writer has created something that seems like a third race of tale, born from the fusion of two genres that are not usually associated with each other.

This anthology is a celebration not only of Lovecraft and fairy tales but of the creative process itself. It is, to my mind, a triumph, and you know why? I'll end on this disclaimer:

INTRODUCTION

No wheels were re-invented in the making of this collection.

vii

—Gary A. Braunbeck, Lost in Ohio

THE PIED PIPER OF PROVIDENCE

WILLIAM MEIKLE

Based on The Pied Piper of Hamelin by Robert Browning

ONCE UPON A TIME, on the shores of a great ocean in the north of the American continent, lay a town called Providence. The citizens of Providence were honest folk who lived contentedly in their gray stone houses. The years went by, and the people grew very rich. Then one day, an extraordinary thing happened to disturb the peace of this sleepy town.

All summer, there had been portents in the sky, and country folk talked of strange beasts roaming the hills to the north and east of the town. Being city dwellers and modern men, the councilmen of Providence would have no truck with such superstition. It was not until autumn that they were forced to pay closer attention to what was happening on their doorstep, and by then, it was too late.

The first indications something was amiss came when the local constabulary started to receive reports of missing cats. That in itself was not unusual in a city where the countryside was lush and wild just beyond the town limits. The borders were like a magnet that drew feline hunters to the woods to explore their wonders. But normally, those *explorers* would return to their homes of an evening, lured by the promise of food that could be procured more easily. Over the course of the first week of October, more and more cats stopped returning home. By the end of the month, there was not a single cat left in the town.

The first baby was bitten a day later.

***

At first, the authorities suspected a wild animal attacked the child, something from the woods that had been given its opportunity by the strange disappearance of the cat population. But it quickly became apparent that whatever had bitten the baby was also the *cause* of the decline in felines.

Old lady Malcolm was the first to see them when, on descending into her cellar late in the evening, she was attacked by six large rats, which bit her most grievously before she managed to fight them off with a broom.

It was not long after the rats grew bold enough to be seen in daylight. Soon, reports came in from all over town of rats in the grain stores, rats in the butcher's meat locker, rats in basements, and rats in the walls.

A council meeting was convened in the Town Hall. John Berryman, the mayor, called the meeting to order . . . just as a *whooshing* scraping noise filled the room. Tapestries writhed, and mortar trickled from loose stone before the sound finally subsided, rushing away to subterranean depths.

"What's to be done?" Berryman asked. "Has anyone called out the dogs?"

"There are no dogs," George Priestley said. "They've all gone. Either run off or scared off." Councillor Bill Timmings laughed nervously and scratched at a fresh bandage on his hand, the result of trying, unsuccessfully, to shoo a rat from his bedside the night before. He held up the hand to show the others.

"The thing was as big as any of the dogs," he said. "And twice as bold. If they're all like that, it's not dogs we need but a miracle."

Fresh screams rose from outside on the streets as if to counterpoint his argument. As a man, the councilors rushed to the window and looked on a scene of terror. Initially, it appeared as though a heaving black carpet of fur was making its way down the thoroughfare, then they saw, only too clearly, the rat pack had broken out into the open.

They ranged in size from only a few inches to great beasts as big as dogs, all with too-red tongues and pink, hairless tails that swayed obscenely in the air. Townspeople fled in the face of this new assault.

The councilmen watched, white-faced, as an elderly lady tripped, fell, and was engulfed, a pale arm waving feebly before being splattered red then devoured in seconds.

The council turned, ashen-faced, from the window, trying to blot out the few remaining pathetic screams.

"What's to be done?" the mayor whispered.

No one answered for the longest time, and they were saved doing so by a heavy knock on the chamber door. It swung open to reveal the most preposterous figure standing in the doorway, a wizened old man, bent with age, dressed in a leather outfit dyed in bright, gaudy shades of red, green, yellow, and purple.

The old man's face was too long, too thin, exaggerating the size of his teeth, particularly the front two, which seemed too large for his mouth and hung over his lower lip. Coarse, black hair fell in a cape down his back from an almost bald head, and pink eyes peered from beneath heavy brows. As he came forward into the chamber, he walked stiffly as if unsure on his feet. His pale pink hands were clutched tightly to his chest, carrying a pair of thin wooden flutes.

"And who might you be?" the mayor asked.

The wizened figure bowed at the waist.

"I am Rattenfänger Van Hameln," he said, his voice a high, thin whine. "And I have come to do you a favor."

***

Of course, the councilmen's first thought was to have the strange newcomer escorted from the chamber, but before they could call for the ushers, a great skittering and whispering rose up inside the walls around, above, and beneath them. The tapestries bulged again, as if many small shapes pushed against them from the other side, and bricks trembled and shook, threatening to fall from their places in a wall previously thought solid and impervious. The councilmen quaked and trembled before this fresh onslaught as the air filled with high, frantic shrieks and squeals.

Just as the noise threatened to reach a crescendo, von Hameln raised the flutes to his lips and stared to play.

The mayor felt it first through the soles of his feet, but soon, his whole frame shook, vibrating in time with the rhythm. His head swam, and it seemed as if the very walls of the chamber melted and ran. The room receded into a great distance until it was little more than a pinpoint of light in a blanket of darkness, and he was alone in a vast cathedral of emptiness where nothing existed save the slow, almost mournful singing of the flutes.

Shapes moved in the dark, small, low-slung shadows with no substance, shadows that capered and whirled as the dance grew ever more frenetic. He gave himself to it, lost in the dance, lost in the dark.

Finally, after what seemed an age, the flutes brought their tune to a close, and reality fell back in place around them. The councilmen blinked, shook their heads, and looked around in puzzlement. Somewhere, far below, the skittering whispers of the rats descended once again into the depths. The attack was over.

Van Hameln stood in the center of the room, a small smile on his lips.

"You have a problem, gentlemen," he said. "And I can rid you of it for, say, ten thousand dollars?"

The mayor was the first of them to come fully back to his senses. "Hell, man, I'll give you twenty thousand if you will just make them go away."

He did not have to wait long for the agreement of his fellow councilmen. To a man, they were most enthusiastic in their desire for the rat problem to be brought to a swift resolution at any cost.

Van Hameln bowed again. "Then I am at your service, gentlemen. I shall return anon, and I shall expect my payment."

He left the chamber, raising the flutes to his lips as

he turned and walked away. The mournful tune floated once more in the air.

A rumbling rose from the street outside.

Once again, the councilmen rushed to the window. The small man walked down the main street, the flutes at his mouth, doing a little jig in accompaniment. Behind him came the black, writhing carpet of rats. They poured from every door, came up through every sewer, their numbers swelling and growing until the carpet became a towering wall of dancing rodents that capered and jigged in time to the tune as they followed Van Hameln down the street.

As the councilmen watched, the strangest thing happened. The small man brought his tune towards a climax. At the same time, the whole street shimmered as if in the grip of a heat haze. The street itself seemed to fade and vanish until they were looking down into a black, bottomless hole, a pit that led to stygian depths. Without a pause in the tune, Van Hameln leapt into the dark.

The rats followed, tumbling in a black wave that crashed on the shore of the blackness and fell away squealing into the deep.

The tune came to an end.

The black hole was broken and scattered by a slight breeze, and in a second, there was nothing to see but the empty street.

***

Although the townspeople were unsure as to what had happened, there was great rejoicing, and an impromptu street party began in the main square. Being politicians after all, the councilmen were conspicuous at the party, ensuring that everyone knew just how *vital* their role had been in ridding the town of the menace.

Drink flowed, food was eaten with gusto, and men, women, and children danced in the street, singing the praises of their *heroic* councilmen. The council lapped up this attention and thus were somewhat deflated when Van Hameln arrived back in their midst.

The small man appeared as if from nowhere after the councilmen had met to formulate a strategy for capitalizing on the newly found goodwill.

"Well, gentlemen," Von Hameln said. "Did I not keep my promise? The deed is done. Ten thousand dollars was the price, I believe?"

The mayor laughed. "You can whistle for it, if you like," he said, somewhat emboldened by a combination of good cheer and too much beer. "The rats have gone. Who is to say they would not have done so of their own free will."

"Free will, is it now?" the small man said. He was no longer smiling. "I very much doubt you know the meaning of the term. But let us have a little test, shall we? I aim to have my payment, one way or another. If I cannot have it in dollars, I shall take it in kind."

The mayor laughed again. "Try to take anything you damned well please," he said, his cheeks ruddy and red.

This time, Van Hameln did indeed smile. "That is very kind of you," he replied. He raised the flutes to his lips and started to play.

"Hey. We'll have none of that," the mayor shouted and lunged forward, trying to grab the flautist. Vn Hameln stepped lightly to one side, easily avoided the clumsy attack, smiled again, and danced a little jig.

Every child in the town started to dance in time.

***

"Hey," the mayor shouted again but this time more in fear and confusion than anger as the children of the town, like the rats had before them, started to congregate behind the small man. The mayor's own son walked past, skipping and dancing. He tried to grab the boy, but every time his hands grew close, the child seemed to *jig* away, just out of reach.

The small man walked down the main street, the flutes at his mouth. Behind him came a writhing mass of children. They poured from every side street, their numbers swelling and growing until the carpet became a towering wall of dancing youngsters. They capered and jigged in time to the tune as they followed Van Hameln down the street.

The small man brought his tune towards a climax. At the same time, the whole street shimmered as it had earlier as if in the grip of a heat haze. Once more, the street itself seemed to fade and vanish, leaving only the black, bottomless hole, a pit that led to stygian depths.

Without a pause in the tune, Van Hameln leapt into the dark.

The children followed, tumbling in a black wave that crashed on the shore of the blackness and fell away into the deep.

The tune came to an end. Parents threw themselves forward in frenzy only to tumble onto the hard stone of the roadway. The black hole was broken and scattered by a slight breeze, and in a second, there was nothing to see but the empty street.

***

The mayor stood over the spot where the hole had been and screamed. "Rattenfänger!" Three times, he called. And on the third, he was answered. The small man appeared in front of him.

"Is there another service I can do for you, sir?" he said with a smile.

"Give us back our children," the mayor said.

"But they were a payment agreed between gentlemen," Van Hameln replied. "You agreed to it. Of your own free will."

"I will have your ten thousand for you," the mayor said, pleading. "Just come to the bank with me now."

Van Hameln shook his head sadly. "It is too late for that, I am afraid. The children have already been taken. That which has been taken cannot be returned exactly as it once was."

The mayor wasn't really listening. "Please. Give us our children back. We'll do anything."

"There is one thing I want," Van Hameln said. "But remember, you give it of your free will."

"Anything," the councilmen cried as one. "Just please return the children."

"Very well," Van Hameln said. "It is done."

And with that, he was gone again as quickly as he had come.

***

The town's children were all found safely sleeping in their beds.

But the mayor was taking no chances. He left town that same night, taking his family to a cousin's home in Boston, where he would be safe from any return of the strange, small man.

They arrived early in the morning. His cousin was waiting at the door.

"I say. You didn't see a cat out there, did you? It's

the strangest thing. They seem to have gone from all over the city, from all over the country from what I have been hearing."

"Father. What's that noise?"

The mayor looked at his son. The boy's face seemed too long, his chin too sharp. His front teeth grew down over his lower lip, and his pink eyes seemed wet with fresh tears.

The boy skipped then started to dance a jig.

That which has been taken cannot be returned exactly as it was.

The sound of twin flutes floated over the city.

THE THREE BILLY GOATS SOTHOTH

PETER N. DUDAR

Based on Three Billy Goats Gruff by Peter Christen Asbjørnsen

IT HAD BEEN so long since Aelrick had heard the sound of human footsteps crossing his bridge he had almost forgotten what it sounded like. He was the last of the trolls, and when the ancient ones had fallen into hibernation and mankind came and knocked down the old wooden bridge, his bridge, Aelrick had known the gates of the dominion had closed forever. The planet had moved on. And mankind, with their ambitions and technologies, had taught themselves above and beyond the dark magic and alchemy they'd once clung to.

His old wooden bridge that gave passage between the flatlands and the mountains was replaced by beams of steel and paths of smooth, bonded stone. It was a blasphemy in Aelrick's opinion. He could not understand why the Ancient Ones no longer concerned themselves with how mankind was corrupting the landscape and turning themselves into the New Gods.

Nowadays, he merely slept beneath the bridge, casually listening to the roar of car engines above as man raced back and forth in his pursuit of defiant convenience, concerned only for himself. Even the trees along the mountainside whispered their displeasure at those ridiculous beasts, and the animals choked and gagged on the breaths of their metal chariots.

And, not that he would admit it, he was deathly afraid of them. So when the day came when the engines ceased and the once noisy bridge was blanketed with a malignant silence, Aelrick began wondering if he might creep his way back up to the surface, back to the gates of his bridge, to investigate.

It was the sound of approaching footsteps that startled him.

It had been so long.

Aelrick spilled out from his nest beneath the cold, iron girders and scrambled his way to the road. "Who's that clip-clopping over my bridge?" he screamed aloud and found himself wondering if those were even the words he'd used to say.

The shroud of mist along the highway parted, and there before the tired old troll marched the first of the Billy Goats.

"Old Fool! It is I," the first goat announced, its voice rolling off the vast expanse of nothing where the roar of traffic used to reside. "I am the Harbinger of Truth and Light. Have you not read about me in the Necronomicon's pages of Revelation? I have come to prepare the way for those who would escape the wrath of the Ancient Ones. I am the Clearer of Paths, and I must cross your bridge and make my way into the yonder mountains so that I may guide what is left of the pure and righteous to shelter and safety."

"You may *not* cross my bridge," Aelrick replied. "Mankind has made a mockery of this world, and I shall be damned to let any of them flee from the wrath of the Ancient Ones. Turn back, lest *you* wish to spend eternity falling prey to the monstrous appetite of Cthulhu himself!"

The old goat snuffed and stomped its feet on the worn, cracked macadam.

"Have you not felt the changes already begun?" the old goat spat. "Have you not witnessed the return of the Colours out of Space? The Ancient Ones are awakening, and it is for *them* to decide who is saved and who is cast aside. I implore you to move so that I may cross!"

The troll gazed into the heavens and found his mind spinning as he now understood the cosmos was also spinning in dreadful misalignment. Had it been so long since he last left his nest to gaze at the night sky? For all his mind, he could not remember a time when the patterns of the stars were not pacifying in their constant celestial locations. Now, they reeled in chaos, vomiting themselves into terrible new patterns. Aelrick grew hypnotized as he gazed upon them, and when he closed his eyes, the spell broke. He turned and faced the first goat.

"You may *not* cross," the troll insisted. "Even mankind knows that goats are deceptive beasts. That is why in man's own misguided religions, you are a symbol of evil. You have disrupted the silence of my home and have awakened me from my slumber. Turn back! Turn back, or I shall have to kill you and eat you for my dinner!"

The old goat lowered his head and started across the bridge. Without warning, the troll produced a dagger and spilled the blood of the animal, slitting its throat from one side to the other with a terrible wave of his hand. Aelrick was smiling as he bit down into the animal's flesh and swallowed his first taste of warm meat while the dying animal watched him.

After he'd fed, Aelrick returned to his nest and dozed off. In his weary mind's eye, he could still see the cosmos circling in chaotic orbits. How had he *not* felt that something was amiss? The crossing of those infernal metal beasts the humans traveled in had practically stopped overnight, yet the enveloping silence had not grabbed his attention for only Yog knew when. With his belly fuller than it had been in centuries, the old troll yawned and curled into a ball, and he'd almost fallen asleep when the approaching footsteps brought him back to consciousness.

"Another intruder!" he sighed. He crawled out of his nest and scrambled up to his bridge as the light of the blood moon crested over the mountain top.

"Who's that clip-clopping over my bridge?" Aelrick demanded.

Once again, the mists along the highway parted, and another goat stepped forward.

"Old fool, it is I," the second goat announced, its voice rolling off the vast expanse of nothing where the roar of traffic used to reside. "I am the Harbinger of Plagues and War. Have you not read about me in the Necronomicon's pages of Revelation? I am the Bearer of Woe and Misery. The trial of mankind has begun!

"It is I that corrupts the lands with wars and rumors of war. I am the producer of maladies that squeeze the life out of man until he panics and begs for mercy. I must cross this bridge and await the judgment of the righteous. I have killed many, many men throughout history, and once they cross this bridge, they will earn the right to judge me. They will slay me if they must. It is their reward for pleasing the Ancient Ones. I must cross this bridge and meet my fate. I ask you to please stand aside."

"You may not cross my bridge!" Aelrick replied. "For the last hundred years alone, I've watched mankind flourish in spite of his wicked ways. Where were the Ancient Ones when mankind blasphemed the world with their dreams of becoming gods themselves? They have plagued the world with terrible machines and filled the skies with the darkness of progress. This is *not* the world as the Ancient Ones had once perceived it."

The second goat snuffed and stomped its feet on the worn, cracked macadam.

"Have you not heard the cries of the suffering? Have you forgotten the mercies of the Ancient Ones? You, too, shall be judged before this apocalypse is over. The Ancient Ones are returning to feast and to reclaim their reign over this world. It is not your lot to defy them or alter the cleansing this world has waged upon itself!"

"Turn back, or I shall have to kill you and eat you for my dinner!"

The second goat lowered his head and began to cross the bridge.

Without warning, the troll produced a hammer from his cloak and proceeded to bash the beast until its skull shattered and its body tumbled lifeless to the ground. As the goat's legs and tail produced their last twitches, the troll proceeded to flay off its skins and hang them along the sides of the bridge to dry. The rest of the goat was torn apart and left on either side of the road for the wolves to feast upon.

"Whatever other intruders happen upon my bridge tonight will have to turn and flee from the wolves," Aelrick said to himself as he scampered down the hillside to his nest underneath the bridge. The troll once again curled into a ball and fell into the deepest of slumbers.

He dreamed of the Ancient Ones and how they once ruled the planet in fearsome wrath with their slimy, phosphorescent appendages and cavernous mouths of soulless blackness. Where had they gone? Where had they been for all these millennia? Were they sleeping at the bottom of some vast ocean floor? Or had they returned through space and time to whatever hell they were birthed from?

It was just before dawn when Aelrick was awoken by the sounds of the third chorus of footsteps. He crawled out of his nest and scrambled his way to the bridge. The sun was just beginning to peek over the eastern mountaintops. And with the dawn came the call of the Ancient Ones, who were undoubtedly cresting from the depths of the cold Atlantic Ocean.

Seagulls screamed, and fish shrieked at their return. And from the west came the clip-clop of the third goat.

"Who's that clip-clopping over my bridge," the troll announced and found his knees beginning to tremble beneath him. The Ancient Ones *were* returning . . . that much was obvious. But had he somehow interfered with their return to glory? Had he somehow callously thrown himself into the wheels of fate? Had he perverted the gospels of the Necronomicon? Surely, the Ancient Ones would forgive him after abandoning their sentry so long ago. He'd remained at his post, after all. Even when man had forged these terrible highways and blighted the landscapes with billboards and skyscrapers and polluted the earth for the sake of convenience, he had remained at his post.

Even when he was no longer effective at stopping them.

"You fool! It is I," the third goat announced, its voice rolling off the vast expanse of nothing. He was much larger than the first two, and his horns curled with sinister perfection. When he spoke, he sounded not like the others, who bleated in the old animal-speak. This goat talked like the humans, and its voice echoed off the stones of the mountainside. "I am the Harbinger of Nothingness. I have come to blot out all that remains of the Old Ways. And you, Aelrick, are as much of the Old Ways as mankind ever was!"

A swarm of rats appeared at the goat's feet. They scampered and prowled about along the cold, desolate highway. Every now and then, the roar of the Ancient Ones bellowed over the mountainside at their rebirth. From behind the rats came the sound of the Human Parade, the last of the chosen survivors who were being led to the Mountains of Madness, where they would remain in sheltered safety until the Ancient Ones could feast upon the blemishes of the earth. It was as it had been written in the Necronomicon's pages of Revelation.

The old troll smiled in dreadful defiance.

"None of them shall pass," he sneered. "This is *MY* bridge! The Ancient Ones have tasked my kind to defend it, and defend it we have for as long as we could. I have never strayed from my post, even when mankind built their metal beasts and tried to run me down. And now they are the ones fleeing, and by their own hand. You cannot save them! Turn back, and turn them back, or I shall eat you all for my dinner!"

The third goat snuffed and stomped its feet on the worn, cracked macadam.

"Can you not see that the Ancient Ones are *here*? On the other side of this mountain is the face of mankind's destiny. Those who are not on the mountain behind you by daybreak will be snuffed out of existence. It is not up to you who lives or dies! These things have been preordained through time and space and existence. For all you know, you are unbalancing the scales of fate. If some of mankind does not survive, the dominion of the Ancient Ones will die as well. You will defile the symbiosis that the universe has created. That is *not* your lot to decide!"

The troll rubbed his chin in deep thought. Before him came the screams and cries of mankind, hoping and praying for refuge from the coming Armageddon. From behind him came the fierce, unforgiving bellows of the Ancient Ones, arising from the murky depths of slumber to once again restore balance to the planet.

Aelrick looked at the goat and smiled a wicked smile.

"Perhaps *I* am a God after all!" he declared. "Perhaps the fate of this world rests in *MY* hands alone. It has been so long since I've been able to stand up against man in his metal beasts as they crossed my bridge. But here they are on foot once again, and the reign of those infernal automobiles is over. It would take so little for me to destroy this bridge, and all of your followers will meet the same cruel and terrible fate as everybody else!"

The third goat lowered its head and began to stomp his way across the bridge. But before the troll could reach him, the long, thin tentacles began to berth themselves from its face. Its eyes rolled back, exposing the terrible, unseeing sclera of an awakening God, and its horns grew out into long, poisonous lances.

Aelrick barely had time to scream before Cthulhu erupted from the third goat's body and gored him into a savage, bloody pulp.

From beyond the mountainside, the Ancient Ones roared their approval.

LITTLE MAIDEN OF THE SEA

DAVID BERNARD

*Based on The Little Mermaid by Hans Christian
Anderson*

OFF THE COAST of Massachusetts is a reef where strange creatures dwell. They were brought here by an Arkham captain as minions of his unholy allegiance to an ancient and blasphemous god. Unpleasant as the beasts are, and they are most assuredly unpleasant, what is worse is they can mate with humans and do so. These half breeds look human, but as they age, they show the other half of their lineage. First, their eyes bulge. Then, their necks grow fat with gills, and their skin resembles scales. Finally, their chins disappear, and they turn green. A frog? Perhaps—but a 5-foot-tall frog with the mind of a human and the cunning of a beast. When they reach this point, the call of the ocean becomes too great, and they return to the reefs beyond Innsmouth. The purebloods are even worse, powerful and ruthless, with the infinite patience that comes from the knowledge that the time is nearing where they will claim dominion over the delicacy called humanity. The humans call them "The Deep Ones."

LITTLE MAIDEN OF THE SEA

One of the purebred Deep Ones, a "maiden," was different from the other creatures. By her species' standards, perhaps she was a simpleton, for she didn't have the instinctive distrust of humans her ancestors had honed over the centuries. The Little Maiden longed to walk on the land. But the maidens who dwelled beneath the sea were forbidden to visit the surface. The priest of Father Dagon had decreed only young princes were to rise to the surface and only in search of a mate. But the Little Maiden was stubborn and would swim to the surface and hide among the rocks, gazing upon the lights of the village that the hybrids said the air-breathers called Innsmouth.

While resting upon the rocks at twilight, marveling at a sunset behind the hills, she noticed a man. The Little Maiden had long been told that humans were vicious brutes, and the reason the young princes went to the surface to breed was to dilute the mammal blood in hopes of tempering the evil in their souls. But the human she saw looked lonely. Suddenly, as if he sensed her gaze, he looked at her. She saw neither fear nor anger in his eyes.

He simply looked at her and then said, "Hello, sea dweller."

She tensed to leap back into the sea at the first sign of attack. The most important function of the maidens above all others was to tend to new arrivals. When the princely spawn matured and returned to the seas as hybrid children of Father Dagon, the maidens aided the transition. And for that purpose, all the maidens were expected to learn the air breathers' tongue. She carefully recalled her lessons.

"Hello air-breather," she croaked.

By such an innocuous start grew a friendship between the old man named Whateley and the Little Maiden. Through the summer, the two met. Whateley talked of clouds, hills, and plants that bloomed and filled the air with fragrances. The maiden spoke of ancient cities hidden beneath oceans so deep that light never reached the turrets.

Summer turned to fall, and one day, the human announced he must stop his visits. The weather would soon make travel from his village in the hills too difficult.

"I shall miss you, Whateley. I wish there was a way to come with you and visit your land," she croaked sadly.

"I'll miss ye too, Little Maiden." Whateley had never learned to pronounce her name—far too many consonants for the human throat.

He paused a moment. "Unless . . ."

The maiden looked at him as he paused. A moment passed where only the sound was of waves crashing upon the rocks.

"Little Maiden, I have a confession. I'm not jes' a farmer. I'm also a bit of a wizard. I have an old book with an incantation that might turn ye into human. Iffen ye could, would ye like to visit my home as a human?"

The maiden nodded in agreement, for an adventure on the land had long been her wish. So the wizard Whateley went back to his home to consult his ancient tomes of forbidden magicks. The two agreed to meet on the second day of the full moon at Falcon's Point, where the Little Maiden would become temporarily human.

LITTLE MAIDEN OF THE SEA

On the second day of the full moon, the ocean reflected a swollen red moon. The Little Maiden swam ashore to find Whateley waiting. "Little Maiden, I must warn ye—these types of conjurin' come at a cost. The spell demands a gift. It demands your first born child as a servant to the ancient gods. Is that acceptable?"

She croaked her agreement—a Deep One barely considered a human child more than a small meal. Its survival was of no consequence to an aquatic denizen who would spawn dozens of offspring.

The night grew still as the wizard began his chanting. Soon, a bluish light surrounded the Little Maiden. She felt a transformation—her lovely green hue drained away as her spine straightened. She felt her eyes recede and the webbing disappear between her fingers. Where a Deep One hunched upon the rocks moments before now stood a human female.

The wizard wrapped her in a blanket. "We'll head back to my farm in the hills and tell the town you're my daughter, back from stayin' with cousins. You'll be needin' a human name. How does "Lavinia" suit ye, child?"

The maiden tried to reply, but human vocal chords were much more difficult to manipulate than she expected. So she merely nodded. Much later, she would discover her "father" had ulterior plans when she came across his copy of *The Aeneid* with a passage underlined about Lavinia, the only child of the king and "ripe for marriage."

So in the shunned hamlet of Dunwich in the year of 1909, Old Wizard Whateley returned from a trip accompanied by his daughter, Lavinia, a somewhat deformed albino who had been staying with his late wife's family "on the coast." Old Whateley's wife had died years before, and there was no one alive who could recall her, let alone recall the Whateleys having children. But there was little doubt she was a Whateley. Who else would have such a strange and unattractive child?

Lavinia certainly gave the town ample fodder for discussion. An albino with crinkled, lifeless, white hair and a slight hunch to the shoulders, a sunken neck, she scurried from place to place with a gait that looked like hopping. She also had an odd predilection for dancing in thunder storms, her pink eyes ablaze with some distant memory as lightning and thunder waged war above her. The Bishop boys started calling her "White Frog" until Brother Asaph, the circuit preacher from Aylesbury, heard them. Brother Asaph had no idea how close to the truth the boys were, tanned hides or not.

As the years passed, the Whateleys, social outcasts to begin with, were shunned even more when it became known that Wizard and his daughter were performing ceremonies on a stone altar atop Sentinel Hill. When asked, Wizard Whateley would simply claim he was "waiting for the stars to be right."

Brother Asaph suspected Wizard Whateley might be worshipping a pagan god there, so one night, he quietly slipped up the hill to see. He came back down white as death. He quit the ministry soon after, and no preacher has visited Dunwich since. On the evening of April 30, 1912, while most of New England prepared for the next day's May Day celebration, the Whateleys were celebrating an older, darker version of the holiday. Wizard Whateley had driven to Kingsport and returned with a burlap sack containing a squirming bundle. And as the sun set, Lavinia lit the Walpurgis bonfires across the hill, chanting the same unholy summoning spell that had driven a good man from the clergy. Once the bonfires were lit, the stolen infant was unceremoniously pulled from the burlap sack. Placing the child on the ancient stone altar, Whately sacrificed the child in the name of ancient beings best not named. Lavinia, as was her wont, stood to the side trying not to look as bored as she felt.

The ceremonies were too frequent, too long, and too lacking in results. Suddenly, as the Kingsport child's blood collected in the runnel around the altar, the sanguine liquid erupted in a spectral green flame. The unholy blaze spread across the altar, and as the otherworldly pyre rose in the night sky, bolts of lightning shot to each bonfire, turning the hilltop into a glowing symbol that had not been seen on the planet in countless millennia. The spectral conflagration leapt from the table and enveloped Lavinia. She dropped to her knees. The flames disappeared and the bonfires went out as one. The only sounds on Sentinel Hill were the distant howls of dogs on neighboring farms. Whateley looked at Lavinia. "Well, Lavinny, looks like you'll be meetin' your obligations for that transformin' spell in about nine months."

A few weeks later, the Dunwich rumor mill was running full speed. Old Wizard Whateley had announced Lavinia's impending bundle of joy, and the gossip mongers were beside themselves trying to figure out who the father was and how Whateley had known so early in the pregnancy. That alone was worth nine months of back fence chats, but then Doc Haskin stormed into the feed store and added to the rumor mill.

Doc Haskin was the only physician willing to visit Dunwich, and word had spread about Lavinia being in a family way, so the Doc had driven down to the Whateley farm to offer prenatal advice. When he got there, he found a strange man dressed in black with a turban. Old Man Whateley introduced him as Dr. Zeloft, a specialist from Kingsport who would be treating Lavinia. Doc Haskin didn't like the Whateleys any more than anyone else, but he felt bringing a new doctor into his town was just rude on Wizard Whateley's part and unprofessional on the part of the Kingsport doctor. What really set the Doc off was the Kingsport doctor never said a word to him. He just stood there, wearing dark-tinted glasses and gloves. The Doc was not the most superstitious resident of the upper Miskatonic Valley, but the silent stranger had given him the heebie jeebies.

Nine months passed by quickly. Lavinia became a recluse, giving the local gossips no chance to pry in search of hints as to the identity of the father. Dr. Zeloft was given a wide berth on his weekly visits to the Whateley farm by the townsfolk and the dogs. Old Man Whateley, in gleeful anticipation, was investing a small fortune in lumber and construction supplies. When asked, he would smile furtively and say that he had to remodel the house for his grandson. From the amount of wood he had been hauling out to the farm, the locals felt he could have built a new house.

On February 2, 1913 at 5 am, a day known in certain religions as Imbolc, Lavinia Whateley gave birth to twin hideous monstrosities. One child was completely alien, a writhing mass of deformities. Dr. Zeloft quietly took that twin into the remodeled area. The second twin was slightly more human—at least the upper torso. Proportionally, if not anatomically, correct, it could at least pass as human if carefully dressed.

Lavinia quietly suckled the child. She was not that familiar with humans, but these offspring stirred something deep within her she believed was called revulsion. She looked at her surrogate father.

"Father? I think it's time for me to go home."

Wizard Whateley looked down at the mother of humanity's downfall. He glanced at the locked door. "Lavinny, you can break the spell as soon as ye be ready."

Several days later, a horse and wagon pulled up to the rotted wharf in Innsmouth. The streets were deserted as if the Innsmouthians knew something beyond their understanding was in their midst. The cracked bell in a squat church tower dully chimed the hour. Lavinia stepped down from the wagon and handed her child to the wizard.

"Lavinny," he started, holding the baby close, "in a few years, the world will be changed, and ye were the one who started things rollin'. Thank you."

Lavinia looked at him with emotionless pink eyes. "Well then, Father, we might just meet again." She turned and walked toward the brackish shoreline, stripping off her human clothing. As she stepped into the water, Whateley watched as her shape transformed slowly. Her shoulders dropped, the white hair fell away, and her back returned to the batrachian curve and color of her people. She turned and looked at the shore one last time, waving her webbed paw, and then dove into the Atlantic.

Wizard Whateley watched her go, a tinge of regret at her departure. He shifted the child and walked back toward his horse and wagon.

"Yer brother will take yer daddy's name, but I need to name you so as the folks in Dunwich have something to call ye. I guess I'll name you after my daddy."

He raised the child close to his face. The child's feral eyes glinted, revealing a shrewdness and malevolence that belied his newborn state. Old Wizard Whateley stared right back at the child.

"Hello, Wilbur Whateley. Let's hightail it back to Dunwich. You and I are goin' to do great things. We're goin' to open the gates for your daddy to return to earth."

THE GREAT OLD ONE AND THE BEANSTALK

ARMAND ROSAMILIA

Based on Jack and the Beanstalk by Joseph Jacob

I TELL THIS tale in hopes my poor mother, suffering from dementia all these years, will survive in relative peace for a few more months, perhaps years, without the pain I've caused her. After my death, this letter will hopefully be unsealed and given to the proper authorities although I know not who they would be.

It started with the barren cow. At this point—November of 1931—we only had one left, and she was growing old but still producing for Mother and me. We were the last of the Whateley clan on this side of the mountains. I say this side since the strange folks from Dunwich (relatives or not) never ventured too far from their desolate farms and rocky soil, and that's never been a problem. Queer folk is what my father used to say about them cousins. I couldn't complain too much, though, since I hardly saw them and Jeb Whateley gave me this cow from his herd for nothing. Family is family, after all.

"It's time to trade in this cow," I told Mother. If we could get some vegetables or meat for her, I'd be happy. I hoped no one noticed the greenish tinge around the udders and the brown stains on her coat.

She was rampant with something, but I didn't want to chance it spreading before I could unload her. I sure wasn't going to eat meat from her. Mother said nothing, staring out the window of our shanty and watching the fields, once ripe with corn and squash and a dozen other crops, now broken up and unused. I had no way of doing the farming myself now that Father was long gone—and my gimp right leg and lame left arm kept me from doing most menial chores.

Three miles up the road stood the trading post. I was sure I'd get something for her. I pulled her along in her slow but steady gait and wished she was a horse so I could ride her to the store and be done with it. Three miles to walk in the heat with a slow beast is unnatural. I was just past the old Marsh farm, fallen into disrepair these last few months since the old man had snapped and beaten his family with a shovel when I stopped. Standing, hunched over in the road before me, was a young man with a long, straggly beard almost down to his navel. He waved an odd greeting, his right hand missing a digit or two, and then shoved his hand back into a pocket. Despite the heat, he was wearing a long, woolen coat and had an odd derby perched on his long, raven hair.

"I say, good day, sir." He spoke like a man thirty years his senior, voice harsh and phlegmy. "Where might you be headed?"

He was definitely from these parts with the thick accent we all had in the New England States, but there was a strange underbelly to his words, as if he hissed them at the endings. I didn't like him and neither did the cow, which stamped her front feet like a bronco. I'd never seen her do that before.

"I'm heading to the crossroads," I said, trying to sound at ease and hoping my voice didn't crack as I spoke.

"Have business there, do you?"

I hesitated with my answer but saw no harm in it. Nothing secret about that. "I'm selling my prized cow."

"Prized, you say?" He came forth, still bent slightly, but as he approached, I could see he was much taller and lithe than I. I guessed at full height, he must be two heads taller, a giant of a man. When he put a hand on the cow, I wanted to yank it away but didn't know why. There was something odd about the man, and he seemed much older than his physical features. I realized it was his eyes: gray and deep and a tad menacing.

"I'm afraid I have bad news for you, sir. Your cow is diseased and likely won't finish the trip to the crossroads."

I began to sweat. "I beg to differ."

He ran his hand across her back, stopping at one of the spots but not touching it. "She's riddled with a deadly fungus. Her meat is already spoiled." He closed his eyes and put his face to the spot, breathing it in. When he lifted his head and smiled at me, I felt nothing but warmth from his formerly menacing eyes. "There are horses coming, you know. Four Horsemen are riding from town to town and leaving devastation behind."

I didn't believe any of this. The man was trying to scare me.

"End times," he murmured through a smile. "You'll see."

"I need to be off, sir," I said rather rudely.

"I can take her off your hands and dispose of her properly."

Dispose? That was unacceptable. I needed to feed my mother. I needed to eat myself. "I have to trade her for food."

When the strange man put his hand on my shoulder and looked at me, I knew I was lost. Looking back at that fateful moment, I realize I was closer to the crossroads than I assumed, under a full moon at midnight instead of a burning sun at noon. The Devil was dancing, however, and the deal was sealed.

The three stones felt hot in my hand as he put them there, and I squeezed them in my fingers and held them for the next hour even as the bent man led my sick cow away.

***

Mother didn't say a word as she held the three round stones in her feeble hands; she continued to stare out the window. I'd been sitting patiently near her since my return home and explaining my actions.

Once the spell was broken, I had run all the way to the crossroads to find the man. He was gone like smoke. The trading post hadn't seen the man, and no one believed my story, I could tell. Mister Gantor, proprietor of the post, smirked when I told him and showed the rocks.

"Those are some fancy rocks," he said and stifled a laugh. "You got some deal there." He took one from me but dropped it on the wooden counter as soon as he did, the heat of it surprising him. He wouldn't be stopped from his ribbing. "He could've gotten two cows for these fancy rocks." When Mister Gantor, now wound up and laughing, turned to pull in some of the employees with his banter, I took my stones and fled.

It was getting late and mother needed to eat, even though I had no real idea what to feed her. I supposed I would have to go without tonight since I'd given away our only possession of value.

"Open the window," mother whispered, so quietly I thought at first it was ruffled parchment blowing in the wind. I took a step away, but she turned her head and fixed me with a glare. "Open this window."

I did as I was told and stepped back, not sure what she had in mind but never one to cross her no matter how old or weak she became. Mother came from a long line of fighters, her family and fathers having met in Innsmouth years ago, a hardy stock of fishermen.

Her arm cocked and flew, and suddenly, the three stones were gone into the coming night. I didn't dare move as she continued to stare at me. "Go find me something to eat."

I took that as my cue to run to the kitchen and pulled myself from her glare, filled with not only hatred but disappointment.

***

My night was spent fitfully, dreams of sea monsters and being trapped in remote, ice-filled caves with strange but almost familiar markings on the walls and the sounds of scratching. I woke, still in the dark, covered in sweat and somehow lying on the floor next to my rumpled bed.

I tiptoed to the living room and was glad to see

Mother wasn't in her chair. It was dark outside. Very dark. Darker than I'd seen in . . . forever?

I went to the window and looked out, but it was as if a wall had been erected a foot from it, blocking out the stars. Bewildered, I ran out the door and stopped short.

There was a black, twining mass, thick as twice my torso, twisting up into the sky. It had a strong but not unpleasant odor, reminding me of a green bean dish Mother had made when I was young and we'd visited the Whateley clan over the hill.

I put a hand to it and felt the warmth. I recoiled when I realized it felt like the stones Mother had thrown out the window . . . and at this exact spot. Impossible.

The sky above, what I saw of it, was cloudy, but it didn't feel like a storm coming. In fact, the clouds hovered directly above where the beanstalk rose into the night. Beanstalk. That sounded right even though I'd never seen a beanstalk this thick or this tall.

The clouds shivered, giving off a queer light. There were definitely shapes moving in the mists, but it was hard to see clear enough when I looked directly at them. And they were getting bigger as I moved my head, taking in the wonder and trying to make sense of the chaos above. Colors I cannot describe flashed only a few feet above my head, sparkling lights and pinpoints around my body.

I closed my eyes and felt the wind on my face. When I opened them, I was high above. I'd apparently climbed the beanstalk although I had no recollection of doing something so dangerous. My farm was a tiny speck below, as if an ant were at my feet. And at my feet? A cloud cover and nothing more. I felt solid ground but could tell not what I stood on. Yes, I'm aware none of this makes sense, and as I read it back, I cannot make it clearer. Suffice to say I was more out of sorts than you, poor reader. I will stop here before you learn of what happened and judge me harshly to ask you to watch after my poor mother while I am gone. We don't have much, but perhaps you'd be so kind as to send her to the rest of the Whateley family so she can spend her last days with kin?

There were others on the cloud with me, vague figures in robes carrying queer items the likes of which I'd never seen and probably never will again in my lifetime. There was timelessness as I stood there and watched the chanting horde as mist swirled and they moved to a brighter light hovering above us and away. They sang out, words I had never heard, and wished I could forget.

I know not what they meant. But such was the chill I received when I heard them and stared into the evil, cloud-like entity they clearly worshipped. That they will forever be imprinted on my psyche and the words spoken in my nightmares until the day I die.

"Ever Their praises and abundance to the Black Goat of the *Woods. Iä!* Shub-Niggurath! Iä! Shub-Niggurath! The Black Goat of the Woods with a Thousand Young!"

I raised both hands to ward off the glow and realized I suddenly had full use of my limbs, no impediments. So enthralled was I, it never occurred to me I couldn't have climbed the beanstalk because of my useless arm and leg, yet here I stood. Was it a miracle? I was suddenly closer to the Great Old One. How I knew this, I cannot say. Before it sat four horsemen, cloaked in darkness and unmoving save the snorting animals.

As I write this, it has been long days since I stood there on that cloud, yet my limbs remain fully functional, and I can move freely. Two strong legs have taken me hundreds of miles from my blighted farm, but it still feels too close. But in my madness and grief, I digress.

***

I went to the figures, but they kept moving inexorably to the creature of power, and I was always a hand's width from reaching them despite how fast I went. And all this time, the chanting would not stop, droning over and over.

"Ever Their praises and abundance to the Black Goat of the *Woods. Iä!* Shub-Niggurath! Iä! Shub-Niggurath! The Black Goat of the Woods with a Thousand Young!"

I touched a dark robe, and it felt like a snake had struck my fingers, the pain was so intense. I pulled back, and something ripped loose from the robes with my jerk. I put the item in my free hand, expecting blood and a missing digit, but my hand was clean.

A small burlap sack, no bigger than a coin purse and jingling, was now in my possession. The chanters kept moving away from me. I opened it, and when I beheld the golden rounds, I nearly cried out in joy. I was a rich man. I glanced at the robed figures again, my greed nearly overtaking me as I thought perhaps another would have gold.

But they were almost to their evil destination, and I had no desire to get any closer. The riders held although their mounts seemed restless.

Now, to descend. I cannot explain how I did so, but

it was as if I simply thought it and I was already on the ground though my arms and legs pained from no exertion of climbing.

The sun was rising, and a look above showed me the clouds dissipating, leaving only the dark, overlarge beanstalk.

I went inside and roused Mother from her bed. Placing the sack in her feeble hands, I told her my tale. When I repeated the words of the chant, she closed her eyes and crossed herself several times. Her eyes snapped open, and she dropped the bag to the bed and told me she wanted nothing to do with my ill-gotten gains. I was messing with old power like the Whateley clan had for eons, like the Marshes and those that hadn't gotten away from the sea. She spoke of Revelations and End Times and Damnation.

I admit I scoffed at her silly talk, sea creatures and monsters from our family's past, old tales from generations ago to explain some hereditary defects in our clan, and fiction from a Bible I no longer believed in. Back outside in the open air and standing near my prized beanstalk, which could feed the community for weeks to come, I opened the burlap bag and gasped.

It was filled with the round stones, dozens of them, and not a single gold piece. In utter frustration, I threw the sack as far as I could, and looked up to see if I could reclimb the stalk and find the real gold.

The sound of ripping ground startled me. Where I'd tossed the bag, I could see the stones leaking out and even moving inches at a time, some slipping into the overturned dirt. Where they disappeared, a new beanstalk, black as night, twisted up from the ground and rose into the sky until I could no longer see the top.

Dozens of them blocked the sun from my eyes, surrounding the shanty as the stony seeds crawled from the sack and sunk into the ground. I heard the horses and the Call of their Riders, and my heart sank.

They would hunt me.

I'd like to say I did what any good son would do and went inside and saved my mother, but you know if you have these pages that I ran. Like a coward, I fled, skirting Dunwich and moving ever inland. I could hear the horsemen behind me, just beyond sight. I've never seen the ocean again, for in my nightmares, the waves call to me. I am afraid of the goats that roam this region and of the Midwest I currently reside in as well for some crazed reason. I imagine it is because of the chanting I still hear nightly. It will not fade, and some nights, it is as though they stand at my window and call me back to the dark beanstalk to join them.

I pray in death I will not join them but go to the one true God.

I've been praying to and wished I'd never stop believing in and hope He saves my soul from the chanting hordes. And from the pestilence and death that sweeps inexorably toward me, borne on the backs of apocalyptic steeds.

"Ever Their praises and abundance to the Black Goat of the *Woods*. *Iä!* Shub-Niggurath! Iä! Shub-Niggurath! The Black Goat of the Woods with a Thousand Young!"

I end this tonight and will leave this suicide note with the desk clerk and the envelope sealed and addressed to my poor mother if she yet lives after all these weeks.

IN THE SHADE OF THE JUNIPER TREE

J. P. HUTSHELL

Based on the Juniper Tree by Philipp Otto Runge

ONCE UPON A TIME, a person could look to the sky and be comforted by the knowledge that things were exactly as they should be. Once, it was that way, but no longer.

The world is blighted, and those who live within it are different somehow. Strange things creep within the woods. Men look about their surroundings, confused and afraid, a note of insanity hinting in their eyes. Prayers go unanswered, and I am afraid they are heard by the creeping things, which laugh and blaspheme.

It began with something as simple as a wish.

In the foothills of the Smokey Mountains, where both my husband and I were born and raised, life was simplicity itself. You lived by the land, and in turn, the land lived by you. Most folks were content; they lived within the means the Lord dealt them.

Olan Miller was our closest neighbor, and he lived a mile away.

Olan and his older brother, Elias, had fought in the war. Elias never made it through his first skirmish; he was run through by a Yankee bayonet. Their daddy, Alvin, died not long after Olan made it home, some say from a broken heart. It was no secret Alvin favored his eldest boy. Most folks thought the idea of him bequeathing all that fine land to Olan was what did the old devil in.

But that's just talk.

Olan was nearing forty and had taken a notion to marry. After a month of courting a young and lovely girl from across the ridge, named Molly Scripps, he married her. Molly was about fifteen and had the sense of one much younger. But that was all right. She was smart enough to cook and help Olan tend the land, and what she didn't know, she soon learned fast.

I took an immediate liking to the girl.

Molly usually hiked up to the house on Sundays and rode with us to church. She was a wonder with my children, and I often felt they were the only reason she made the long trek through the woods.

Why, she acted like a kid herself, running and chasing the girls. Olan refused to enter the Lord's House and kept to himself on Sundays.

I suspected he took to drink while Molly was away, but I never said anything about it. Molly was so enamored with my children I had to ask her what her and Olan's plans were in that regard.

"Well, I don't rightly know," she told me. "Olan got an injury down there during the war and says that he ain't up to doing it no more."

Served me right for being nosy. I changed the subject. That night, after the girls went to bed, I told my husband, Isaac, and he said Olan took a bullet right in the testicles. The bullet blew one completely off and mangled the other. The doctors had to castrate him like a gelding.

For the second time that day, I wished I had kept my mouth shut. It set me to thinking, and I got a little sad about it. Molly was young and quite beautiful, hair like corn silks and skin as white and pure as the face on a porcelain doll. Olan was a good-looking man even if he was rough around the edges. They would have made beautiful children together. But they seemed to love each other, and I guess that's enough to sustain through any tribulations.

Some time passed since I asked her about having children, so it caught me off guard when she brought it up one day while we washed clothes under the shade of the juniper tree.

A sizable and steady branch flowed between Olan's property and our own, creating a natural property line. Olan planted tobacco on his side, and Isaac had corn on ours, leaving about twenty feet on each side of the branch barren. Both men kept their side of the creek cut down and free of vegetation except for that old juniper tree. It was about sixty feet tall and a bit ragged, but it provided a pleasant shade.

After Sunday worship, Molly and the girls often conspired to coordinate our washing days so we could all meet up at the creek. The girls would mostly frolic in the water, catching crawdads and splashing each other, leaving Molly and I to the work.

"Do you think the Lord will see fit to bless me with a child?" she asked.

"Well honey, I can't rightly say. I reckon stranger

things have happened," I said, not wanting to hurt her feelings. So innocent and naïve, she near broke my heart.

"Olan told me it ain't gonna happen and for me to get them fool ideas out of my head. He said the Lord ain't so much on the giveth, more about the taketh away."

I didn't know how to respond to that, though I thought it had the taint of blasphemy to it. Then again, I suppose I could see Olan's point of view. Men folk were awful proud about such things; proud of their tools whether used on the farm or in the bedroom.

Molly was washing one of her Sunday dresses, a white one that Olan paid a pretty penny for, and going at it on the scrubbing board like she was racing the devil. She seemed frustrated—I knew Olan's words had stung her—and in her anger, she skinned her knuckle.

She jerked her hand back, inspected her knuckle, and grinned at her carelessness. A single droplet of blood fell onto the white fabric, and it blossomed like a rose opening up to kiss the sun. Molly was transfixed by the spreading stain. "If I could only have a child as white as snow and red as blood," she said, smiling while fat tears welled in her eyes.

***

As the years passed, things continued as they always had, and Molly seemed content to be childless. I guess you could say she shared mine, and I was more than happy to oblige. Three girls were a handful, and Molly was all too glad to keep them occupied whenever the chance arose. I don't know who enjoyed it more: Molly or my girls.

And then came the day that little imp of a man came around peddling his poison.

IN THE SHADE OF THE JUNIPER TREE

He came up on a covered wagon pulled by two mules one evening in the late summer, and my girls rushed to look at it. The word "Necronomicon" was painted on its side in bold red letters. The little man got down from his wagon when he saw us come down from the porch. He was a squat and bespectacled man, whose top hat and fancy tie looked like they had seen better days. His white shirt was near saturated with sweat, producing the beginnings of the latest in a long series of stains. The little man held his hands behind his back and started talking. He was a fast-talking Yankee and claimed he was from a university in Arkham, Massachusetts. Miskatonic, he called it.

My husband pointed to those red letters on his wagon and asked him what kind of word it was. The man laughed and said it was the only word that mattered.

"Yes sir, that word is the name of a book, maybe the finest ever written," the toad-like man said.

"I wouldn't reckon it's no better than the Good Book," my husband told him.

"Oh no, there's not anything sweeter to soothe the nerves than the Psalms, sir. But this here book can do things. Miraculous things."

"Well, let's take a look at this miracle book," Isaac said.

"I can't do that. It is a very old and rare book. I am merely selling copies of certain passages to suit your wants." My two youngest daughters, Elle and Sarah, were hiding behind me and clinging to my apron, shy at the man. My eldest daughter, Mary, stood beside me and pulled at my sleeve so hard my neck nearly cracked.

"Momma," she whispered. "That man smells like a fish." I shushed her but had the same thought the moment I caught wind of him.

The little man pulled several papers from a fancy leather satchel and handed them to Isaac. Isaac recoiled as soon as he looked through them, curling up his nose.

"Godammit, mister—you been soaking them papers in a pond or something? Hell, they ain't even in English." He quickly handed the papers back to the man and ran his thumbs under the straps of his overalls. That was his signal he was done chatting on the matter.

"Latin. It's in Latin. Well, most of it anyway. That's what I did at the university, translated the book into English. It didn't . . . work right. It's been said that the original words were carved onto stone back when the world was nothing but swamp and gas. It has been translated ever since, passed on through various cultures and societies, weakening a little with each rewriting. I guess the Latin is the last pass the old boy can stand. But those words aren't too hard to say, and I would be glad to give you a quick tutoring."

Sweat stood on the man's forehead, and he wiped at it with the back of his left hand. The fingers were webbed, and the whole hand had a sickly blue tint to it. All three of the girls gasped in unison.

"I think you better ease on down the road a ways. We ain't got no use for witchery here, friend. Fact of business, I think you're gonna be wasting your time lingering in these parts all together. We are simple folks around here. Simple *Christian* folks," Isaac said with that familiar tone of finality.

"Very well, sir. But what if you were to have trouble with your crops or one of those fine daughters comes down with the pox, wouldn't you like some insurance for some future calamity?

"Simply tell me of your dreads and worries, and I will copy an appropriate passage from the book. For a reasonable fee, of course," the man said, pushing his luck and my husband's patience. Isaac's ears were getting red.

"Look here, shitbird, the best thing for you to do is climb up on that wagon and get the hell off my property. I've asked you nice-like. If I have to ask you again, you're gonna have to use them stinking papers to wipe up the shit I stomp out of you."

"What is that saying you people have? You can lead a horse to water, but you can't make him drink. Well, in the end, you will beg to drink." Without another word, the man quickly hopped up onto the wagon seat and made his way down the road. The way he jumped into that wagon gave the impression that he was well practiced in being run off. I admonished Isaac for speaking harshly in front of the girls, but I was glad he did.

"Lord, I hope Molly's got enough sense to run him off," I said.

"If Olan ain't laid-up drunk, I imagine he'll do a fine job of it. And even if he is drunk, I expect he'll 'rouse when he hears that Yankee's mouth."

He had a good point, and it laid my mind at ease. But what a queer thing for a man to peddle: pages copied from an old book, and one not even in English.

***

A month passed since that peddler come by, and we

had plenty other things to occupy our minds: crops had to be harvested and prepared for the winter, wood needed to be cut and stacked, and the girls trekked two miles a day to school and back. Mary was ten and old enough to look after the other two, but I walked with them anyway that first week. Those girls were more than a handful, and I missed them dearly during the week.

We didn't see Molly during that month and often wondered about her. Our weekly churching was put on hold, being that the preacher, L. B. Collins, had caught himself on fire trying to testify to some moonshiners. I aimed to ask Olan if she was okay, but Isaac said he had hired his tobacco farming out to colored field hands. On our monthly wash day—a chore I did a lot quicker without the girls—a large and jovial black woman greeted me down at the branch. I was puzzled, so I enquired about Molly. The woman laughed a great bellow that echoed across the hills.

"Why, Miss Molly is with child," she said.

"What?"

"Oh yes. She said I might see you or your girls. She told me to tell you that she wanted to told you herself, but Mister Olan got her taking it easy."

"Well . . . I swear." I wanted to ask her how in the world that could be with Olan's "problem" but didn't have the nerve. "Could you tell her the girls and I might come down Saturday to visit?"

"Yes ma'am. She done told me to tell you to come down anytime."

"How is Olan taking the news?"

"Mister Olan's beside his self with joy. He done give up the devil's elixir and took to studying the Good Book," she said.

IN THE SHADE OF THE JUNIPER TREE

Two miracles in one day, I thought. A man with Olan's problem might suspect their wife of slipping into adultery; apparently, Olan had seen it for what it was: a true miracle. Poor Molly would never do such a thing, but some men are prone to jealousy and let it cloud their minds no matter how outlandish. But to inspire Olan away from the drink and into the Bible, that was indeed a double dose of good news.

I told Isaac the news, and he seemed happy for them. He joked and said Olan must have a little juice left in his root. Isaac never let on, but I knew he'd taken a shine to Molly. When I told the girls, they—of course—went wild and started thinking up names and schemes. They chattered all evening, so much so that Isaac had to half-heartedly threaten them with a belt.

That Saturday, me and the girls marched down to see her. She was in high spirits and hugged me until my breath was strained. Even Olan gave me stout hug. We all talked until it was near dusk. As she embraced me again before we left, I smelled a faint odor I hadn't noticed before. Something indistinct, but it reminded me of rank water.

I put it out of my mind and gathered the girls for the walk home.

***

Nine months passed quickly, and spring arrived. The girls were out of school, and planting needed to be done, but thoughts of birth and babies occupied our minds. What a fine time to have a child, I thought: born in the season when the Lord's good creations sprang from the desolation of winter.

One evening, while we sat on the porch after a hard day of work, we heard a panicked hollering come from down the road. It was Alvernia, the colored woman Olan hired to help Molly. I had grown quite fond of her, and we moved our wash area upstream a ways where flat rocks stretched into the sun. Alvernia claimed one of the Negro field workers had seen a haint dancing round the juniper tree late one night. She laughed it off but said it was not wise to take any chances.

I didn't mind; the work had to be done regardless of the location, so I placated her.

She was standing in the middle of the road about fifty yards away, bent double with hands on knees. I ran to her. Alvernia's mouth was swollen, and one of her eyes was shut and matted. I wondered if Olan had mistreated her.

"What is it?" I asked. "Is it the baby?"

"Lord Jesus. Something's wrong."

I took off running down the road. "Tell my husband to keep the girls at the house," I shouted over my shoulder.

Molly was lying on the bed, cradling a bundle to her bosom. She looked up at me and smiled weakly. Her skin held a bluish tint, and her eyes were yellowed.

"What's wrong, honey?"

"Nothing at all. Look here," she said. Kneeling down close to her, I had to strain to hear, her voice was so low. She held out the bundle to me. "Ain't he beautiful?" I caressed the folds of the blanket, gently digging to look at the child's face. There was nothing there.

"Oh Lord, Molly. What happened?"

"Why nothing. Is that not the most beautiful thing you ever saw?"

She smiled, but her eyes were wild. "Just like I wished for. White as snow and red as blood," she said and began giggling.

"Why yes, honey." I slowly laid the empty wad of blankets close to her exposed breasts. "I do believe it is."

She tucked her left breast into the folds, taking great care to position her nipple just right. "He sure is a hungry one," she said. She laid her head back on the pillow and shut her eyes.

"You just rest now, Molly. Everything is going to be fine."

I laid my hand on her forehead, and it told me what I already knew. She was ablaze with fever. I walked outside to get some sense out of Olan. I found him leaning against the smokehouse, pulling hard at a jug. His eyes were rimmed with redness.

"What happened here, Olan?"

"Damned if I know. She delivered yesterday morning, but it weren't alive. It was a white mess of gristle and blood. I told the colored to bury it underneath that tree by the creek." And with that, he took a long pull from the jug and began laughing. "God has damned me for a fool, and I have damned Him for a cheat."

"Hush that ignorance. You need to sober up and go fetch Doc Wells, or Molly ain't likely to make it through the night." He looked at me with the dumbness of a cow. "Go. Now!"

To my shock, he bounded up and trotted to the barn.

I went back into the house and found some molasses and sulfur, which I mixed together and fed a spoonful to Molly. She barely stirred, but she swallowed the mixture without choking. I used the trusty concoction in winter when Isaac, the girls, or I happened to come down with a feverish crud. I hoped it would work for Molly. A fire blazed in the hearth, and I threw an iron into it, intending to wrap it in a blanket and place it at Molly's feet when it got warm enough.

A sizable pot hung above the fire, suspended by a spit. At least Alvernia had the good sense to try and get some food in Molly, I thought.

Spying inside the pot at the bubbling stew, the smell nearly socked me off my feet. I took a ladle and stirred at it, curious to see what was producing the stench. It was full of bone and sinew; the liquid was a thick, milk-colored slime. A red eye floated to the surface.

I fell back and stifled a scream. Molly whispered some nonsense words, and I went to her, laying my head close to hers. As I concentrated to understand her, the door slung open. Alvernia stood in the doorframe, swaying back and forth, holding an ax handle.

"Get away from her, Miss Thora. She is the mother of devils," she said.

"What—" I said before she cut me off.

"Miss Molly delivered damnation to the world, and—Jesus save me—I helped her."

She took a slow, uneasy step toward me.

"When Mister Olan saw it, he started laughing a high-pitched laugh just like a child would and told me to bury it under yonder juniper tree. He ran out to the smokehouse, and I watched him flop down on the ground with a jug of whiskey in his lap, crying and screaming at the sky. He been there ever since.

"I delivered me plenty of childrens into this world, and I never seen a thing like that. It was white with snow-colored coils wrapped all around it. And it was cold, colder than the creek after spring thaw. Miss Molly insisted to see it, but I told her: 'No, Missus, the Lord didn't see fit to let it live on this Earth right now. He done called it home to Him.' Didn't know what else to say. Just something to soothe her grief a bit. She got mad, saying awful things about the Lord, and snatched that bundle away from me. She smiled at it and held it to her breast. Miss Molly craned her head down and took a bite out of the thing."

She paused moving for a moment, as if she had just made a decision, and then flipped up the ax-handle into both hands. She continued talking, and I didn't interrupt; I hoped it would buy me some time to figure out what to do.

"After a minute or two of chewing at it, she told me to throw it into a pot and cook it. I say, 'no ma'am, that child needs a Christian burial.' She gets mad again and cusses me and the Lord both. She said the paper from the book called for eating the child. 'Flesh of my flesh, blood of my blood, Iä, Iä, Shub-Niggurath.' That's what she said to me; I won't ever forget it."

Alvernia cinched up her grip on the ax-handle. The fingernail of her thumb picked and fidgeted with a splinter. I looked around carefully for something to use as a weapon. A poker stood by the hearth, but it was ten feet away.

"And then she jumps up out of the bed and backhands me to the ground. I been hit before, hit by strong, rough men, but never that hard. She knocked a jaw tooth plum out of my head. I lay on the floor dazed and watched her dump the contents of that bundle into yonder kettle. I thank God I blacked out then."

She took the end of her apron and wiped bloody spit from her mouth. She wobbled but never took her eyes from Molly. I looked over to the bed, and it was still; the rise and fall of breathing was absent. I needed to go and check on her but was afraid to make any movement.

"I come to some time later, and Miss Molly and Mister Olan were sitting at the table eating. Mister Olan went to that kettle for a second helping and said: 'that colored lady can sure cook.' He was drunk as hell and nearly fell down on his way back to the table. Miss Molly was pale and sweating to beat the devil, and I saw her lay back down in the bed. When I felt a little strength come back into me, I ran out and got you.

"They were things along the road. Things whispering to me with voices like dead leaves scraping along the ground. I couldn't see them, but I felt them watching me."

"I think she's dead." I said.

"If she ain't now, she's gonna be." She raised the ax-handle above her head and lunged at Molly. I dove at her and tried to wrestle the weapon from her hands. Our struggle was short-lived; she was at least a hundred pounds heavier than me. She shrugged me off and popped me in the forehead with the butt end of the handle. I fell straight back but remained conscious.

Alvernia looked at me and said she was sorry. She raised the ax-handle high over her head until the end of it scraped the ceiling. As she tensed to bring it down, a sound like thunder shook the house.

Directly following the rumble came a smaller, higher-pitched bark. Alvernia fell to her knees. Blood poured from her throat. Isaac stood in the doorway; a smoking pistol sat alert in his hands.

"What in the name of Hell?"

Alvernia's hands dug at her throat, her mouth working fiercely as though she were trying to say something. And then finally, she fell. Isaac rushed to my side, gingerly looking me over for injuries other than the obvious pump-knot growing on my forehead. I told him I was alright, and he helped me to my feet. The world spun, but I held to Isaac. He helped me walk over to inspect Molly.

She was dead. I cried for her. Cried for all of it.

I decided to say nothing about the boiling pot and what lay within. Molly should rest in peace without that business plaguing her name. I asked Isaac if Olan had passed by the house, and he said he hadn't seen him. Something was pulling at me; I looked down at Alvernia's hand clutching a fistful of my dress. She was on her side, her mouth opening and closing like a dying fish. Her other hand worked out from underneath her side and pulled a crumbled paper from the fold of her apron. I knelt down to her, trying to listen, but the only sound that came was a gurgling whine. The whine turned into a deep rattle, and she moved no more. I took the wrinkled paper from her dead hand.

It had strange writings and symbols drawn onto it, and I remembered the nonsense of the strange little peddler. Marked beside some of the queer words were a few in English: something about black goats with a thousand young and suckling the ghosts of the dead. I wadded it up and threw it into the fire. The flames retreated from it.

"Can you go out and see if you can find Olan? Last I saw of him, he was heading to the barn. I expect he's passed out on the ground somewhere between here and there." Isaac left to look and left me to think.

I went to the stewpot and poured the liquid out the back door, trying my best to keep the bones and such from slipping out. The weeds hissed and withered when the liquid flowed through them. It thundered again. I looked to the clear sky, puzzled at the source of the thunder. I turned back to the tiny thing inside the pot—what was left anyway. It was an impossible mess, but I made out a few features before my nerve gave out: a tiny hand capped by curved, clear claws; a white, bulbous skull with more than two eye sockets; and something very much like leathery wings unfolded from its sides.

Grabbing a blanket from Molly's deathbed, I dumped the thing into it and tied it up. Isaac stumbled through the door. He was terrified. In our years together, I had never seen my husband cower from anything. But now, he looked like he had stared the devil straight in the eyes.

Reflecting back on it now, maybe he did. I went to him.

"What is it?"

"I found him . . . like you said . . . lying out by the barn door . . . "

Isaac was shaking.

"For God's sake, what's wrong?"

"He's dead. Something stepped on him."

His legs gave way, and he dropped to the floor. I told him to sit there and rest for a while. I walked outside toward the barn. I wanted to see for myself. Olan laid face first in the dirt. As I got closer to him, I noticed that his back looked funny, misshapen. I looked down at him. A two-foot-wide semi-circle-like depression had sunken into his back. It was a hoofprint.

I turned back toward the house and saw a great white bird perched on the chimney. It was larger than an owl and looked like it had a mouthful of snakes. Thunder rolled once more, further away, and the bird-thing spread its wings, which stretched the entire length of the house. A crown of blood-red fire floated above its head. The snakes in its mouth writhed, and I heard a voice like water pouring over rocks. It sang:

> "It was my mother who killed me;
> It was my father who ate of me;
> Iä, Iä, Shub-Niggurath.
> All my bones in pieces found,
> Heaven and earth now be bound;
> Iä, Iä, Shub-Niggurath."

It flew off in the direction of the thunder.

***

Alvernia's corpse was taken by the other Negroes who worked for Olan, and I told them to make sure she got a proper Christian burial. I even slipped them some money so they could buy her a nice dress to be buried in. They gave me queer looks, and I can't say that I blamed them. They weren't stupid, and I suppose that bullet-hole in her neck made them suspicious of the white folk around here.

Molly and Olan were buried in the shade underneath the juniper tree. I lay the bundle containing Molly's dead child on top of her in the pine wood coffin. The community grieved for the family as Isaac and I feigned ignorance of the details of that horrid night. Had anyone else known they had eaten the flesh of a stillborn child . . . well, I don't know what would have happened.

We had a new preacher, an educated young man from Virginia by the name of Preston Sharp, who gave a poetic benediction. After the service was over, he looked at the juniper tree and ran his smooth fingers over its trunk. Strange symbols had been carved into the wood, markings matching those on the paper that wouldn't burn. Reverend Sharp said he had seen something like them before. In his travels spreading the Good Word, he had found the wreckage of a wagon at the foot of a steep bluff. A strange book lay amid the debris, but all of the pages were missing.

A few feet away from the wagon, the skeleton of a man lay spread-eagle on the ground. It was picked so clean it shined in the sunlight. As he looked more closely, he noticed symbols—like the ones carved on the tree trunk—etched into the bone. He tried to recite a prayer over the man's body, but the cicadas' hum drowned out his words. He heard a voice like water churning over rocks. It sang to him.

> "Mine mother will slayeth me,
> Mine father will eateth me,
> Iä, Iä, Shub-Niggurath;

IN THE SHADE OF THE JUNIPER TREE

You will pray over bones cast by death,
The words of God betray your breath;
Mother of life, Shub-Niggurath."
***

And now, here I sit, alone with nothing more than the memories of the beginnings of the last days. I often wonder about that little peddler: If the one page he gave Molly could do that much damage, how many more had he spread throughout the world before he died?

I can only speculate, but I suspect it was enough to turn this world into waste. Isaac was never the same after that night—nor was I. At night, he often sat with a far-away look in his eyes, and I would wipe drool from his mouth.

I lost all three of my girls through the years: Mary to pneumonia, Sarah to the pox, and Elle to something in the woods. The men-folk say it was a bear that got her, but a bear doesn't leave a person empty and dried like a corn husk.

After the girls died, Isaac got worse. He rambled about a black goat with eyes like the sun. Ten years ago, he finally put an end to his dementia and hanged himself from a limb on that cursed tree. I am old now. The seasons have grown together, forming something new, something colder. The people, once so proud and good, have taken to madness and murder. The stars do not sit right; and if you look long enough, you can see them moving.

Last night, I heard a singing outside my window. The words were strange at first, but the longer I listened, the clearer they became.

J.P. HUTSHELL

"It was my mother who murdered me;
It was my father who ate of me;
Iä, Iä, Shub-Niggurath.
You who buried flesh under the tree,
Thy time has come, be bound to me;
Iä, Iä, Shub-Niggurath.
That is not dead which can eternal lie,
And with strange aeons even death may die."

I sit waiting and watching as the world dissolves around me.

THE HORROR AT HATCHET POINT

ZACH SHEPHARD

Based on Rumpelstiltskin by the Brothers Grimm

THE LOCALS CALLED the cliff Hatchet Point because it was shaped like an axe blade jutting into the sea. The man in the robe and his dwarf companion called it something else because they knew things the locals didn't.

The perfect night they'd been waiting for was upon them: The clouds were dark sacks full of writhing pythons, the wind a banshee's breath. Hatchet Point cleaved oncoming waves in a spray of black water while distant lightning illuminated the foaming sea.

"Set it down there."

The frail, hunched-over dwarf lowered the sack from his shoulder.

As it touched the ground, something inside emitted a bleat that could scarcely be heard above the storm.

The robed man turned his back to the wind and consulted his book. His lantern light glowed like the lure of a deep-sea predator, a pale yellow against the sky's vast darkness. As he reviewed the steps of the procedure, his companion moved to the edge of the cliff and leaned over.

A lightning strike lit the crashing waves far below, showing the dwarf a glimpse of something dark beneath the water's frothy surface: It was a vague outline that could have been a reef, a whale, or nothing more than his imagination.

"Come, imp," the robed man said. "I'm ready to begin."

And so he did.

Standing at the edge of Hatchet Point, the robed man recited the lines of the ritual: long, archaic words strung together in a spider's web of forgotten language. As time passed, his voice seemed to anger the storm, drawing the lightning closer with every forbidden phrase spoken.

There came a rumble that nearly knocked the dwarf from his feet, as if massive hands beneath the waves had grabbed the roots of Hatchet Point and were dragging it into the ocean. The robed man ignored the quaking earth, raising both arms as he bellowed the final line of the ritual:

"Rise, Father Dagon, Herald of the Great One! Rise and guide those who would serve you!"

The dwarf tossed the sack over the cliff, creating a splash far below, and after that, there was nothing to do but wait.

Time passed, and the robed man's outstretched arms grew tired. A curtain of rain came in from the sea and overtook them. By the time it hit, the ground had long since stopped shaking.

"Miserable abyss!" the robed man said and kicked his lantern over the cliff. "It didn't work!"

The dwarf gazed into the waters below, one hand on his pointed chin as the hungry waves swallowed the lantern's light. "Yes, Master. It would seem the ritual is flawed."

"You!" the robed man said, jabbing a finger at his companion. "This is your fault. You prepared an improper sacrifice."

"The text called for that which gives love and security."

"And you brought a goat!"

"It was a pet to a small girl who loved it, and its milk was sold to pay debts. The sacrifice was hardly in error. Perhaps the incantation was wrong."

"Impossible! I translated the text myself."

"If you'd let me look it over—"

"Enough!" The robed man turned away. "I tire of these repeated failures. You will review the ritual and determine a more fitting sacrifice before we try again."

"But the sacrifice—"

"Was *wrong*. Now go, and get it right this time. I don't care how long it takes you."

Before the dwarf could speak again, his master departed. He stood there alone at the cliff's edge, waiting for a lightning strike that would once more illuminate the waters below; when it came, the dark shape beneath the surface was no longer there.

***

It wasn't in the library. It wasn't in the treasury. It may have been in the king's chambers, but the dwarf hadn't yet gained access to that place and wasn't sure he could—his spells and illusions weren't proving potent enough to fool the minds of the royal guards, and he certainly didn't have the physical strength to overpower them.

So he continued wandering the high halls of the castle, hiding from knights and counselors and nobles as he searched for secret passageways and hidden rooms. Signs of his presence gave way to talk of a haunting ghost, and the dwarf used these rumors to deter those who might discover him.

For weeks, he found little of interest between those white-stone walls until one day, during his search for the thing he was certain the king possessed, he came upon a closed door and heard a soft whimpering. There was no guard, and the lock was simple enough. The dwarf cast a minor spell and let himself in.

She was seated on a low stool before a spinning wheel, weeping into her hands. A single lantern glowed at her feet, its weak light casting sharp shadows against the wall. The young woman's hair was long and dirty, closely resembling the mound of dry straw at her side.

Intrigued, the dwarf stepped inside and shut the door. At the sound of the latch's click, the woman looked up, showing eyes that were moist and red.

"You're not my jailor," she said.

The dwarf ignored her, hobbling over to the spinning wheel. He frowned and gave it an exploratory spin.

"Who are you?"

"Just a curious soul who heard your cries from beyond the door."

The young woman straightened her posture, her eyes opening wide. "You can get through the door?"

"I can do a great many things if I've a mind to." The dwarf picked up a handful of straw, rolled it in his hand. "Why are you locked in this room with no more company than a wheel and straw?"

"My father boasted that I could spin straw into gold, and now, the king wants proof."

"But you cannot do it."

"Of course not. No one can."

The dwarf was no prophet, but his intellect was such that he could oftentimes see the outcome of certain actions many steps in advance. Because of this skill, he detected an opportunity in that small chamber and was able to set a plan into motion.

"Don't be so sure," he told the young woman and held up the bit of straw he'd been toying with. She took the shining object from his hand and marveled at what it had become.

"You can do it!" she said. "You can save me!"

"Indeed I can. But what might I receive in exchange for my services?"

"I would give you my necklace. It's been in my family seven generations."

The dwarf appraised the charm though he cared little for its value and even less for the fact that it was nowhere near as old as the woman believed.

"Very well. Stand aside, and your work will be done."

The dwarf took to the spinning wheel, and before morning came, all the straw had been transmuted to gold. He vanished while the young woman slept, knowing he'd have cause to return soon enough.

***

The robed man waited in a quiet and lonely place, where wisps of fog slithered between gravestones like the tentacles of deep-sea horrors. Before long, the dwarf joined him, emerging from behind a mausoleum under the silver moonlight.

"Master, I've spent many days scouring the castle of King Jordan and may have found what we require to complete the ritual. Unfortunately, it will take time to procure."

"How long?"

"At least nine months if things go as they usually do."

The robed man, coming to understand the dwarf's meaning, nodded slowly. A smile crept up his face, exposing two rows of wicked teeth.

"Very good," he said. "Be gone then, and return when you've progress to report."

The dwarf left with his master's blessing. Alone in the graveyard again, the robed figure started a fire to cook his dinner; he choked only once during the meal and from that point forth was very careful with the finger bones.

***

When the dwarf arrived in the castle on the second night, the young woman was weeping again. She told him that the greedy king, who had promised to release her once she'd completed her initial task, was now demanding that another pile of straw be spun to gold. The dwarf was more than happy to aid her a second time in exchange for a ring he threw into the canals the moment he left.

Then came the third night, when the young woman was assigned a third pile of straw. She had no items left with which to barter.

"I will gladly assist you one last time," the dwarf said, "and you need not pay me now. All I ask of you is your firstborn child, should it ever come to be."

"My child? But—"

"If you refuse and this straw is not gold by morning's light, the king will have you beheaded, will he not?"

"Yes . . ."

"Then it seems the decision is a simple one."

And so it was: The young woman agreed to the dwarf's terms, and he spun one last pile of straw to gold.

The next day, the king was so impressed with the young woman's work he released her from her prison and made her his bride. She was afforded all the luxuries of royalty and was never again asked to spin straw to gold, for she'd made the king rich enough for ten lifetimes.

The marriage ceremony was beautiful, and several weeks later, the queen was with child.

Nine months after, the child was born.

The following night, as the queen slept, a shadow visited her chamber. When she awoke, her child was gone.

***

In the graveyard of the slithering mists, another moonlit meeting was called.

"Do you have it?"

"Nearly, my master."

"Nearly? What do you mean? News throughout the kingdom tells of an infant prince gone missing. I assumed it to be your doing."

"You assumed rightly, Master. But my task is not yet complete."

"I don't like the sound of this, imp."

"Worry not—we've three nights until the conditions are perfect once again. I need time to sort out a few matters."

The robed man reluctantly conceded to his companion's judgment. He turned away, and when he turned back to say one last thing, the dwarf was gone.

***

The queen rocked in her bedchamber's chair, staring blankly at a flickering candle. Behind her, the dwarf hopped down from the window's ledge with a deliberate noise.

"You!" she said and shot to her feet. "Guards! He's return—"

The dwarf gestured, silencing her.

"Please," he said, "there's no need for that. I come in peace."

The queen tried screaming, but no sound emerged. Unable to hear her own voice, she whipped into a panic.

"If you'll promise to be quiet, I'll gladly lift the spell. That way, we can talk about getting you your babe back."

The queen stopped in her tracks and nodded vigorously. The dwarf released his spell, and she gasped with relief.

"My son . . . " she said between heavy breaths.

"Yes. While it's true he's rightfully mine, I've found the jaws of guilt gnawing at my mind of late. As such, I would feel better about all this if I knew you had a fair opportunity to win him back."

"What must I do?"

"Name me."

She gave the dwarf a puzzled look. "Name you?"

"Guess my name within the next three nights, and the child is yours."

"And if I fail? What more do I lose?"

"Nothing. I simply feel as though I took advantage of your unfortunate situation those many months ago, and I'd like to set things right."

Fearing the offer might be withdrawn, the queen greedily accepted. She started right away by rattling off every name in her memory. In time, the dwarf grew tired of her failures and announced his departure. He recommended that the queen engage in some research before he returned.

When the dwarf returned the following night, the queen had a list of obscure names from far-off lands, which she'd read from the covers of her husband's most prized books.

"Heinrich?"

"No."

"Sarataki?"

"No."

"Molotok?"

The dwarf sighed, shook his head. He hardly listened to the next few guesses, but soon enough, something caught his attention.

"Wait," he said. "Repeat the last one."

The queen consulted her list. "Alhazred?"

The dwarf licked his lips, looked away. He scratched the tip of his crescent-moon chin.

"Is that your name?" the queen asked.

"No," the dwarf said. "Not even close. Forgive me, but the hour is late, and sleep calls."

He disappeared out the window, not to be seen again that evening.

***

"Where. Is. The. Child."

"Do not fear, Master. The sacrifice will go as planned."

"And if this woman guesses your name?"

"She will not."

"For your sake, I hope you're correct. You were a fool to offer her this opportunity. Your conscience will be your undoing."

"Worry not, Master. There will be no disappointment."

There followed more assurances from the dwarf, but his master didn't hear them. With the perfect night rapidly approaching, he had other things to worry about.

***

The dwarf normally came at night, but on the final day, he arrived in the queen's bedchamber in the afternoon. He told her he wanted to afford her more time to make guesses, but in reality, he simply had other plans for the evening.

"I've brought more names," the queen said. "I stole a look at my husband's most guarded book—the one written by the mad Arab, which drew your attention last time." She couldn't help but smile, being pleased with herself for having read the dwarf's insecurity on the previous night.

The dwarf shifted on his stool, avoiding eye contact. "Proceed."

The queen recited many names, but it wasn't until she reached the third sheet of her list that the dwarf started paying close attention. He moved to the edge of his seat, growing excited with her subsequent guesses.

"You are Shub-Niggurath, Black Goat of the Woods!"

The dwarf shook his head sharply and urged her to try again.

"You are Nyarlathotep, the Great Messenger! Azathoth, He in the Gulf! Yog-Sothoth, the Key and Guardian of the Gate! Father Zel'Tahga, Herald of the Great One!"

This last name struck the dwarf strongly. He stopped listening and reviewed what the queen had said, rolling the word around in his mind, guessing at its spelling and proper pronunciation. Yes—that was it. He was certain.

After a time, his attention returned to the present, where the queen was still listing names.

" . . . Rumpelstiltskin, Flayer of the—"

"Yes," the dwarf said. "That is my name. Rumpel . . ." He trailed off, not recalling exactly what she'd said. "Very good. You have successfully outwitted me and shall be rewarded accordingly." And with that, he gave the queen instructions on where to find her lost son. He then left her chamber, never to return.

***

Hatchet Point was as it had been nearly a year earlier, with a dark, violent storm whipping the world into chaos. There were rains in the distance, but they hadn't yet reached the cliff, leaving the dwarf and his master dry.

"You've brought the child," the robed man said. "Let me see it."

The dwarf dropped his sack on the ground. Something inside honked.

With a look of angry confusion in his eyes, the robed man pushed the dwarf aside and ripped the sack open. A goose thrust its beak out and nipped one of his fingers.

"Miserable abyss!" he said, flicking the pain from

his hand. The dwarf secured the sack before the bird could escape.

"You brought a goose! You were supposed to bring the child! Is this what I waited nearly a year for?"

"Indeed it is, Master. As I told you on that night long ago, our error was not in the sacrifice. The ritual called for that which gives love and security, and the goat surely fit that description. This goose does so as well, for it was beloved by a small child, and its eggs were used as currency by the family."

The robed man spun away and yanked at his hair. "You're a fool, imp! If this sacrifice is no better than the last, how can the ritual possibly succeed?"

"It will succeed because I obtained from the queen exactly what I'd been searching the castle for."

The robed man faced the dwarf again.

"My sources had informed me that King Jordan possessed a copy of Alhazred's *Necronomicon*. I wasn't able to get at the book myself, nor was I able to bribe anyone who could—but while I was roaming the halls one day, I stumbled upon a different opportunity.

"It was not difficult to manipulate the girl into a position of royalty and win her firstborn. Once that was done, I gave her the chance to reclaim her babe and listened as she recited the Old Ones' names. Soon enough, she came upon he who was described as the Herald of the Great One—we call him Dagon, but that is the name given him by mortals. To the others of his order, he's known as Zel'Tahga. Your previous incantation was wrong, Master."

The robed man turned away. He rubbed his cheeks with both hands.

"The incantation," he mumbled, his voice lost under the blast of the storm. "Yes—yes! That's it!"

And so, without so much as thanking the dwarf, the robed man recited the ritual, substituting the new name into the final line:

"Rise, Father Zel'Tahga, Herald of the Great One! Rise and guide those who would serve you!"

The dwarf cast the sack into the night, and the pair was left to wait.

A rumbling came as it had before. The dwarf peered over the ledge, and within a bolt's flash, he saw the sea popping and exploding as though a thousand sharks thrashed beneath its surface. He wondered what the storm must look like to the marine creatures below, staring through their blue-black skylight at the flashing chaos overhead. The dwarf imagined the sound of crashing waves to submerged ears and envisioned himself as a tiny speck within the perpetual night of the ocean, floating weightlessly in the blue void while something larger than any castle strode silently across the seafloor behind him, a quiet and terrible shadow in that quiet and terrible place.

When the lightning flashed again, the waters had changed—waves crashed violently into the edge of Hatchet Point as they always did, but their motion was no more than what might be seen on an ordinary day. Something was wrong.

"Imp," the robed man said. "Tell me what's happening. Now."

The dwarf scratched his head, staring into the waves below. "I—don't know, Master. You pronounced the name perfectly, to the best of my knowledge. The sacrifice, it must have—"

The master screamed in agony as the quarrel struck his shoulder blade. He turned to see the king standing there, the blue and gold of his tabard flapping in the wind. He carried weapons for combat but wore no armor, indicating he'd left the castle in a hurry.

Rather than reloading the crossbow, he dropped it and drew his sword.

"That book was not meant for mortal eyes," he said, striding forward. "Not mine or anyone else's! Do you realize what you could have raised here this night?"

The master tried to conjure a spell but wasn't fast enough. There was a brief, purple-green flash as the incomplete magic fizzled harmlessly from his fingertips, and in that same moment, the king's sword bit deeply into his collarbone. He screamed and fell and could not rise again before the king ran him through.

"And you," the king said, pointing his sword at the dwarf. "You are the one who abducted my son!"

Knowing he could never summon a spell in time, the dwarf chose to defend himself with his tongue.

"My lord, surely the queen explained to you the circumstances. I'd won the child fairly, and yet, I gave her an additional opportunity to win him back simply because—"

The sword shot through his belly in one quick thrust. The king yanked it away, and the dwarf fell onto his side at the tip of Hatchet Point.

"The souls of this land are fortunate," the king said. "Had you performed your ritual with competence, you'd have unleashed an evil that would spare none—not even its supposed worshippers. What did you expect to do after looking into the yellow lamps of the

Herald's eyes? You'd be driven mad if you weren't devoured first."

The king shook his head. "Farewell, dwarf. May your body rot in the realm of your beloved."

With that, the king placed his boot on the dwarf and shoved. The frail, bleeding figure rolled over the cliff without a fight, crashing into the waters below.

The king cleaned his blade on the other man's robe, sheathed it, and walked away. He mounted his horse and was quickly gone, glad to be free of the eldritch feeling that permeated Hatchet Point.

It wasn't long before the rains came, their cold beads splashing the robed man's face and waking him. Though the wound in his gut was mortal and he would not survive the night, he had enough strength left to drag himself to Hatchet Point's edge, where he peered over and searched for his lost companion.

When the lightning flashed, the dwarf, who could spin straw into that which brings love and security to all, was nowhere to be found. Instead, the robed man caught sight of something else beneath the sea: It was a dark shape, larger than the kingdom's largest castle, and when the light that had shown it faded, all that was left was a pair of dim, yellow lamps climbing steadily to the surface.

THE MOST INCREDIBLE THING

BRACKEN MACLEOD

Based on Det Utroligste (The Most Incredible Thing)
by Hans Christian Anderson

MARCUS CARTER WAS happy to finally be out of the August heat. The theater hallway was not necessarily cool but was somewhat air conditioned and a welcome respite to the tropical late summer humidity infecting the New England climate like a fever. Ahead of him, a queue of people lined the backstage corridor, practicing adroit movements, warming voices honed by years of careful discipline, and, like him, clutching items of handcrafted elegance. Behind him, many more waited, all possessing some form of wonderment to submit to the judgment of the producers and posterity.

The cattle call for *The Most Incredible Thing* had been made after last season's finale of *America's Finest Talent*. The prize at the end of this new show was the same as any promised by the host of other reality programs: an exorbitant sum of money and a brief period of notoriety. But Marcus knew his success would be different. The winner of *The Most Incredible Thing* would gain more than fleeting fame. He would be elevated, revered, culturally embraced. He would be Marcus. Like Galileo or Einstein or Oppenheimer, his would be a single name that would echo through time.

He took a half step forward as the line inched ahead. Clutching the box cloaked with a black velvet shroud, he glanced around again at the people who thought any talent they could perform with their bodies could possibly win. The idea this might be any other talent contest disheartened him. There were shows for physical and artistic talent; this was about changing the way people thought—making the world an entirely different place with one thing of perfect beauty and refinement.

"So what have you got under there?" the man in line behind him asked. Marcus clutched the box a little tighter and looked his questioner up and down. The man stood there, hands empty and hanging at his sides, looking like he'd intended to audition for one of those outdoor survival shows. He wasn't singing scales or standing on his hands while reciting some jejune verse. He just waited, doing nothing.

"It's the most—"

"Yes, yes. The most incredible thing." The man waved his hand dismissively.

"What about you?" Marcus asked.

"What about me?"

"What's your thing?"

The man smiled. "You'll see."

Marcus turned back, trying not to feel unnerved by the presence behind him. He didn't care what useless talent anyone else had to offer. No one could top the box. No one.

The line moved forward another step. The distant sound of laughter and intermittent applause carried down the theater hallway. He'd always dreamed of being talented. As a child, Marcus took piano and guitar lessons and dance lessons and even a few martial arts classes. As a young man, he'd enrolled in writing workshops and photography seminars and learned to paint. But nothing he created elevated him above the standard practitioner of any of those pursuits. He was painfully average and always had been. Whenever he'd failed to impress with either his grades or his acumen, his mother sarcastically pronounced, "Well, it's a good thing he's pretty." Of course, everyone knew he was plain. At least that's how he interpreted his less-than-exceptional romantic performance. Sure, he could get dates. But he rarely got *second* dates and even more rarely got laid. *The Most Incredible Thing* would change that. When everyone saw what he'd created with his hands—with his mind—women and men both would flock to him. He'd have his pick. When they saw what he'd done, he'd be handed the keys to the kingdom. The rewards of being an Edison, a Gates, or a Jobs awaited.

After his first dream of it, he'd awoken in a panic. It had all felt so real to him he searched his apartment for the missing device. But of course, it was nowhere to be found; he hadn't yet built it. The memory of its form faded, leaving only the recollection of parts to gather. Succeeding nights and additional dreams passed, and he began building the box, not understanding its function until further somnambulant visions enlightened him like an unfolding tale. The box had taken months to fashion. Months of growing fear and frustration as the invisible—but compellingly felt—end of the project eluded him. And when it was finally finished, the call was announced on the television as though the universe had been waiting for just the right moment for him to unveil his creation. As though the stars had perfectly aligned and offered all the secrets of the ancient universe to him.

With a finger along the outside of the velvet drape, he traced the design engraved in the top of the box. He felt along the single straight line up the center, backtracking to take each of the shorter five detours off the main branch—two strokes on one side, three on the other, like an evergreen twig or a primitive cuneiform. A tingle danced up the back of his hand into his wrist as he caressed his creation. Behind his eyes, a flash of his original inspiration played out like a vision. He marched forward a single, glacial pace at a time with the other contestants as his mind wandered the hallways of the dream monastery resting on a forgotten plateau—the lonely place upon which he'd based his creation. Navigating each darkened passageway more by feel than sight, his fingers dragging along the walls, reading the frescos like Braille, sparking flashes of inspiration in his mind until finally, he came to the central chamber where the full blueprint for his apparatus was handed down to him as a revelation. From atop his throne, the priest in the yellow silk mask raised a hand to him and spoke.

"I said, next! You, there," a voice ripped him back through time to the present. Marcus stared through the back stage door at the woman with the clipboard gesturing for him to step forward. "Come on. You're next. We don't have all night." Marcus followed her to the edge of the curtain and peeked out. Bright lights backlit the judges at their table facing the stage. Behind them, he heard the murmur of an unseen audience as a performer finished her act. Her final note echoed through the hall, which erupted with cheers and applause. When the adulation died down, the judges spoke to the singer, assuring her that she was indeed very talented, and based on their assessment, she would be going on to the main competition. "Congratulations!" one shouted.

"I thought this was just an audition," Marcus said to the stage manager.

"It is. It's a live audition in front of an audience. Didn't you read the materials?"

"The what?" Marcus remembered being handed several sheets of paper to sign when he'd first arrived. He'd signed them and handed them back perfunctorily, not caring what he was signing away. Only that the world be allowed to see what he'd made.

"Never mind." The woman drew a finger down her checklist and said, "Marcus Carter, right?"

"Yes'm. That's me."

"When I give you the sign, you walk out and do your thing, okay? What exactly is your thing, anyway?" Marcus held up the box. "Okay. A magic routine. Whatever." The stage manager touched a finger to the side of her headset and barked something about needing an exhibition table. By way of reply, her headset emitted a short blast of chirps and beeps.

"All right, Kreskin," she said. "You're up." With a

hand in the center of his back, she shoved him out into the light. "Just relax, and you'll do fine."

Marcus stumbled forward, greeted by a polite smattering of applause from an audience clearly disappointed he was not another dancer or warbly singer. He took a deep breath and stepped forward into the spotlight. He reluctantly set the box down on the newly placed presentation table. Taking a deep breath, he introduced himself. After a moment of banter with a surgically beautiful judge, she asked, "Well, what have you got for us, Marcus?"

"I made *this*," he said, pulling the shroud away with a practiced flourish, revealing a glass and brass box. Its hyperbolic geometry defied notions of weight and solidity. Despite the glass and metal, it looked as though it might float away or disappear in a puff of smoke if a breeze blew too hard across the stage. A pair of rotating arms adorned the front between two, foot-tall rococo doors. Marcus caressed the copper touch-strip symbol along the top of the box, and the arms began moving, sweeping around and clicking a quiet Arabic *iqa'at* musical rhythm. When they came together the first time, the right door of the device opened. A discordant melody began playing in time to the whipping metronome arms. Out spilled a red luminescence, bathing the judges in a crimson bath of radiance that exposed all their scars and stretches. No trick of makeup or camera angle could prevent them from appearing as they really were before the object.

Stalking from the door, a lone clockwork man in Bedouin clothes twirled in a gentle arc, clutching to his chest a tiny, leather book emblazoned with minuscule Arabic script. The light shifted from red to white as he opened the book and beheld its contents. Following the man, a pair of black, faceless creatures swept out to lead him away with tickling fingers and beating wings spinning him into the door on the left. The swinging hands on the face of the device clicked and swept as more characters danced out of the doors, each successive group greater in number and character.

Dreams and nightmares spilled from the box, gracefully moving from right to left in a carefully choreographed reproduction of the sublime creatures of his dreams. Each set of beasts that emerged was more elaborate than the last—curling tentacle and blinking eye and gnashing, great teeth in hungry, consuming mouths—until finally, thirteen brilliant points of light emerged from the doors and paused, shining in a small constellation above the box. Beneath the stars appeared the figure of a golden pharaoh holding crook and flail.

The audience, which had been holding a collective breath, gasped and sighed at the sight. The judges stood up and applauded. The looks of astonishment on their faces meant more to Marcus than their ovation. Behind him, he heard the stage manager let out a long-held breath.

He'd won.

He might have destroyed the narrative arc of the season, but he was sure they'd find a way to feature his creation as a show of its own. He'd take them back through the process of how he'd made the box. He could tell them all about its inspiration—the dreams of the dusky man who helped him conceive its mechanical wonders. And when they knew everything about how it had been made, he'd show them the final thing it did—the one amazing feature he was holding back.

"That was remarkable. What . . . What is it?" a judge asked.

"I call it the Clockwork *Kitab al-Azif.*"

"Well, I'm not sure how we can follow that up. I don't know about the others, but I think you may have created the most incredible thing. You are definitely progressing to the next round." The crowd applauded. Marcus stood in stunned silence. The next round? The *next* round! How could they think this is anything but the show-stopper it *is?* Marcus heard the stage manager behind the curtain bark, "Cut to commercial," into her headset. *No! Not a commercial. This is my time in the spotlight. I've won!*

The contestant waiting in the wings behind Marcus stalked out onto the stage. Marcus had the urge to yell at him, to warn him away from *his* moment. This contest was over. Everyone else could see it; why couldn't he?

"Excuse me, sir," the woman with the clipboard said. "But you need to wait your turn," she said before stopping dead in her tracks and backing away with her hands held up. A low murmur of nervous laughter rippled through the audience. Marcus turned back to his box and slid his finger along the strip, turning it off and sending the stars and pharaoh back inside. Before he could whip the velvet cover back over his device, he heard a shriek from the judges' table, followed by a collective gasp from the audience.

Marcus spun around to give the contestant a piece of his mind. "Get off my stage you—" The man raised the fire axe over his head and swung it down hard.

Marcus stood frozen in place, wanting to throw himself in front of his delicate creation but unable to move to confront the inevitability of the axe. It crashed through the top of the box and lodged inside. The jarring clatter of shattered glass on the floor and a screech of metal on metal echoed across the stage as the man pried his axe from the clockwork box. The table upon which it sat toppled, sending the box crashing to the floor. The man swung the blade down again and again. Marcus felt each blow land as the impact of the axe vibrated through the floorboards, into his feet, and up into his heart. He stared, frozen in shock, as his work was reduced to nothing.

The audience sat in stunned silence, uncertain how to respond without the blinking lights above them that commanded laughter, applause, silence. A few people called out their derision and others their support. It wasn't until a pair of armed security guards appeared at the skirt of the stage that it seemed most spectators realized this was not a part of the act. A low murmur rose from the orchestra seats as several people declared their intention to get away before things became worse.

Outside, Marcus heard a distant peal of thunder. There hadn't been a forecast of rain, but it was only appropriate the sky weep for his loss. His blueprint for the box had been his dreams. He knew those dreams would never return—he would never be able to build another thing like his music box. He fell to his knees among the ruins of his ambition and began brushing the debris toward himself as though he could wish it all back together. "All gone, all gone," he whispered.

The guards shouted for the man to relinquish his

axe. The man stood tall, held the red-handled tool above his head, and proclaimed, "If I can destroy a thing, I am greater than it. I am greater than that box. I am greater than its creator. *I* am the most incredible thing!"

A judge plucked his microphone from the lapel of his shirt and, holding it up to his mouth, spoke deeply and calmly, trying to placate the man. "Yes. Yes. You have done a great thing." The other judges held up their hands and backed away toward the wings.

"No!" Marcus shrieked. The man smiled and winked at him as though weighing whether he should cut Marcus down as well.

The thunder grew louder. The audience hushed as the judge did his best to talk the man into surrendering. "To destroy such a work of art is indeed the most incredible thing we've ever seen. Please, put the axe down, and let us declare you the winner."

An ear-dulling roar shook the auditorium, and the lights went black. The audience shrieked. Without the spotlights shining in his eyes, Marcus could see them pushing and shoving to get into the aisles and away. A booming voice from backstage carried over the panic; the crowd hushed and stilled as the pharaoh from Marcus' dreams stepped out of the gloom. Dressed in a golden-colored suit, he seemed to materialize from the blackness. Several stage lights above him flared like the stars from the box, and he stepped into the ring of radiance. The effulgence of the dark-skinned man eclipsed that of Marcus' box, and he felt ashamed to look into the face of his inspiration. He diverted his gaze to the shadow spreading out from behind the dream figure.

He couldn't understand what he beheld, however. The crisscrossing patterns of the spotlights gave the man's shadow an amorphous appearance—three-legged with a tentacle for a head and arms as long as he was tall, ending in great claws.

Marcus despaired.

The other contestant dropped his axe and fell to his knees on the opposite side of the kingly figure. The man in gold looked down at the contestant and smiled. "You can ruin a clockwork box, but the spirit within it cannot be crushed. Released? Yes. But that which is eternal can never be broken by man."

The man in gold touched the contestant with a finger, and Marcus' mechanical figures, full-sized and flesh and blood, emerged from the wings, surrounding them. The mad Arab with his book and countless other figures, winged and tentacled, snapping jaws and clacking claws, tickling, chomping, and stomping fell upon the contestant, breaking and tearing him.

Marcus' mind broke in concert with the other man's body, and he laughed madly as the crowd shrieked in terror and scrambled for the emergency exits, trampling one another to escape the horrors visiting the stage. Marcus looked down at his ruined box, dulled and empty doors hanging open. He tried to scoop up as much of it as he could, to cradle his beloved device, but his arms passed through the debris, and it remained in pieces.

The dark man turned his attention to Marcus. "My little clockmaker," he said, his voice shaking the walls of the ancient theater.

"We have taken our vengeance upon the destroyer of your device. And now, bow down to your lords, the

Outer Gods resplendent." It smiled at him with a gaping mouth filled with far too many teeth. A droning musical note reverberated through the hall. The spotlights above the golden man shattered and rained down fiery shafts of light that pierced through the veil of his appearance, revealing the shadow-glimpsed beast beneath, and the rest of Marcus' mind slipped.

He scrambled on his hands and knees through the jagged wreckage of his device toward the backstage doors. None of the other contestants, long since fled, barred his way. He crawled then ran down the hall toward the double doors through which he'd first been ushered to present his marvel to the world. Bursting outside, an icy wind blew, chilling him. He ran for home, glimpsing the shambling beasts of his box in the shadow of every alley and corner—some waiting, some devouring, all indescribably horrible and hungry and terrible in their debasement of form and movement. Marcus stopped and stood immobile while delicate August snowflakes colored his black hair white. Across the Charles River, above the darkened skyline in the distance, clouds churned and blazed with flashing lighting, illuminating the descending, great maw of some ur-god older than the stars its chaos eclipsed.

A great, descending tentacle mouth screamed with the unfathomable obscenity of the audient void.

And he saw that it was the most incredible thing.

LET ME COME IN!

SIMON YEE

Based on The Three Little Pigs by James Halliwell-Phillipps

THE WOLF WALKED into the cemetery, looking for something edible he could scavenge in the open graves. At the end of the war, there were a lot of bodies put in the ground in haste. Sometimes, the cemeteries did not have the manpower to bury the dead deep enough in the ground, or they would pile bodies under a mound for the economy of space. The taste of putrescence was never good, so the wolf was not big on eating carrion, but beggars couldn't be choosers. Somewhere, when evolution had set things on an even platform between man and beast, a war had broken out, engulfing the world into a cataclysm. The Great War, "they" called it, had destroyed humanity and most of the anthropomorphic denizen, leaving a wasteland for none to claim. The wolf was a survivor and walked the desolate plains carrying a duffle bag full of weapons collected on the battlefields either to use for barter or for self-protection.

LET ME COME IN!

The scent in the air was stale and old. The wolf looked around at the headstones, the type with a vertical face that stood more than two feet off the ground. Not a good sign. It meant the cemetery was an old one that housed corpses dead before the twentieth century, potentially with inedible, embalmed flesh. The wolf huffed and puffed in disappointment.

Then to his surprise, he got a whiff of something delicious in the air. Maybe a stew or pot roast cooking slow over an open flame? His mouth watered in the most salacious manner. The scent led him out of the cemetery and into an open grove, where he saw a thatched cottage made of tightly wrapped straw. A cloud of white smoke puffed from the center opening. The wolf dropped his duffel bag and knocked on the door. Waves of pain emanated from his gut as he waited. The door had an odd white marking in the shape of a crooked J with entwined circles.

"Hello, is anyone there?" the wolf inquired. Despite ravenous hunger, he had not lost his sense of decorum. The sound of small footsteps came toward the door, and a pig opened the peephole staring at the wolf. The pig looked pale with an opaque shade of sickly green seething underneath its pallid skin. Its big, bulbous eyes scanned the wolf from head to feet. "Pardon my intrusion, but I'm a weary traveler looking for a meal. I fought in the Great War against the humans and beg you for a bite to eat." The wolf smiled, showing his sharp teeth. The pig recoiled and sneered then spat a greasy, white discharge and closed his peep hole.

"Go away, corpse eater! I know your kind, and you only want to eat my bacon and chops," the pig croaked from behind the door.

"Please let me in!" the wolf begged. "All of our kind have an alliance. You can trust me."

"That alliance died along with the last human. Now, there is nothing but wasteland and the memories of a meaningless war. You only offer my death if I fall for that trick. So fuck off!" cursed the ornery pig.

"But little pig," the wolf said, losing his patience, "little pig, let me come in!"

"Hell no! Not by the hair on my chinny chin chin!"

Despite being a wolf, by nature, he did not want to eat the pig. He was no longer a base animal living feral in the woods. No, he was civilized and had a sense of ethics to guide him.

"You don't scare me! I belong to the heirs of Ib. Vengeance is mine if even the hair on my chin is touched. My brothers and the Great One who watches over us will see to that."

"I don't know anything of Ib or your brothers, but you will let me in now!" the wolf demanded.

"Fuck off, you hairy piece of shit," the pig shot back. "I'll not be intimidated by some desperate wolf looking to bully his way into my house."

The wolf zipped open his duffle bag and pulled out a grenade. He had enough of being Mr. Nice and trying to negotiate a meal. If the little pig wanted a big bad wolf, then he would get a big bad wolf. The wolf stepped back behind a tree for cover and tossed the grenade into the opening on the roof that spewed the white smoke. A second later, the pig ran out of the cottage as an explosion inside collapsed the structure to the ground. The horrified pig looked at the wolf and ran deep into the woods.

The wolf jogged to the cottage to see what food the

pig left behind. Unfortunately, the straw caught fire, and the remnants of the pig's home became an inferno before the wolf could find anything. The wolf huffed and puffed with frustration. *I need to find out where that pig went,* the wolf thought to himself as he tracked the scent and footprints.

The trail led to another cottage made of dried sticks bound together with mud and rope. The wolf sniffed the structure but could not smell anything edible except for the pig inside. No, make that two. His nose and ears picked up the presence of a second pig whispering to the other about the wolf. The soldier in him wanted to honor the alliance and not feast on the lower beings like pigs or cow. Sure, he didn't mind killing them, but the thought of eating the people he fought for and with seemed contrary to his sense of chivalry. Humans were okay to eat; they were the enemy after all.

The door to the stick cottage had the same white symbol he found on the entrance to the straw house. The wolf started to wonder what it meant and found it somewhat eerie to look at. It was not something he was accustomed to seeing from pigs or any creature he had encountered before the Great War.

"I know you're in there, little pigs!" The wolf leaned against the door with his shoulder.

There was shuffling of feet inside the cottage followed by subdued mutterings. Then, the pig spoke. "You tried to kill me with a grenade, wolf. My brother does not want visitors who try to kill their kin. Don't try anything foolish. He was in the war as well and is armed just like you."

"Oh really," the wolf mocked. "Well then, you

should have no fear from me. I mean to come in and have a bite of your food. Be nice, and open the door. It is getting dark, and I am so very hungry."

"No, you are not welcome here!" screamed the pigs.

"Little pigs, little pigs let me come in!" the wolf demanded.

"Not by the hairs on our chinny chin chins," the pigs replied.

"I'll huff, and I'll puff, and I'll blow your house . . ." the wolf said but was cut short by gunfire that pelted the doorframe from inside the house. The wolf ducked and ran back behind the trees for protection. The door of the stick cottage swung open, and a grisly looking old pig with a large, drooping left eye peered out of the house with a rifle. Several shots chipped away at the tree bark above the wolf.

"All I wanted was something to eat, you pigs," the wolf cried as he unzipped his duffle bag. He pulled out an old M47 Dragon anti-tank missile launcher he had been carrying with him. There was only one shot, and he hoped the appearance of the M47 would inspire enough fear in the pigs to quiet their antagonism. As he set up the bipod attachment to the missile launcher, a bullet clipped his ear, making his head jerk back. The wolf checked the wound with his hand and felt the bloody remnants hanging on a small tether of flesh. The wolf yelled in a furious rage, causing the pigs to flee into the forest.

The wolf was blinded by pain and fired the M47 Dragon at the cottage. In a split second, it was eviscerated by an explosion that shook the surrounding trees. The wolf was knocked prone, and when he finally recovered, tiny pieces of wood and mud stuck to his fur. Feeling upset and frustrated, the wolf followed the pigs' trail into the woods.

The woods opened into a dark field with a brick tower on top of a colossal rock monolith set against the bright gibbous moon. The wolf narrowed his eyes and could barely see the silhouettes of the two pigs running into the tower for safety. His attention drifted to a mysterious figure, cloaked in a billowing, dim robe of the night's shadow and standing at the edge of the monolith. Whoever was there did nothing but watch as he advanced to the base of the giant granite mass. The wolf discovered stairs that zigzagged up to the tower. As he started up the steps, he smelled the sweet scent of roasting meat.

Blinded by hunger, he forged his way on in a heated rush. The shadowy image of the person at the edge of the monolith was gone when he reached the top of the rocky monolith. A plume of smoke billowed from the top of the tower. The wolf went to the tower door and knocked. As with the previous cottages, the wolf found the strange white sigil painted on the door. This time, the markings were more distinctive and done with an artistic style.

"Little pigs, little pigs, let me in!" the wolf bemoaned, his wet tongue flaccid over his lips. The wolf paced back and forth, waiting for the pigs, but there was no response. "I'll huff, and I'll puff, and I'll blow your house down."

It was then he heard a soft drumming behind the door, followed by a squeal of something that initially sounded like a pig's whine but changed halfway into gurgling croak unlike anything he had heard. The wolf hesitated, wondering what was going on behind the door.

His blood turned to ice as a disconcerting thud of what sounded like wet flesh falling on cold stone correlated from his mind. Slowly, under the continuous drumming noise, a crackling and sloshing sound flowed from behind the door, unnerving the wolf. The hair on his back stood erect, and his tail curled between his legs. The wolf used all of his willpower to keep himself from whimpering, but the feeling was too overwhelming. Even in war, this didn't happen to him. His base nature sensed a presence of something evil that repulsed him.

The wolf went to the edge of the cliff and looked down at the stairwell leading to the dark forest below. The thought of leaving was stopped by the alluring fragrance of cooked meat that wafted past his nose. The wolf ground his teeth and turned to the tower.

"Damn you pigs," he grumbled to himself.

The wolf decided it was best to climb the tower and make his way through the chimney to where the food was cooking. He might be able to avoid whatever was happening behind the door if he did. The wolf was fortunate the bricks on the tower wall were not laid in a flat formation but instead jutted out in random perpendicular fashion for an aesthetic quality. As a result, his feet and hand-like paws were able to get support during his ascent.

Once he got to the chimney opening, he lowered himself down by bracing his feet and back against the walls. The wolf heard the pigs chanting in guttural voices below in a language he was not familiar with. Vibrations from the drumming resonated from the brick wall through his back, almost shaking him loose in the chimney and into a freefall.

LET ME COME IN!

The wolf came to the base of the chimney and felt the heat of the fire underneath him as he smelled the spiced, roasted meat. The wolf twisted his body and saw chunks of simmering beef floating in a reddish brown gruel in a black kettle on a spit. It was then his hunger got the best of him, and he lost the pressure keeping him wedged in the chimney. The wolf fell into the pot, screaming and howling at the top of his lungs as the searing liquid soaked his fur. With all his effort, he jumped out of the pot and rolled into the ashes. His hair was singed and matted down in places. He tried to sit up, but his hands and feet were scalded.

The wolf looked and surveyed his doom with tears running down his swollen muzzle. He saw several grotesque-looking pigs dancing naked around a stone statue of something that resembled a large lizard or dragon. Painted on their bodies was the inexplicable white symbol he kept seeing on the doors. A translucent gossamer tether connected the dancing pigs to the statue as a ribbon would a May-pole, and a misty vortex of iridescent colors swirled above the statue with a dreadful collection of protoplasmic dendrite tendrils descending toward the wolf. A greasy, gelatinous body of flesh trickled down behind the ropey web with a partially surfaced red eye. The wolf screamed as he was pulled toward the fleshy, malicious mass. An orifice under the eye opened with a violent hemorrhaging of black ichor sputum that splattered onto the floor in awful, viscous pools.

One of the pigs stopped dancing and yelled, "It hungers, it hungers! Iaa, Iaa, igfa Bokrug tssu mngui Iaa, Iaa!"

"It's you!" the wolf exclaimed in recognition as he

acknowledged the bulbous-eyed pig as the one from the straw cottage. "I only wanted something to eat . . . Please stop this! Oh GOD! Help me! Please stop!"

The wolf struggled and jerked as he entered the hungry orifice. The pig sneered with contempt at his doom. "Not by the hair of my chinny chin chin."

THE FISHMAN AND HIS WIFE

INANNA ARTHEN

*Based on The Fisherman and His Wife by the
Brothers Grimm*

FROM THE WAY the Director-General's anterior tentacles writhed on his desk, like earthworms dropped onto hot beach sand, I suspected this conversation wasn't going to go well.

"What do you want this time?"

I hated this. Luella should be here, speaking for herself. But the new regime was reluctant to deal with human women in close quarters. Something about the way they smelled, I'd heard, although I never thought fish had a sense of smell. I was only taking in a breath when I had to talk, and sometimes, I waited so long, little pinprick lights danced around in my vision. That certainly improved the appearance of the Director-General, but fainting alone in a room with one of them would be the last thing I ever did. Not because he'd be offended—it was simply a question of instincts taking over. He'd be sincerely sorry afterwards.

"It's not me, you understand, Director-General. It's

Luella, my wife, who is making the petition. I'm here on her behalf." *Just like the last three times*, I thought.

I knew what would happen next and braced myself. Fortunately, the Director-General, like the rest of them, did poorly at reading human faces. The Director-General's mouth widened until his whole narrow, misshapen head looked like a cracked watermelon, the triple rows of triangular teeth top and bottom glittering in the dim light. There was some kind of tongue in there too, but I never could bear to look too closely. I couldn't act affronted; the Director-General was, after all, *smiling*. He *liked* us, me and Luella. That wasn't something to squander. It made us among the most privileged of humans.

God, it was an awful position to be in. But it was better than the alternative.

"We of the Directorate deeply appreciate the services past and present of the Gilman family." The Director-General's voice gave a whole new dimension to the term "oily." His smile, however, was less grotesquely expanded than usual. "But . . . "

"I know, Director-General, I know. It's just that Luella . . . she feels we've given a great deal of loyalty and devotion to the new regime. It's not as though she—I mean, we, are asking for much. We remain at the Directorate's disposal, as always." In every sense of the term. Some days, I wished they'd just get it over with.

The Director-General's huge chair squeaked, groaned, and squished horribly as he leaned back, his body bulging to either side. You'd never believe, seeing them on land, how fast and agile they were in water. The chair was custom-made, carved out of multi-hued coral. "This is turning into something of a habit."

I didn't say anything. Agreement was assumed.

"First, she asked for the public acknowledgment of the Directorate and the right to walk on the street with the First Race as equals. That was gladly granted, under the circumstances. Indeed, it might have been granted unasked." He pondered; I could tell how deeply he was thinking because his eyes retracted slightly. They didn't have eyelids, but you could learn their expressions with practice.

"After that, she requested you be made full members of the Order of Dagon rather than mere servitors, a more difficult request. It came with certain privileges. You alone among humans are allowed to live near the water. You alone among humans are allowed to swim, traverse the sea in boats, and fish in the harbor. Not every officer in the Order thought that was appropriate, but they agreed the Gilman name did carry some entitlement."

My mouth was getting dry; the Director-General had never talked for so long. Human speech was difficult for them. They affected a style they'd learned in the 1830s, when my great grandfather had first contacted them in the South Pacific and, along with the Marshes, made the pact which had inevitably led to this outcome. I had to listen very carefully because the multi-syllabic words slurped and squealed from the Director-General's asymmetrical vocal anatomy.

"Then, a mere four weeks ago, she requested you be allowed to move into the Marsh mansion overlooking the city. She argued that with the Marshes having Descended, the mansion couldn't be left empty. Several of the highest ranking officials of the Directorate had considered using the mansion themselves. I had to employ considerable persuasion."

Since he'd paused for some moments, I swallowed hard. "The mansion wouldn't be comfortable for the First Race, Director-General."

"We planned some remodeling." Doubtless that remodeling would have included sprinkler heads like the one he now triggered by pulling an elaborately worked gold chain, soaking him in a fine spray of sea water. It would be a shame; the mansion boasted hand-rubbed teak floors. Luella and I were very comfortable there although it seemed an inopportune moment to say so. After a full minute, the Director-General released a long sigh that reeked of rotted fish. "And now. What does she want now?"

"She wants . . . she thinks that we should be officers of the Order of Dagon in full standing, Director-General."

The Director General sat without moving, studying me with those eyes. Only the pulses in his gill flaps betrayed his emotions.

"That would give both of you authority over some members of the First Race."

"Only the younger ones, Director-General. She feels that . . . that . . . it makes no sense for us to have the trappings without the responsibility. As members of the family who—"

"I understand." The Director-General heaved himself out of his chair. "You will return in four hours." His movement to the narrow dock that ran along the open side of the three-walled room was a combination of hunching and crawling, like a charging bull sea lion. But he reached the dock and dove off it within seconds.

THE FISHERMAN AND HIS WIFE

I left the Director-General's office, passing several desks occupied by servitors, as the few humans who survived and agreed to swear the first oath of Dagon were called. They kept their heads bowed as required, but I caught two of them giving me glances as I went by, their eyes filled with mingled envy and resentment. I wore the sweeping robes and oddly worked gold jewelry my status allowed, garb that evoked the grudging respect of the First Race. They knew who I was, and Luella, like the earth's moon, basked in reflected light.

Outside of the building, I stopped, scanning the truncated and crumbling skyline of what was once Boston and wondering what to do with myself. The cities no longer had streetlights or electricity. The clock of the Arlington Street Church still chimed the hours, however, so I could gauge my return time. I walked a few blocks to the wharf and stood gazing out at the black ocean, starlight glittering on its surface. No ships were tied at the moorings or anchored in the harbor, and no lights, bells, or buoys interrupted the expanse of water. All the ocean was enemy territory, at least as far as humans were concerned. But for me, it was something a bit more.

I didn't like brooding over the past; I didn't like remembering all that had been lost on and after July 16, 1927. Humanity never knew what hit them, but then, they had never realized how vulnerable they were. Forty-five percent of the earth's population lived on the coasts of the six inhabited continents; in the United States, it had been fifty-three percent. Even those who lived far inland were usually close to a river or lakes with rivers leading to the sea. Those also became unguarded and open gateways for the invaders, millions upon millions of them, all striking at once. Some said if mankind hadn't retired so many of its armies and destroyed so many of its weapons after the Great War, we might have prevailed. I tended to doubt it. The First Race had the backing of powers that humanity had long forgotten. I was in a unique position to understand exactly what the human race faced and how little hope they had.

Trying to escape my own memories, I walked in circles around the dark city blocks, risking a turned ankle on broken concrete and occasionally aiming a kick at a skittering rat. Cats occasionally stared at me from an empty window frame or debris-littered step. They lived on the vermin that had taken over the city and didn't seem to mind the First Race; perhaps they liked the smell. Dogs loathed the invaders, and the feeling was mutual. I hadn't seen a dog for ten years.

When the church clock told me the four hours had passed, I went back to the modified warehouse on the wharf where the Director-General had his office. The servitor let me inside, and I waited patiently. Suddenly, the water off the edge of the dock exploded as the Director-General burst above the surface. He landed on the dock with the geyser of seawater he'd made raining down on him. As many times as I'd seen it, the spectacle still gave me chills. This was how they had come, in all their force, erupting in one moment from every coast and river and waterfront on Earth. No—humanity hadn't stood a chance.

The Director-General hunkered and slithered back to his coral throne. "Agreed." He extended a flipperlike hand containing two small boxes. "Take these. You are now first level officers of the Order of Dagon. You will be taught the passwords at the next congregation." That meant tomorrow; the Order's upper echelons assembled four times a week.

I bowed, but only slightly, and took the boxes. As I straightened up, I saw the Director-General giving me a look that seemed appraising. I knew why although I was surprised he would notice. It was a long walk to the massive mansion built at the peak of Beacon Hill. The Marshes' immense wealth had mystified Bostonians at the time, who gossiped about pirate gold or white slavery in the Orient. Had they known the truth, they'd have burned the opulent home to the foundations. When I entered the front door, Luella came running out into the foyer, her bare feet pattering on the shining marble.

"He said yes, didn't he? We've got it, don't we?"

I held out the boxes. "We've got it."

She flung her hands up in an exultant shout. "Dagon be praised! You know what this means, don't you, Henry? We'll be allowed to access the books, the books in the sanctuary."

"For what purpose, Luella? Isn't this enough?" She gave me a contemptuous look and turned in a swirl of robes. My clothing was monastic compared to hers; she'd had servitors embroider every inch with gold thread and wore so much of the odd, distorted gold jewelry that I sometimes wondered how she could move. I followed her into the grand reception hall, where the long, glossy table was set for dinner. "We're almost equals and peers with the First Race now, Luella. Let's not get greedier."

She turned on me. "*Almost*? And you're satisfied with that?"

"I'm satisfied to be alive. Aren't you? Would you rather be like them?" I waved a hand at the two silent, dour servitors, part of our staff of twenty. Luella just stared at me. "Fine. Read the books if that's what you want so badly. I know you've been studying the glyphs for years. Is dinner ready? I'm hungry."

I went to my end of the table and sat, and a servitor placed a covered plate before me and lifted its lid. At the smell, I recoiled. "What is this? I thought the cook was braising a salmon."

Luella, just seated in her chair, made a little sound of disgust. "This is beefsteak, and it was costly and very difficult to get. I'm sick of endless fish, Henry, aren't you? You used to love a good beefsteak."

I stood up, pushing my chair back roughly from the table. "No, I'm not sick of fish, and I don't want this." I took some bread from the table and left the room, barely registering Luella's stricken expression.

Upstairs in the master suite, I pushed open the bathroom door and stood outside the angle of the mirror's reflection. Luella seemed more fascinated by the heavy glass pane each day. She spent hours in here, turning this way and that, holding candles at different heights and distances, pulling and pushing at parts of her face. I hadn't looked at my own reflection for some time; the servitors shaved me. I had already lost most of my hair at an even younger age than my father had, and I'd never been particularly handsome to put it kindly. Now, I took a deep breath and walked over to the mirror. I wasn't surprised by what I saw, especially after the way the Director-General looked at me.

I'd always known I would change. My father had, his eyes growing more protuberant, his hands and skull and body thickening and distorting. He was almost unrecognizable by the time his throat and mouth had evolved enough to pronounce the words he'd needed to say, the words that started it all. I stood beside him out on Devil's Reef when it happened. That was the last time I had seen him, but I knew we'd meet again, and I knew the first question I would ask him when we did. It appeared that might be happening sooner than I'd expected.

I would change—and Luella would not. She was a Gilman by marriage only. Somehow, she had gotten the idea that if a human was accorded enough favor from the First Race, he or she could be transformed and share their immortality. It might be true; my father had hinted at something like that, but I had yet to see it actually happen. Even if it were possible, I couldn't imagine why a woman as vain as Luella would aspire to look like the Director-General. I had a long time to get used to the idea—and there were certainly some compensations. I'd always believed women valued different forms of compensation than men did although Luella was making me wonder. But she was denied almost every common feminine pleasure. I hadn't slept in the same bedroom with her for years. If she missed her husband's company, she never let on.

Luella took a little longer than I'd expected to make her next move. I think the books were more challenging than she anticipated, and even she knew better than to ask for them right away. She seldom came home, if you could call it that. She ignored the mansion with all its luxuries and servants that she had coveted during the years we lived in a tiny bungalow among the remains of Hingham. We'd been deeply grateful to be overlooked then, seeing what was happening to those humans who went into hiding and carried out pointless acts of petty rebellion. I had the task of keeping a census on the servitors, who had accepted amnesty in exchange for loyalty and virtual slavery. Some of them had children, as though starting a family was a charm to maintain peace and stability. I knew the First Race was considering some kind of cross-breeding scheme in the near future, like the one tried in the previous century, but I kept quiet. There were some servitors who might consider it a fair price for additional freedoms and status.

In other words, I had plenty to keep myself occupied, and I welcomed it because I didn't want to watch Luella galloping toward doom, whipping her steed harder with every step. I didn't want to know what she was thinking and planning as she pored for hours every day through the arcane books in the Temple. I was amazed that she could read them; the glyphs were arranged on the page according to a geometry unlike any human logic and seemed to be scattered randomly. Even learning how to sequence them correctly was an art that utterly defied the rational mind, and the glyphs themselves evoked deep emotional disturbance in humans who merely looked at them. But Luella had mastered them so well, I wondered if she might have some Gilman or Marsh blood somewhere in her genealogy. It did crop up in unexpected places since the experiments of the 1840s.

Six weeks after our admission as officers of the Order of Dagon, I came downstairs to find Luella in a state that was poignantly familiar. She was pacing the foyer, back and forth, muttering. The words were not English, or human for that matter, but she didn't seem to be talking to herself so much as rehearsing a speech. She stopped when she glimpsed me on the broad, curving steps.

"So you're finally awake."

I came down at this time every day. "Have you left me anything for breakfast?" I was trying to be humorous.

"Is that all you can think about? I believe the cook has made you something out of crabmeat." She went back to pacing, brow furrowed, muttering steadily.

"Luella—is there something going on that I should know about?" I waited patiently until she finished some section or stanza and turned back to me.

"Oh, by all the eternal gods, Henry, don't you pay attention to the moon anymore?"

"I know tonight is the full moon. And that means . . . ?"

She met my gaze directly, and I had to take a step back. The madness glittering in her eyes was powerful. If Luella hadn't been away so much of the time, and if I hadn't been trying hard not to pay attention, I'd have seen this coming. She walked toward me, her expression fervent.

"Henry . . . tonight is the night. I'm going to ask for what we really deserve, you and I, a reward that truly means something."

"Luella—"

"No, Henry, hear me out! We're not true equals in the Order; we're barely tolerated interlopers, and you know it! We'll never be their equals. No, we must surpass them, become greater than the First Race!"

"Surpass them? Luella, that's insane. I can't go to the Director-General and ask for that! I'm not going back to the Director-General at all. Enough is enough! If we appear ungrateful for the gifts we've already received, we'll be flung back into the ranks of the lowest servitors, and that's if we're lucky. I'm not going there again."

She drew her head back, shriveling me with scorn. "Of course you're not. This time, I'm making the request. And I'm not going to the Director-General. I'm making my petition to one who is far more powerful than any of the First Race."

"What are you talking about?" It was a rhetorical question; I just couldn't believe she was serious.

"I've learned all the chants and invocations of the ritual. I'm summoning Father Dagon. I know he'll grant my request. We've served the Temple and the First Race faithfully and well. We've sacrificed everything for them."

I ran down the steps and over to where she stood, grabbing her by the shoulders. She was too proud to back away or try to shake my hands off. "Luella, you can't. You don't dare be so presumptuous."

"You whimpering *coward*! We've earned this. You're such a boot-licker, you wouldn't have asked for anything if I hadn't kept after you. We'd still be scavenging the beach for scraps in Hingham!"

"I can't let you do this, Luella. I'm your husband. I'm obligated to stop you for your own good . . ."

She laughed. "You'll stop me? How? The words are in my mind, Henry. I can perform the ritual anywhere."

I let go of her. She was right; unless I drugged her

or murdered her myself, I couldn't stop her. "This is too much, Luella. You can't keep on pressing your luck like this. Of all the humans on earth, we have the least reason for complaint. Things will never go back to the way they were. It's foolish to keep wishing for more."

"Don't you want to be as powerful as they are, Henry? Don't you want to be immortal?" She watched my face as I struggled unsuccessfully for a reply then said with contempt, "Oh, that's right. You've already got that honor, haven't you?"

I turned away and walked toward the arched doorway into the reception hall although my appetite was gone.

She was right about one thing: I was a coward. I couldn't stay with her when she prepared to perform the ritual at midnight. The full moon hung low in the sky, its leprous yellow light seeping through clouds like rotted veils. The sea beneath it was black and featureless, its surface seeming oily and unclean. I sat outside the partly open doors to the reception room, staring down at my hands. My fingers were getting thicker. It was harder to clasp them together. I shuddered when I heard Luella's voice speaking the inhuman words, imitating the squeals and gurgles of their arcane syllables—*Iä! Iä! Cthulhu ftagn! Ph'nglui mglw'nafh Cthulhu R'lyeh wgah-nagl fhtaga* . . . how could she pronounce them so perfectly? She had always been a good singer and clever with languages, but . . . the air was becoming so humid, it was hard to breathe. Drops of water were condensing on the walls and running in short little rivulets. There was a tangible stench, like a storm-battered beach covered with dead fish and seaweed under a blistering hot sun.

Strange how those smells were bothering me less than they used to.

For all that, I still covered my head with my hands, hunching down, when I heard his voice. I'd heard it before, in the Temple, but this was different. It was as though the thunderous roar of a tidal wave had been shaped into speech. Was Luella really standing upright before him? I couldn't bear to look. I heard Luella's voice speaking, at first defiant then frightened. I heard his response, first in their language then in English—

"So. You would be as a god, human?"

I could tell from the sounds there were at least a dozen of them, and Luella screamed but once. After that, there was only the hideous sound of tearing flesh, and bones ground between teeth of metal and stone, that went on and on. I blocked my ears, but I could no longer close my eyes easily, and I saw the single line of blood that trickled out the door into the foyer, moving this way and that like a blind worm feeling its way across the floor. But it ended finally, and at last, I knew I was alone on the first floor of the great house.

I wiped tears off my cheeks; the way things were progressing, they were likely the last tears I'd ever shed. Poor Luella. But maybe it was just as well. I sighed, *finally*. It hadn't been much of a marriage anyway.

THE LITTLE MATCH MI-GO

MICHAEL KAMP

Based on The Little Match Girl by Hans Christian Anderson

THE WORLD IS DEAD.

Humanity is dust, snuffed out by the arrival of the Old Ones and frozen solid on the plains of old Terra. The star spawn has risen and hurled Earth from its orbit into the deepest, darkest regions of space, where Mankind has perished in grueling, suffocating anguish, cleansing the universe of their foul presence.

Little did Professor Eckhart suspect his actions would have such vast consequences when he unwittingly released the Old Ones from their captivity, following his experiments with ancient texts and a certain unholy artifact from before the dawn of Man.

A life of study and gathering information led him to first acquiring and then understanding how to activate said artifact, but nothing could have prepared him for the dying hours of humanity. It was glorious in all its horrifying splendor, choking the infection of life from the sacred surface of the planet while the star spawn resumed their rightful place at the top of creation.

The suffering of billions of souls marked the birth pangs of the new order and initiated a time of prosperity. No longer would the seed of apes soil the world with their presence or defecate on the order of things with their self-proclaimed place at the center of creation.

Everything was dark now.

No sun, no moon, no skies to blot out the pitch-black emptiness of space through which the little frozen speck of a planet had been hurled.

It was heaven.

Not for the little Mi-Go.

While the rest of its brethren had returned to Yuggoth, it alone had been left behind on the icy surface of the newborn world. A new era had dawned, but there was to be no rest for this little one.

Find Ghatanothoa, they said. Bring the light to Ghatanothoa, and let the prison crumble.

Hideous Ghatanothoa trapped beneath Mount Yaddith-Gho in sunken Mu. Free him, and set him loose on the universe.

Poor little Mi-Go.

Stranded on a world frozen solid with no markings left intact, it could not locate fabled Mu. Flittering hither and dither, it searched the peaks and depths of the dead planet, looking for the gargantuan entity, but all in vain.

Too much had changed for little Mi-Go to figure out, and no help was forthcoming from its brethren.

To return empty-handed would mean death, so the little Mi-Go fought to keep its antennae from freezing solid and beat its wings ever faster to prevent them from icing over.

So cold.

So lonely and cold here now that life had gone.

The little Mi-Go dashed through crumbling cities, circling the skeleton skyscrapers and downtrodden ruins, looking for any landmark it would recognize. Often, it had to hide when a rogue Moon-beast approached or the huge Dholes wormed their way across the landscapes. A few times, the titanic shape of an Old One moved across the continents, and the Mi-Go trembled along with the world.

Mu was nowhere in sight.

Exhausted, the little Mi-Go landed atop a pile of frozen dead. The mound of Man-corpses began to shift, and Mi-Go almost lost its balance.

Tall ruins surrounded the plaza, and the Mi-Go fluttered its wings in despair. How would it ever find the entombed Ghatanothoa amongst all this snow and ice?

It broke off the head of a nearby corpse and brought it up toward its antennae. Had this ape-seed known the location of fabled Mu? Could it be snatched from the ape-seed's brain?

The little Mi-Go opened up the head in excitement, but the joy was short-lived. The brain had been destroyed, broken beyond any hope of getting information.

It despaired and threw the useless hunk of meat and bone against a broken wall, shattering it into a red-grey mist.

It picked up a smaller specimen of ape-seed and opened it up, but it was the same. They were all the same—as useless in death as they were in life.

Bringing forth the artifact it had been given, the antennae moved nervously. It was only to be used for freeing Ghatanothoa, but if the little Mi-Go perished, who would search the dead world?

The artifact felt warm to the touch. A raging star caught within a fragment of another universe to be released by the touching of spheres. So much heat.

An alien nebula filled the black heaven as Terra tumbled through the void, and carbon dioxide fell like snow upon the mangled ruins. The antennae of the little Mi-Go sagged. It was so far from home and had so much to search. Too much for a little Mi-Go.

If only it could unleash the raging star—just for a little while. Just to chase away the cold and ice so it could resume the search.

It was strictly forbidden. Non-existence would be the punishment were any other Mi-Go to find out. But they were far away.

The Mi-Go paused a while, spreading out its antennae to search for any sign of intrusion. Then, it triggered the artifact.

A blinding light shone forth, and the violent fury of a star unleashed engulfed the plaza. A huge bubble of gas rose toward the heavens, oxygen and carbon dioxide freed once more, while the ruins were baked and shook like leaves in a storm. Even protected by the artifact, the little Mi-Go cringed back, drawing in its antennae lest they be singed in the blazing heat.

The mountain of dead rolled and heaved like the sea in a gale. Flesh boiled away from bone, spraying everywhere, before bones darkened and turned to ash in the blink of an eye.

The little Mi-Go sank into the broiling mass of

Man-flesh, beating its wings desperately to escape and navigate the scorching air.

It was so pretty.

A sea of burning corpses amidst the glowing ruins of obscene buildings. The little Mi-Go felt moved through space and time to a happier place. A time of conquest and joy—a time of stealing the brains of ape-seeds and sending them into the depths of space, hunting the humans through the dark corners of their soiled planet.

Oh, to once more submerge the antennae in hot, steamy brain matter and slurp the raw, full taste of terror from the primitive beings.

And then it was gone.

The light disappeared, and darkness once more swallowed the plaza although the surrounding ruins glowed bright. The huge bubble of heat began to collapse at once, re-freezing both the vaporized meat and the atmosphere, which combined to an organic sludge falling on the plaza and Mi-Go.

The little Mi-Go waved its antennae around in an attempt to take in the last remnants of heat before it radiated out into the cold nothingness of space. The bone-ash covering the ground froze solid once more, and the little Mi-Go shifted its footing to not get caught.

Then it was off once more, leaving the sad, dark plaza to search for elusive Mu.

It flew across solid oceans, passing over wrecked warships and giant trading vessels, always reaching out with its mind—probing the depths for any sign of the hideous entity.

Suddenly, it picked up something—something

huge and abnormal—and it flew with all the speed a little Mi-Go could muster toward the anomaly. There—in the middle of the ocean surrounded by nothing but ice, a structure rose toward the stars.

The little Mi-Go waved its antennae in joy and paced itself even harder.

Then, everything turned upside down. Space would not fit inside the alien city and became folded in strange ways. The little Mi-Go was too exhausted to realize the danger until it was almost on top of the bastard buildings.

This was not fabled Mu rising once more. This was not the prison of Ghatanothoa. It was the nightmare corpse-city of R'lyeh!

The little Mi-Go fled, darting across the icy plains of the ocean in a frantic attempt to escape before the atrocity within took any notice. Would that blasphemous horror even perceive a creature as small as the little Mi-Go? It had no intention of ever finding out.

Black, smoky tentacles stretched from accursed R'lyeh across the heavens toward the little Mi-Go, but it was too minute to warrant more than passing interest, and they were soon retracted. The timeless evil had no use or plan for a creature such as the Mi-Go.

Once more, it chased across the dark, ice-covered world, searching for sunken Mu. It searched the slopes of mountains, the vast corpse-fields of cities and the deep, secret caverns of the world.

Nothing.

Nothing but nightmares and abominable things from beyond the stars. Not what it was searching for.

In the middle of yet another frozen ocean, the little Mi-Go could fly no more. It landed without grace or dignity, its cold, slimy body sprawled across the ice as it caressed the artifact and clicked its claws in sorrow.

It could not go on. There was no hope.

Only one more time. Only a little bit of heat to keep the cold at bay. Just this once.

Antennae rose toward the stars, searching in vain for a glimpse of familiar suns, but this was an unknown part of vast space.

It clutched the artifact in frozen feelers and tried to lift one iced-over wing.

Then, it released the inferno once more.

An enormous amount of ice vaporized instantly, creating a geyser of steam that shot many miles into the air and carving out a gigantic bowl in the frozen sea. Battered by steam on all sides, the Mi-Go plunged down into the cavity, not daring to fly right away. The conflagration followed, and the bowl became a shaft.

For many miles, the Mi-Go plunged through the vaporized ice until finally it impacted on the seafloor, fluttering its wings just in time to avoid a terminal impact. A shroud of roaring flame followed, and for an instant, it was blind. The shaft grew to a cavern, and the heat baked the seafloor solid beneath the claws of the little Mi-Go.

It raised its antennae and took in its surroundings. A dome of ice kept growing, and wonderful heat still poured forth. It noticed huge, dark shapes in the ice that soon revealed themselves to be whales, now cooking and burning as they emerged from the frozen tomb only to melt away and join the water vapor in a new journey toward the black sky.

The little Mi-Go was reminded of foggy Yuggoth, where they all danced at the rim of the great crater, calling upon Shub-Niggurath.

It could almost see them now. Thousands of Mi-Go buzzing around, dancing and celebrating, calling forth the Darkness From Beyond.

Oh, to behold the splendor of Yuggoth once more instead of this forsaken shell. To once more fly free and dance and celebrate the coming end of everything, hunting the spawn of the outworlders and offer them up as a prize.

And then the artifact went dark once more.

The visions of Yuggoth disappeared, and freezing emptiness returned.

All alone, imprisoned by the dome of frost, the little Mi-Go could face the cold no more. If death would be the price of failure, then so be it. The artifact could not be used too often. It would destabilize the captured star, and strong wards were in place to secure the confinement.

Desperate, the little Mi-Go held the artifact up toward the shaft above, trying to catch the glint of a star in its dark surface, but it was too deep beneath the surface. The frigid cold seeped into the cavern, cooling the Mi-Go and putting a glazing of frost on anything still moist from the steam.

Then, it released the slave-star.

And when the visions faltered, it set it free once more. And again.

And again.

The gibbering beings orbiting the plummeting Earth would witness a small speck of light flaring up through a hole in the ocean.

Again and again it flickered, bringing a soft glow to the ice and sending up trails of steam as the planet spun madly through the darkest, most hostile regions of space. Mere sparks in the blackest of nights, fighting a lost cause, until finally, it went dark.

The world grew silent.

***

Many eons later, a stray Moon-beast stumbled upon the shaft in the ice and fell down.

On the bottom, it found a huge cavern, and in the middle, glazed over by frost and ice, lay the poor little Mi-Go. Its wings were frozen to the floor, its claws clutching the artifact and its frail antennae spread out forever—frozen solid as the body itself—still carrying the thought-image of distant Yuggoth. Still preserving the last glimpse of joy.

The poor little Mi-Go was dead.

Then eaten by a hungry Moon-beast.

FOLLOW THE YELLOW GLYPH ROAD

SCOTT T. GOUDSWARD

Based on The Wizard of Oz by L. Frank Baum

DOROTHY GROANED AT the pain in her side and realized everything hurt. The sky seemed different. It wasn't the same color it was before the storm. Pushing herself up, she looked around. The barn's roof was on the ground, sans barn. The cornfields were gone along with everything else. She knocked on the doors of the storm cellar. It sounded dull and hollow. "Hello?" *This can't be good.*

Dorothy brushed dirt off the door handle and pulled. It gave easily with a squeal of hinges. She peered into the doorway. There was no basement laden with food and water and survival gear. Just dirt. A tear rolled down her cheek, leaving a clean streak. Where was the house? The well? The corral? She scanned the flat, pock-marked landscape covered in grapefruit sized holes with scored edges and scrub weeds. Where was her family?

Blocking the oddly bright sun with a hand, she surveyed what remained. A soft buzzing filled her ears, but no matter where she turned, there was no visible source. She ran to the barn's roof and scrambled up, tearing tiles and tar paper free. Using the battered weathervane for support, she checked around again. Not even a little height changed her view of the desolate countryside.

Clouds danced across a deep purple-veined sky. Darkness pooled in the depths behind them. She felt the presence of something. Something ancient and filled with rage lurked, waiting to pounce. A gust of wind assailed her, and Dorothy shrieked as she lost her grip and slid down the rooftop. The tiles dug into and ripped the overalls covering her legs.

Dorothy winced seeing her fingers damp with blood. Her legs throbbed with pain. She pushed herself up and groaned. Around her, the dust stirred in miniature eddies, spraying debris. Dorothy blocked her eyes again.

"I'd kill for some water." Dorothy walked back to the bulkhead doors. The last time she remembered seeing her family, the storm was coming. Sirens were wailing across the countryside, screaming the tornado warning. Uncle Henry and Aunt Em were hustling from the house, arms laden with food and bottled water. Dorothy dry swallowed thinking of a bottle straight from the fridge, sweating in the afternoon heat.

"Toto," escaped her lips in a soft whisper. She'd seen him running from the barn, red ribbon tied to his collar. Now, like everyone else, he was missing. "You want to get out of this? You want to die out here?" She looked around again. "Wherever here is." Her thoughts turned from "Woe is me" to "How am I going to live through this?"

She opened the bulkhead doors and laid under them. It was cramped but cool. Despite the images of spiders and beetles crawling across her cheeks, Dorothy forced her eyes closed. Just for a moment.

"This will work for sleeping." She stood and stepped from the shelter. "Food and water." The sky was vacant, no birds; in fact, there were no animal sounds at all. Not even a chittering squirrel. Her mouth watered thinking of the squirrel pie and dandelion greens her aunt used to make.

She set off walking. Turning often, looking everywhere for any signs of life, another house, remnants of another farm, anything. Whistling didn't help; her lips cracked and bled with the effort. Eventually, she turned back, hoping it was the right direction to her shelter. It was getting cold, and though she couldn't see it, she swore the sun was setting. It was the only explanation for the cold.

Dorothy screamed when the bike fell from the sky. A deadly present delivered by a maniacal Santa. The horn on the handlebars squawked once and fell to the dirt. The basket was shredded.

It belonged to her English teacher, who had been riding it down the street, peddling for her life, literally, as the storm overtook her and sucked her off the street into the depths of the funnel cloud. There'd been a quickly extinguished scream and a spray of red before she was lost from sight. The bike stood in sheer defiance of being dropped from the sky. Motion caught Dorothy's gaze as something thick and viscous dripped from the basket.

She took a step closer. The bike seemed to shudder and then tilted into a fall. She rushed forward, catching the handlebar with a grunt, and pulled it upright. Looking into the basket, a scream escaped and softened to a tear-choked wheeze. The bike slipped from her hand and clattered against the dusty ground. The remains of her dog were splashed inside. The only part recognizable in the fur and grizzle was the new collar and bow she'd bought him days before.

Dorothy choked back the fear and the sadness. She needed the bike but couldn't look down at the remains. She cut the basket loose and left it in the heat and sand for whatever insects might exist and watched the last drop of blood fall from the bike. Riding it across the scarred ground would be difficult. But survival was difficult.

In the morning, if there was a morning, she'd gather up anything useful from the barn roof and head out. An owl had nested there over the summer; maybe some of the eggs survived. It was a dream she'd save until morning to either confirm or devastate. The darkness fell like a wet blanket, dripping and oozing inky blackness coating everything.

The explosion of odd glittering insects was more surprising than the bike falling from the sky. They poured from the ground and lit up like fireflies. When the first one latched onto her arm and bit, Dorothy screamed, letting the bike fall and running for the bulkhead. By the time she opened the door, there were more than a dozen on her arms, chewing and biting and sucking at the blood. She ripped at them like leeches from the swimming hole and pulled the doors closed.

She saw the "faces" of the insects in her mind: miniscule, deadly, and filled with hate and rage. Their small eyes seethed with hunger, mouths overstuffed with needle-like teeth, puckering and trying to find some more of her arms for food. Dorothy closed her eyes and curled into a ball. She did her best to shut out the buzzing and the clangs of the insects flying into the metal doors. She fell into a troubled sleep and wished her overalls weren't shredded from the barn's tiles.

***

Dorothy bolted up, slammed her head against the door, and fell back into the dirt. The strange screeches were getting louder, closer. After rubbing her newest injury, she fumbled in the darkness until she found the handle and pushed. The door swung open, letting in the painful bright of morning. Through the long hanging clouds, outlandish creatures flitted on reptilian wings, their faces masks of insanity that resembled insect and birds in a grotesque cross-stitch.

She stared at them then turned away, fearing they might see her watching. Or worse, feel her mind slip away a little bit more. Her stomach growled. As she stood and did her best to straighten her clothes and brush some of the dirt off, an odd, briny breeze oozed past. She thought of fresh lobsters, bowls of melted butter for dipping and crispy fried clams.

She held her hands across her abdomen to mute the rumbling. The creatures in the sky swooped and soared over the barn roof and, as suddenly as they appeared, flew off. Dorothy watched them then crawled from the shelter. She let the door fall from her fingers and slam back into the frame. She winced at the noise and waited to see if the flying things came back.

When the "coast" was clear, she headed toward the

roof. The sky was an off shade of blue with swirls of red. Like it was caught in sunrise. But the actual heat of the morning betrayed the colorful display. Under the V of the roof, it was dark and cool. The perfect hiding spot for anything waiting to jump out and scream at her or drive a knife through her neck.

But it was empty as the countryside. No killers, no flying lizard things, and, sadly, no eggs. The creatures had flown off toward what she assumed was the west. And that sea breeze had to come from somewhere that wasn't a crazy desert. With a heavy sigh, she went to the bike, stood it up, and although the front tire was a little warped, she headed off, following the creatures and hopefully finding a fried clam shack along the way.

***

The scorched and pocked earth gave way to rocky terrain. After a few minutes of fighting the gravel and dirt, Dorothy abandoned the bike and set off on foot. She hoped the change in the ground meant she was getting closer to water. Water meant food; water meant living for another night. But what would happen when the insects came out again with their evil little mouths, wanting to chew and bite? She put the thought from her mind and focused on walking, being careful of her steps so she wouldn't twist an ankle or worse.

She tried counting to get some bearing on the time and figure out how long she'd been traveling. Counting her steps was futile. She stumbled and tripped too often. After what she guessed to be about four or five hours, the rocky terrain became grass—sparse at first but then filled in. Finally, there were trees, horrible trees, with evil, glaring faces formed in the bark. The branches shook and twisted in defiance of a windless afternoon. A small, wooden fence kept them at bay, and a path was formed between the sides of the orchard. Lumpy, reddish fruits hung from the branches. *Might be crab apples or really fucked up pears.* She climbed over the fence, looking between the trees, checking for anything flying or crawling. The eyes of the trees creaked as they followed her. She reached for a fruit, and the tree swatted her, knocking her heels over head. She landed hard on her back.

As she sat up, the tree unearthed itself. Thousands of roots squirmed from the soil, like the wriggling fingers of the undead, reaching out for her. She screamed and ran, oblivious to the lumpy fruit held tight in her hand. The roots followed and chased, entangled her feet, and she fell chin first into the dirt. Her teeth clacked together, and she tasted blood. The fruit rolled away.

Dorothy flipped over and fought against the roots wrapping around her legs, worming up past her knees. More trees uprooted and approached, each wooden face twisted in fury. The trees parted, and a lone figure stood in the distance, upheld by a cross of wood. It dropped the distance to the ground with a terrible grunt and rending of flesh. It ran toward Dorothy, arms swinging madly, hay and blood dribbling from the shirt keeping it all inside.

As Dorothy screamed and scrambled back, the vines loosened and slipped from her legs. Whatever was coming toward her frightened the trees; she could tell from the frozen screams trapped in the bark. She heard the rustle of straw with each step and swing of the arms. The splatter of its blood hit the trees and was greedily licked off.

When terror surpassed fear, she stood and ran, knowing the thing on the posts was gaining. Each long stride brought it closer. Soon, it would be on her. She pictured it straddling her chest, her arms pinned with a straw-stuffed arm. From a distance, she could see its eyes, the color of night with a thousand stars in a spiral around unknown galaxies. When fight took over flight, she grabbed a crossbeam from the fence and spun. She drove the beam forward, the formed end cutting through the air and impaling the scarecrow thing through the gut.

She stepped back with heaving breaths and watched it struggle on the post. It slumped forward, the movements getting slower. Blood and straw spilled from the wound. Dorothy took off at a run, slowing only to grab lumpy fruits and continue down the road. As she got further from the orchard, the trees pulled off their fruit and lobbed it at her. She slowed again to gather up as many as she could carry then continued along the dirt road until it, like everything else in the bizarre world, changed into something else.

She pinched her arms over and over, hoping to wake up from the nightmarish dreamscape. "I am so not in Kansas anymore."

***

"This isn't happening." Dorothy slowed as the road changed again. She sat on a rock and watched as the road twisted and turned for no reason, like it was turning into a giant, etched rune in the ground. The gravel of the road merged into thick, green blocks covered in yellow and brown lichen. The road disappeared into the horizon after crisscrossing a field of bright red flowers. The buzzing in her head was gone, but a new sound replaced it. The soft purr of cats? "I have to be dreaming."

She set the fruit down in a loose pile, keeping one in her hand. Trying to judge the time, Dorothy guessed it to be around noon. She smelled the fruit—no scent. The meat of it was firm, the skin red and yellow blotches and no set shape.

She reached into her boot for the Swiss Army knife and cut into the fruit. Inside was white and laden with odd-colored seeds. She detected something sweet, closed her eyes, and bit in. The fruit was delicious, and she relished it. Juice dribbled down her chin; she wiped it with her fingers then greedily sucked at the fluid. Dorothy devoured the remaining fruit, focusing more on the juice than the food. Feeling energized, she left the cores by the rock and set out.

There was something wrong with the road, and she knew it after the first few steps. It led in no particular direction, turned into itself on several occasions, and other times stopped at the intersection of another of its own paths. In the tall grasses that grew around the road, more than once, Dorothy thought she heard rustling. Nothing appeared. Nothing leapt out to snap awful teeth or rake at her skin with its claws.

The road had an odd energy. Sometimes, she'd see sparks between the stones as though the static from her movement was being transmitted through the moss on the green rocks. Hearing something deep and metallic and screeching, Dorothy stopped and crouched down under what she hoped was cover from the tall grasses. Examining the stones in the road, hidden beneath the lichens, Dorothy saw a pattern. She scraped with her hands and eventually her knife to reveal some kind of rune. Energy pulsed along it and jumped to the next stone in its path. Then came the distinct sounds of footsteps. But like everything else in this place, it didn't sound right. Two regular steps followed by one very large, labored step.

She stood, folding the knife, catching her reflection on the blade for a moment and stuffed it into her pocket. On the road ahead of her only a few feet away was something absurdly wild, a crazed creature out of the three-legged race at the state fair. The right side of it was a bipedal lion, face caught in a warped roar. The mane appeared combed back from its face, dirty and matted. Vicious claws sprouted from its one arm and one free leg. The other side was part man but made of metal. It had an axe held tightly in a gloved hand. Each movement brought a squeal of metal.

Red eyes glowed from the center of the metal head. The one free leg moved haphazardly, disjointed. And whatever it was, was joined at the hip, one right and one left leg fused together in an abomination of flesh and metal. A mechanical cry erupted from the metal side while the lion part let out a pathetic, choked roar.

Dorothy took off through the grasses. She had nothing to fight this monstrosity. There were no more fence posts. She could hear the *whoosh* of the woodsman's axe clearing a path through the grass. It was slowing, and each time she risked a glance, it seemed like the halves fought against each other. The lion raked its claws across the already scratched and scarred chest plate of the tin man. It hop-ran with an off gait, the lion trying to run one way while the metal man surged forward. The outer legs moving easily, followed by the forced lope of the fused middle.

She ducked into a crawl, hiding in the grass, moving when she dared. She didn't risk a glance back for fear of seeing the thing too close behind. She tried to keep the path, or what she remembered of it, off to her right and crept, stopping often to listen. Labored breaths, metallic groans, and painful cries always seemed over her shoulder. The grass wouldn't hide her forever.

Dorothy quickened her pace, thinking the beast sounded tired. *Why does a metal thing need to breath?* She half stood, but it was nowhere in sight. Maybe it had fallen while chasing her. She needed a weapon if she wanted to live to see home—or what was left of it after the storm.

She took off at a slow run, hoping she was still moving in the same direction as before. She stepped on the tiled road again, her foot sliding in the yellow moss. A cat with golden eyes and long, iridescent fur that fluctuated color came out of the grass and sat in front of her. Dorothy reached out a hand to pat it and pulled back, remembering where she was. The gold eyes followed her movements then looked up at her, curious at first and then bored.

"Follow me," it said and walked down the road. It purred when it walked, and without analyzing her decision, Dorothy followed the cat. She watched the soft, gentle steps and the way the fur rippled in the breeze. She stopped, smelling it again. A breeze from the sea? Looking around, there was no hint of the ocean or a harbor. Just an endless, grassy plain that someplace far ahead merged with another field of red flowers.

"Excuse me, Mr. Cat."

"Miss," it said.

"Sorry, Miss Cat." Dorothy jogged to catch up. "Can you tell me where, how, what, and why?"

"No. Just follow me."

"But I'm following a talking cat down a strange road in a place I don't know." The cat stopped and turned to look at Dorothy with golden eyes.

"I don't explain. I tell the lost ones to follow me, and I lead them through the maze before something comes out of nowhere and lops their head off with a giant, bloody axe."

"There was a storm. I was running for the storm cellar, and I woke up here. Little flying bug things were biting me, and I killed a scarecrow." Dorothy rubbed her arms, remembering the pain.

"So the storm brought you?" Dorothy nodded in response. "Do you know why?" She shook her head. "The storms always have a reason." The cat continued on. "You're in between. Your physical being is . . . elsewhere. Your consciousness is here." Dorothy rushed to walk beside the cat. She looked into the grasses swaying to the unknown breeze and saw dozens more cats, sitting and waiting.

"You're saying I'm asleep. This is all a messed up dream?"

"No, I'm not." The cat stopped and sat, started to clean itself. "What I'm saying is: Part of you is here, and the other part isn't." Dorothy felt tears brimming. The confusion was overwhelming almost as terrifying and disjointed as the conjoined Lion/Woodsman.

"I fell asleep watching a movie. And the storm siren woke me up. You know what I was watching, cat?"

"Yes I do."

"This is a nightmare. I'm asleep in my bed. I got hit in the head or something, and my uncle must have carried me to my bedroom."

"Sadly, no." The cat continued walking. "Follow me; don't dally." They walked in silence for what seemed an eternity. The light in the sky never changed, never brighter, never darker. The cats in the grass paid them no mind. Dorothy thought hard while she walked, trying to figure it all out. Sometimes between steps, she'd watch the arcing lights on the stones.

"You're going to hurt yourself if you keep thinking like that," the cat said.

"You can hear my thoughts?"

"Of course I can. Cats can't talk. Have you seen my mouth move once with a word?" Dorothy tried to shut down her mind, focus on the road ahead. "Much better thank you." They walked; Dorothy didn't watch the stones or stare at the sky. She even stopped looking over her shoulder. The road ended abruptly at the sea of flowers. The cat stopped.

"Walk straight, don't stray from the path." Dorothy looked, but there was nothing discernible cut through the flowers. "Stop questioning and accept. It will open up to you soon. When you come to the great, green city, stop. All your questions will be answered soon."

"How soon?" Dorothy asked, turning to look at the cat. It was gone from the road, as well as the road. She stood alone in the vast sea of flowers and tried to find the path.

***

Through the red flowers swaying on unfelt breezes, there were no more cats. No more nightmare creatures. Her stomach growled once again, the stolen fruit eaten . . . hours ago? Or was it days?

The flowers stopped, no explanation, no thinning of the field. Neat grass took their place, and cut like a dirty scar through the center was another road. This time, the bricks were yellow and glowed with more glyphs and runes carved on them.

Far off in the distance, she heard another rumble, constant and faint. Much louder than her stomach—or so she imagined with each step. The winged creatures from the barn fluttered overhead. Great insect heads, feathers the color of the dead scarecrow's eyes, reptilian wings with awful claws that captured the wind. For a moment, Dorothy thought she heard a gull. "Gulls means ocean that means food."

Soon, she heard the crashing of distant waves. The sky was polluted with the flying creatures, but they paid her no mind. For the first time since she arrived, Dorothy saw the moon sitting low in the sky, a jagged rip torn through the center. It was cracked, immense chunks of rocks stagnant in the sky near the rift. Then, she saw the tall spires and great dome of the city. Like everything else in this place, it wasn't right.

The spires moved up and down; the giant dome swiveled occasionally. Dorothy ran for the building, for a balloon ride home or at the very least a good night's sleep and a hot meal. The endless time spent in this landscape was fatiguing her body and mind.

"This place has thrown its worst at me." She stopped and took a deep breath. The spires and domes seemed to be sinking. "No!" she screamed and ran faster. The great grinding and rending that filled the chilled air disturbed the flying beasts. Agitated, they dove and climbed. They were feeding. As Dorothy got closer, she saw the torn apart bodies of the Woodsman-Lion. The lion part smiled, finally at peace. Pained, mechanical wheezes filtered out of the Woodsman, his axe nowhere to be seen. She covered her mouth running past. The dome was definitely sinking. Each step, each desperate breath was taking away her chances of getting home or waking up.

Dorothy slid to a stop, bent over, hands on knees, breathing deeply. Continuing down the road, she slowed to a walk. *Yellow brick road.*

"This is a fairy tale!" she screamed. She ripped grass from the ground, flung it into the air, screamed and hollered until the tantrum passed.

She felt silly at losing control. After, Dorothy looked around to make sure no one saw her, before she arrived at the city. Only it wasn't. It was a great and massive creature, older than space and time. The green dome of its head looked up at her through a thousand sparkling eyes. The spires of its wings moved with each massive breath. It was sinking through a portal. And through it, Dorothy saw Kansas and the farm and more. Tornadoes destroyed everything in their path. Storms raged, pelting everything with softball-sized chunks of ice. Lightning bolted out, blasting everything. The raw power jumped and arced.

"It really is the end." The portal widened as the Elder God began his descent to her time and place.

"No child, it is the beginning." His deep, booming voice filled her mind. Through his many eyes, she saw the farm, her family like lifeless rag dolls caught in the winds of the twister. The barn and house were shredded, and the debris shot out like bullets.

"Step through, and come with me." Dorothy turned to see a dozen cats on the yellow brick road, eyes pulsing gold in time with the bricks.

Taking a deep breath, Dorothy stepped off the edge of the cliff. The wind buffeted and spun her. She slowed nearing the portal, a giant, star-filled hole where the shoreline of this place should be. Dorothy felt the freezing chill of space as the oxygen was ripped from her lungs.

"I don't understand," she gasped.

"Mortals were not meant to travel the portals."

Dorothy plummeted toward the remains of the farm. Strange creatures were there. Clouds of fire and massive piles of crawling flesh with dozens of eyes that gibbered madly. Of the farm, the only thing still standing was the windmill.

"That's odd," she thought, and the world went dark.

THE GUMDROP APOCALYPSE

PETE RAWLIK

Based on Red Riding Hood by Charles Perrault

AS THE WOLF used the oar to push them away from shore, he heard the little girl in red let out a whimpering cry. "Grandmother is dead." She said it as if they hadn't been there, hadn't seen what had happened, hadn't suffered the consequences, hadn't been on the run for days. "Grandmother is dead," she said again as if trying to convince herself.

The lumberjack put a comforting hand on Red's shoulder. She was called Red, though that was not her name, because real names, as her grandmother taught her, have power. Red shrugged the man's hand away.

"Grandmother is dead," she cried, "and it is entirely your fault." There was venom in her voice. "You were warned!" Red screamed, "You were told the rules, told only to eat the food we brought with us, not to eat anything in the house itself." Red pulled back her cowl, letting night reflect back from her eyes. "I warned you about Grandmother, told you she was a witch, told you not to interfere with my lessons. You said you knew about witches, that you could follow the rules. Do you think you can upset the order of the universe and not suffer the consequences?"

"I ate a gumdrop, one gumdrop!" the man pleaded.

"And now Grandmother is dead, the moon-lens is cracked, and the dark young prepare the forest for the coming of their mother." She pointed at the great orb and the jagged scar that ran across it. Smoke from the devastated forest stained the shattered sphere orange. "You ate a gumdrop, and now the Black Goat comes to claim that kingdom which is rightfully hers. Yes, Grandmother was a witch, a world witch, and like us all had her part to play. Since time immemorial, we have dwelt in the Enchanted Wood and performed our stories for men and Gods of Earth alike. Now, our home is lost. We flee, we things of myth and fancy, like zoogs and trolls in the morning sun, all because you ate a gumdrop."

The wolf watched as the lumberjack curled up, made himself small, while Red sat back and took some pyrrhic satisfaction in verbally abusing the man. The wolf moved the boat into the center of the river. They picked up speed as the current caught the tiny skiff and pushed it along. It was days to Ulthar and not far after that to the River Skai. The Skai would take them to the basalt city of Dylath-Leen and beyond that the Southern Sea. If they could make it to the sea, find passage to Kadath, perhaps the Gods of Earth could be implored to come to their aid, to take up arms against Shub-Niggurath, the Black Goat of the Woods. Perhaps.

Suddenly, the girl in red turned pale, whipped her head over the side of the sloop, and wretched violently into the wine-dark waters below. The lumberjack moved to help her, but the sick girl waved him off. "Over the river," she coughed, "Over the river and through the woods, to Grandmother's house . . . I'm too far from the path, and while I'm used to crossing the river, I've never gone downstream before. I think . . . " She whipped her head back over the water and gifted whatever she had left in her stomach to the fishes. "Where did we get a boat?"

The wolf shrugged. "It was there at the river. No one was watching, so I took it."

Red nodded as her eyes closed. "Of course you did; what else would you . . . " but she was asleep before she could finish.

The wolf kept to the center of the river. Great shadows crept along the riverbank, their source always just out of sight. Wolf knew they weren't bears, but that's how he thought of them. They were monstrous things, massive, lumbering beasts with legs like tree trunks and arms like thick whipping vines. They moved in herds and thundered through the forest, trampling all that stood in their way. Nothing was safe; the whole landscape fell before them. Why the river seemed to keep them at bay, he had no idea, but it did, and he used it to their advantage.

Once the river left the wood, those who served the Black Goat ceased to follow. Not long after, Red's basket of food ran out. Wary that they were being hunted, they stopped where possible and gathered wild berries, marsh mallows, and such. Five days on the run and they had little to keep their strength up. Red was feverish; she had never left the wood before, never left the path, never been anywhere else before.

It made her sick. Sweat soaked the cloak, and the lumberjack kept at her forehead with a damp cloth. Despite their best attempts, Red drifted in and out of consciousness, moaning the whole time about her dead grandmother.

A week on, and the moon hung in the sky like a piece of broken biscotti. They could see the towers of Ulthar, the city of cats, and the great force that gathered outside its gates. It was an army of cats. Tabby cats swarmed through the makeshift tents. Prides of lions roared orders at subordinate platoons of Siamese, Manx, and Persians. Cheetahs functioning as couriers ran from unit to unit. A lone Smilodon stalked through the camp, scattering most of the others. Only the Saturnine cats, their jellied skins prismatic in the light, and those horrid gray feline-things from Uranus stood their ground against the extinct monster.

A cohort of lynx decked out in armor and armed with steel claws surrounded them and then guided them into and through the camp. As they pulled the boat out of the water, it shrunk until it was no bigger than a large hat. They carried it with them, and the further they went from the river, the smaller it became. Once back on dry land, Red's weakness dissipated, and as they approached a green pavilion, she was able to walk on her own. By this time, the boat had shrunk so small that Red popped it into her pocket. Inside the tent was a harried little cat with large, tired eyes and a limping gait. In places, his coat had become thin, and the skin revealed beneath was pale and squamous. Behind him stood a man who wore nothing more than a simple cassock. After they settled, the cat began purring and rubbing up against the man's leg, who after a brief pause began to speak. "My Master bids you welcome, and wishes he could offer some hospitality, but alas, neither he nor any of the other cats are in a position to be hospitable. The best we can do is give you meager supplies and move you on downriver. A flotilla of refugees is gathering in Dylath-Leen. They sail for fabled Kadath in six days."

The lumberjack moaned in protest, "What of Ulthar? Is there nothing the Patriarch Atal and the others can do?"

The catspeaker shook his head. "The city ordered an evacuation; only we few remain. We cannot hope to stand against the Black Goat herself, but we shall do our best to keep her young at bay."

The wolf begged. "Can we not seek refuge in the city? Would that not be a better place to make a fortified stand?"

The cat yelped, and a puzzled look came across the man's face as he opened his mouth to speak. But whatever he had intended to translate was lost amongst a roaring thunder that suddenly filled the air. A great shadow fell across the land. The amassed feline warriors, the guardians of Ulthar, charged forward, hissing and spitting at unseen foes. The master cat himself launched over the trio and slashed at a tentacle of malevolent darkness that twisted through the camp and struck at them.

The trio ran while all about them, the horde of cats screamed, fought, fell, and died as the capricorn forces cut them down. They followed the river and tried not to cry out as the wine-dark waters turned red with blood. As they reached the walls of the city, they moved to bypass the abandoned metropolis, but there came a great cracking, a rending peal that set their very teeth aching. The wolf looked back. The sky turned black, and the moon-lens had shattered completely. In its place, a great, slitted eye stared down at them in hunger. The gaze of the cyclopean orb was palpable, and beneath it, the three felt ill. Desperate to be out of its sight, they scurried inside the walls of Ulthar and took refuge within its towering temple.

Once inside, Red collapsed, exhausted and fearful, muttering, "My, what big eyes you have," before she passed into unconsciousness.

Red could not say how long she slept, but when she awoke, both the wolf and lumberjack were gone. Far below, on the field of battle, the forces both feline and capran lay strewn about, all quite dead, or at the least mortally wounded. In the sky, there was a hole where the moon-lens had once been. It had no color, that hole. She thought it should be black, but it wasn't; it was simply a hole, a hole in the sky. On the horizon, beyond the fields, beyond the blasted wood, something titanic lurched. It was a smoky, gelatinous thing that spawned tendrils of vapor and things more substantial that reached out and tore through what remained of the Enchanted Forest. Red shuddered and turned away when a trio of sclera opened up and stared in her direction with horizontal pupils.

She wandered through the temple, searching for her missing companions. She found the wolf in the temple larder, passed out between two half-eaten cakes, a small pile of chicken bones to one side. At his feet were a dozen empty bottles, ales mostly, but one or two larger decanters of wine. A round of cheese had been cut; a great knife was still embedded in the pungent mold. Slowly, a thought crept into Red's mind, wormed inside, took root, and blossomed. Red took up the long, sharp utensil and smiled wickedly. "My, what a big mouth you have!" Red, wielding the knife, went to work on the wolf, carrying out the rending her grandmother had so often shown her how to do.

It took hours to bone the wolf and mince the flesh then fold it into the dough. After she stuffed the pies into the oven, she waited, letting the aroma wash over the room, and down the hall, and throughout the tower. Red waited, and in time, her quarry came to her. The lumberjack stumbled into the kitchen, in his arms a great conglomeration of jewelry, including necklaces, tiaras, bracelets, rings, and the like. He came in following the smell, intoxicated, mesmerized, seduced by the aroma of his baked companion. He went to the oven and, with some difficulty, refusing to set down his treasures, pulled the great doors open. He marveled at the great pie within and thus never heard Red come up behind him. Red shoved the huge man from behind, and he tumbled into the fire still clinging to his trinkets. As she shut the door, Red muttered, "My, what big hands you have!"

Somewhere deep within the alleys of the city, something stirred, a building shifted, a block rose up, and a parapet sank. Red ran up the stairs, sprinting feverishly to the top of the tower, chanting an ancient couplet. Blood had been spilled in the temple of Ulthar, and great magics were in play. It was no simple spell Red had begun, not hearth magic, not hedge magic, not even ha'penny magic, but blood magic and the blood of fables at that.

THE GUMDROP APOCALYPSE

Red took her knife and cut a line across her palm. As she did, the minaret tilted, shifted, and rose up into the sky. Buildings folded in on themselves, the fortifications shook themselves free of the earth, and the great city of Ulthar walked. For all its size, all its vast, bulky constructs of granite and sandstone, the city of Ulthar moved across the landscape sleekly, silently with strength of purpose. It moved as a cat would, but a cat the size of a city is hard to hide.

On the horizon, the Black Goat of the Woods reared up and hissed at Ulthar. The city roared back and charged, each loping step clearing miles. In the tower, young Red took off her cloak and cast it aside. She had learned much from her grandmother, learned more than the old witch had meant to teach her. She took the boat from her pocket and made it big, big enough to climb into, big enough to carry her away, and she flew from the tower on raging winds.

The two gods brought their ancient conflict to the Dreamlands, and as they struck at each other, the foundations of the world shook, cracked, and split asunder. The oceans rose up and swallowed the already devastated lands. Cities fell, and the Land of Dreams came to ash. And as they destroyed one world, the young girl, this young world witch, caught the energies that spilled from the battle. Caught them and used them to spin another.

She was a gnat flying between two warring gods, stealing from them what she could. She took those dark energies, those ancient magics, those eldritch forces, and with them wove a cage. She spun it out of their own power, and because of that, it had power over them when nothing else could have. She circled round and round, and a great globe formed about the beasts, and still they raged at each other. It took hours, perhaps even days. The girl lost all track of time, but eventually, the two ancient forces became tangled in the web of their own making and ceased their battle.

They turned attentions to the little thing flitting about in a wooden boat, but by then, it was too late. She had stolen much of their power, and as she grew strong, they weakened. The god-things, Shub-Niggurath and Ulthar, the Black Goat of the Woods and the Cat that Played at City, opened their once great maws and roared at the little girl who had taken so much from them and wouldn't give it back.

And as she sewed up the last hole and set the moon back in its place, she roared back at the things that had once been gods, "My, what big voices you have!"

CURIOSITY

WINIFRED BURNISTON

Based on Bluebeard by Charles Perrault

SONIA KORBAN KNEW right away that Charles Blaubart was a little different. They met at a social gathering sponsored by the Internet dating site they'd joined. He strolled up behind the insufferable fool droning on to Sonia and began making ridiculous faces behind the guy's back. Sonia kept her composure as Charles faked his own death several times before Mr. Dull finally went on his way.

Charles hummed the familiar beat to one of Sonia's favorite songs and whispered, "Can anybody find me somebody to love?"

"So," he said, sliding into the seat across from her, "what names have you picked out for our children? Please tell me you aren't one of those people who favors state names like Dakota or Nevada for children."

Sonia burst out laughing. "No, no. I prefer good old-fashioned names. I can't imagine why anyone would name their kids that way."

"Well," he mused, "I supposed it might be to commemorate the state the parents were in when the child was conceived."

Sonia smirked and volleyed back with, "If that were true, wouldn't there be a hell of a lot of kids named Intoxicated running around?"

Charles clutched at his heart and began to moan in feigned agony.

"That is just awful. Good Lord, woman, are you trying to kill me?" He smiled his big, dimpled grin at her, and it was all over. He was the one.

***

A year later, Sonia sat in stunned silence, a pile of student paperwork and a history book in front of her. This was the first time Charles's opinion surprised her. She'd been correcting essays for her Greek mythology unit and casually mentioned discussing the story of Pandora. She'd been pleased because the class had connected the story to others in which women were blamed for the ruination of man. Charles piped in at the end of her description with his own sexist remark.

"Well, of course she couldn't help looking. One, she was told not to. And two, women always need to see for themselves no matter what the danger. Their curiosity gets the better of them."

And so, here she sat, looking at him as though he were a complete stranger.

Sonia leaned on the stack of essays and asked, "Do you actually believe that?" she asked. "Of all women? Do you think I'd be so consumed with curiosity I'd eventually crack and take a peek?"

Charles smiled at her mischievously and shot back, "You bet your life I do."

CURIOSITY

This led to their first official fight, ending only when they both agreed to disagree, and the subject was shelved.

***

Two months passed. Charles was planning another trip to his family's cabin deep in the woods just outside of Dunwich to do some research. He worked in antiquities, often acquiring and translating bizarre texts, scrolls, and carvings for some even stranger clients. It was time-consuming work requiring a great deal of concentration, and the cabin, he said, was the ideal place. Sonia's need for background noise while working was often deemed distracting.

However, this time it was school vacation week, and he was willing to put up with her noise. In fact, he said her presence was desired. Odd, she thought, but flattering.

"Do you remember the discussion we had a couple of months ago? The one about women's curiosity?" he broached shortly after getting on the highway.

"Of course." She was annoyed he brought it up.

"How would you like to prove one way or the other who's right?"

Sonia bristled at his proposition. "This is your plan? You finally decide I'm worthy of joining you at your precious secluded retreat because you want to prove I'm a nosy bitch? It's insulting!"

They were both silent for a while. Charles finally spoke.

"I'm sorry. I really do want you with me. It only crossed my mind last night we could add an element of mystery to the week by playing this game. I didn't mean to upset you. I honestly thought it might be fun;

that's all." He reached over and laid his hand on hers. "Do you want me to take you home?"

Sonia let his hand stay there and stared out the car window, mulling it over. She was perturbed but believed him. She didn't want to be mad, and she wanted to spend the week together. But there was some truth to his comment she couldn't ignore. She was dying to see his cabin.

"No," she said, "I'm fine. Let's have a nice time together." She turned her hand over and gave his a loving squeeze as they continued on their way.

***

Sonia gaped at the house when it came into view. The cabin was enormous and definitely didn't fit the image she had of a rustic getaway. Yes, it was isolated in the woods. And if not for the strange-colored patches of algae on the water and the slight fishy odor, the lake would be picturesque. But this was a monstrous Victorian home seemingly dropped into the woods. It reminded her more of the "cottages" in Newport, Rhode Island. There was wrought iron topping every peak and valley on the façade. It was a deep green, camouflaging it in the surrounding forest. The front doors were etched glass with oddly swirled, almost aquatic images depicted in the slightly warped panes. Overall, it was a masterpiece of craftsmanship and the creepiest looking place she'd ever seen.

"Cozy," she stated flatly. Charles peered over at her and started to laugh.

"That's the last word I'd use to describe this place. I always imagine the Munsters coming out the front door to make it less scary."

"Why do you come up here at all if it bothers you?" she inquired.

"I don't know. Tradition, maybe? Or because it allows me to focus and get the job done quickly so I can go home? Either way, I don't procrastinate, and I get my work finished."

Sonia let it drop.

***

As Charles gave her the tour, she discovered the interior proved to be more welcoming. Someone, Charles perhaps, had transformed each room into a Pottery Barn catalog page. Everything was clean, crisp, bright, and new. The upstairs bedrooms proved to be as lovely, like some breathtaking, upscale inn. The third floor walk-in attic was Charles's workspace. It had lots of windows and a separate door that went further up to the top of the front turret. This was the only room displaying a smattering of old photographs. The people in each appeared austere, with big, bulgy eyes. They reminded her of Don Knotts in *The Incredible Mr. Limpet* in mid-transformation. If these were his relatives, then Charles had clearly gotten all the good genes in the family.

After the walk through, Charles sorted the groceries they'd brought into an amazing kitchen. They settled their bags into the master bedroom, and each set to work. Charles went up to his office, and Sonia chose the enormous kitchen table, correcting schoolwork and writing future lesson plans. She'd been working for an hour or so when she decided to poke around the kitchen and rustle up some lunch. Between what they brought and what was already there, the choices were seemingly endless. But cooking was not her forte. In the end, she made a simple meal of grilled cheese sandwiches and canned tomato soup.

Charles meandered downstairs to join her. He opened a bag of potato chips to go along with the soup and sandwiches. He munched away, sitting across from her, clearly still engrossed in whatever he'd been doing. The glazed look finally cleared, and he smiled lovingly at her.

"Thanks for the lunch, Hon. I'm always forgetting to eat when I'm here." He looked at her for a second, a little furrow deepening between his eyes. "Everything okay? Are you bored yet?"

She grinned. He knew her so well. Although it had only been a few hours, she was already crawling out of her skin.

"I'm a little antsy, but you expected that. I was planning on poking around after lunch if that's okay with you?"

A shit-eating grin spread across his face, and she knew it was something to do with his bet.

"Okay, smartass, what's the bet? That I couldn't help but wander around the house and yard? That isn't curiosity; that's boredom."

"Close but not quite. Don't get mad; you're the one bringing this back up. And you're right; looking around a new place is perfectly normal." He paused and chewed on his sandwich, obviously trying to decide if he should continue. When he saw she wasn't truly upset, he went on.

"What if, on the other hand, you were told you could have absolute free reign to go anywhere you liked, inside or out, except for one room? What if you were expressly forbidden to go into that specific room?

Wouldn't that drive you nuts? Wouldn't you want to know what the hell was in there? And wouldn't you have to take one tiny peek to see what the big deal was all about?"

Charles seemed genuinely excited over her thoughts on this matter, almost giddy with the idea of undertaking this foolish experiment. For herself, boredom lurked around every corner of this place, and he was offering her the prospect of doing something peculiar and potentially entertaining for the week. It overrode any anger or misgiving she'd had earlier.

"Which room?" she asked.

***

The rules were straightforward. Sonia could go anywhere in the house and on the grounds save for the room at the top of the turret. Although that door was kept locked, Sonia was in possession of the house keys, which included one to the forbidden room. They'd agreed to the honor system to monitor the game.

To intrigue her more, Charles moved his work into the downstairs den, leaving the door to the turret unguarded all day long. And as an added temptation, he was also in the habit of taking a long walk each afternoon to help clear his head. She'd be left in the house alone and to her own devices. If Sonia made it to the end of the week without going into the room, she won. If she caved, even asking to see the room before going home, he won. The winner got dinner at his or her favorite restaurant and, of course, unlimited bragging rights.

***

The first few days went well. Sonia kept busy shuffling her way through class papers, going for walks, practicing cooking, and catching up on reading. And then she started to get bored. Really bored. Charles was holed up in the den, bumping and thumping around in there for hours.

Her mind began to wander, and her thoughts were about the house as well as the room at the top of the turret. There couldn't possibly be much up there. Based on what it looked like from the outside, it's fairly small. *And I'll get to see the inside at some point. Won't I?* She reviewed the rules and began to wonder if that were true.

What if he wanted to continue the bet each time she visited? And if that were the case, was there more to the selection of the room than a random choice? She considered whether Charles had planned this before they'd left and how he'd conveniently avoided this room on the tour. It became more plausible the longer she thought about it. And this led her to wonder what he might actually have hidden away in there.

By midweek, the room was nearly all she thought about. She tried coming up with various diversions to keep from dwelling on it. Worse, she could tell by the glint in Charles's eyes he knew it was driving her nuts. It was like poison ivy. You know you're not supposed to scratch, but the more you think about it, the more intense the need becomes. Worse yet, she swore on several occasions she'd heard faint noises coming from somewhere upstairs. The groans and moans of the old house were now adding to the unending torment of trying to focus on anything else but that room.

On the second to the last day, Charles said he needed to go into town to pick up a few supplies to restock the kitchen. He was lounging on the couch, and nothing changed in his voice, but she knew it was a test of her resolve when he asked, "Do you want to drive in with me or stay here?"

She stared over at him, trying to determine how she felt about this question. Should she be annoyed or not? They'd both agreed to this wager and both simply hated losing at any sort of challenge. She decided to play along.

"I'll stay if you don't mind. How long do you think you'll be gone?"

This time, Charles turned in her direction, grinning. "Oh, probably a couple of hours. I may poke around in some of the antique stores while I'm there. Sure you don't want to come?"

Sonia stuck out her tongue playfully. "Nope, I'll be fine on my own. Go. Enjoy. Because you're going to lose this bet."

"Okay, if you say so, Babe. You've certainly lasted longer than I expected." A dark expression fell across his face as he intoned, "Just remember, if you go in there while I'm gone, you'll open a portal that'll lead to the destruction of mankind."

After a pause, both of them started laughing.

"Oh, right, sure. I'll remember that," she said, waving. "And the pc term is now humankind, Honey."

"Humankind. Got it. Do you want me to pick you up anything while I'm gone?" he asked on the way out.

***

Sonia was sprawled across the couch, attempting to read a magazine when she heard it. A thumping sound coming from somewhere upstairs. She didn't have to get up, she knew. She looked over at the clock. Thirty minutes had passed since Charles left. This was a setup. It irked her a little. Mostly because she'd managed to push down any thoughts about the room until the thumping started.

The noise grew louder. He was really banging away up there. How the hell was he managing that? Computer program? Was it recorded? *When?* Except for a couple of walks, she'd been around all week.

A heart-stopping shriek came from upstairs. Her body turned to ice, and she needed to clutch at the couch to keep from falling. She felt lightheaded. Every nerve in her body strained at the urge to run. *What the hell was that?*

Then, the house fell completely silent except for the ticking of the mantle clock. The blood behind her right eye pulsed in time with the sound, as though it might explode out of her skull at any moment. Her heart slowed as the initial shock wore off. A slow rising tide of anger bubbled up through her body. *I could've been on the stairs when that scream went off. I could've fallen and broken my arm or leg. Or neck! What a reckless asshole!*

***

Fuming inside, she got up from the couch to get a drink. The house remained still. She looked up the stairs toward his study and the secrets within. What did she really know about Charles and this house? She'd never met his family. His parents were elderly and lived in a retirement community in Florida. They sent holiday cards and casually chatted with him on the phone at Thanksgiving and Christmas. He wasn't close to his siblings, and they were scattered across the country. She wasn't even positive how many he had. Two brothers and a sister? Or was it the other way around?

And now that she thought about it, why was he out buying items to stock the kitchen? He didn't come up here often, maybe once every two months as far as she knew. Canned and dry goods made sense to a certain extent, but there were plenty. This could be a mild obsessive/compulsive thing of his, but he never kept the kitchen at home this organized. Hell, their furniture wasn't this nice!

A worm of dread began an icy tunnel in her stomach as Sonia thought about how much she didn't really know about him. He seemed like such a loving, thoughtful guy, but . . .

You've never met his family, coworkers, or friends.

She'd never really thought about it before. *Just who the hell is Charles Blaubart?*

What if he wasn't the person she thought? What if he was coming up here all the time? And what if the sounds she'd heard weren't recorded? She'd always been puzzled by television interviews of people who knew murderers and serial killers. Nobody ever seemed clued in. The whackos were always described as nice, normal, a great neighbor, a wonderful son, boyfriend, or husband. Was she now in that same situation? Was Charles getting a sick thrill keeping her in the same house with a victim?

Sonia was at the top of the stairs and outside the study before she realized it, pondering the dark possibilities.

Entering the study, she crossed the room and stood in front of the turret door, trying to make up her mind. She pulled out the key ring and banged on the door with her other fist. *Okay, fine. You happy, Sonia?*

Nothing but your overactive imagination. She was about to walk out of the room when she heard a faint whimpering coming from above. *Holy shit! Somebody's in there!*

Screw the bet; that noise was a response, not a recording.

The key danced around the lock in her trembling hand before it clicked, and Sonia turned the handle. She pulled the door toward her, revealing a darkened set of stairs and a hatch to the forbidden room.

There was no light switch, so she climbed the stairs in darkness. As her eyes adjusted to the dimness, she saw something carved into the panel of the hatch door above her head. It appeared to be a series of random gouges. She turned to double check for a light switch when she caught sight of the same symbols etched on the back of the door below. She'd been so fixed on what lay behind the door she never actually looked at the back of it as it had opened. *What the hell is with the Blair Witch crap?*

Itching for a flashlight, she hesitated for a moment before pushing up the panel and sliding it over. Bracing a hand on either side of the opening, she continued up the stairs.

It was still gloomy, but the room received light from small windows high up on one wall. The room was devoid of furniture and bizarrely decorated. A series of random and haphazard lines were drawn on the floor. Each wall had a set of gigantic letters scrawled across it, forming what looked to be a series of repeated nonsense words. No one was in the room. And none of the walls seemed to be aligned properly. From the outside, it looked perfectly normal, but from the inside, it was angled so obscenely her mind wouldn't comprehend.

Turning back toward the hatch opening to leave, she heard a shuffling noise and whimper behind her. Whipping around, the room swirled and shimmered like heat rising over a gas grill. A hazy, misshapen figure formed in the oscillating light. It was monstrous in shape and appearance. Huge hands hung from limbs too long for its twisted, bulbous body. It reared back its withered, pinched head and emitted an earth-shattering shriek.

Run, run! Goddamnit, run! Paralyzed, she couldn't seem to get her feet to budge.

Whatever it was took a few shambling steps in her direction as it completed coalescing. She started to move, flinging herself in the direction of the hatch opening and landing half in and half out of the entry. She began frantically dragging herself through the hole to get down the stairs. The floor rumbled under the weight of the beast as it lumbered forward to stop her.

Get to the door! Get to the door! Ice and fire sliced into her leg as the talons on the beast's claw-like hand closed around her right calf. With a vicious twist of its wrist, she was yanked back. The bones in her arms jolted as she clung to the edge of the hatch. A white-hot bolt of pain shot up her leg as it snapped under the beast's grasp. A terrible shrieking sound was shaking her body and filling her ears. It took a second to register she was the one making that noise.

It took another moment for her brain to believe what her eyes were seeing. Charles was standing in the doorway! *Help me, Charles! Please help me! For the love of God, do something!* But what came out of her mouth was nothing more than guttural sounds and screaming.

He leaned against the door. "Didn't I say it would end this way, with you destroying the world? You are the last one I needed, Sweetie!" He smiled, did a little soft shoe shuffle, all the while insanely humming *Another One Bites the Dust*. He abruptly stopped his capering, a look of sincere regret registering on his face. "Damn, I miss Freddie Mercury," he declared. Sonia gaped at the man she loved only hours before. And then through a haze of agony, she watched as Charles transformed into a monstrosity. Huge. Clawed. A massive, red tentacle instead of a head. Everything tilted, and her mind snapped.

"I win," it said and started laughing hysterically.

All of the strength left her body. Sonia was jerked back through the opening and disappeared into oblivion as the sky began to darken.

THE ICE QUEEN

MAE EMPSON

Based on The Snow Queen by Hans Christian Anderson

GRETCHEN HOLDS A scuffed baseball comet over a five-gallon drum of planted winter beets.

"Will beet-earth survive?" she asks, signaling the start of our game.

I've got the rocket. It's not a real toy. I've made a triangular hand puppet out of an old rocket arugula seed packet. The word "rocket," still visible, compensates for how hard it is to recognize from the shape alone. We searched a lot of rooms in this high-rise, checking for toys after the lockdown, but couldn't find a single rocket. Kids like us, boys and girls both, threw their rockets away. Rockets failed. They couldn't save us from comets that fired back.

I fly the seed packet triangle on an intercept course, careful not to brush the red-veined greens of the beets poking out of the soil. You don't mess with food. Every part of a beet is edible.

"Mission control, this is Captain Kyle. I am in firing

range." Gretchen brings that baseball down toward beet-earth, as slow as she can. Waiting.

"Ka-pow," I yell. If Mom weren't gone, she'd lecture me that there isn't any sound in the vacuum of space. I know. But Gretchen likes sound effects.

"Foosh!" She tries to hide the baseball in a closed fist. "It explodes. We're saved! Way to go, Kyle."

Out the window behind her, I can see the snow that doesn't stop falling.

It's been over a year since the mile-wide comet/ship crashed into Arizona and kicked so much dirt into the atmosphere that it triggered this endless impact winter. The scientists, like my mom, and the bloggers and newscasters warned it would get cold afterwards and there wouldn't be enough food.

Gran and everyone else here in the city bought all the canned vegetables and dried grains they could carry. They bought seeds and soil, gallon drums and window boxes, and heating pads and fluorescent lights and generators.

We can't leave the high-rise. Mr. Slim and his gang keep it locked down tight to keep out looters and the aliens.

The rooms that have been converted into indoor gardens are like playing outside with all the dirt and green and light and heat. It's like sneaking back into the summers we grew up in, when my mom and Gretchen's parents were alive and you could order pizza or Chinese or anything just by making a call.

The phones stopped working about two weeks after the cable TV and internet a good nine months ago. The heat and lights still work. Mr. Slim and his men set up generators after the lockdown. We collect snow from the roof for water and strain it through cloth as it melts to take out the sediment—the pieces of Arizona, dirt, and people.

I don't see any lights in the other buildings through the window behind Gretchen. They didn't have the sense to lock down as fast as our building did. Mr. Slim and his gang acted quickly. They had guns and rooms already set up for growing something called weed. The grown-ups fought over it until it was gone. Maybe Mr. Slim still has some somewhere. He deserves it if you ask me. He knew a few of us could keep eating if he did what had to be done.

His gang didn't kill the old women or children who happened to be at home the day he took control. I guess he knew it would take extra hands to keep everything watered and catalog the other people's stuff. The gang needed folks like Gran to tell them which seeds to stockpile that grew quick and hardy indoors in the winter and didn't take much space to grow.

Gran's old enough to remember something she calls Victory Gardens, when she was younger and there was a war and it was important to grow food everywhere, even indoors. She told Mr. Slim what to choose. Beets, kale, radishes, ball-shaped carrots, and tomatoes. And she explained about mason jars and canning. That helped out too.

Gran adopted Gretchen after her parents died during the lockdown. Gretchen's like the little sister I never had—just two years younger, eight to my ten, though sometimes it can seem like a bigger gap because she doesn't understand everything's that happened. But that's why Gretchen can still laugh and smile. And that's gold as tomatoes as far as I'm concerned.

Gran thinks we're crazy for playing in the garden rooms so much. If we broke anything, we'd be in awful trouble, and you do not want to be in trouble with Mr. Slim, but we can't resist. We're always careful.

Gretchen moves over to a window box of kale and signals that another baseball impact event needs to be averted.

"Comet sighted," I confirm and plot the rocket on an intercept course, confident that kale-world, at least, can still be saved.

***

Gran stares out the window as the three of us sit and eat another night's ration of one cup of beet soup, watching the snow. "The snow bees are sure swarming tonight." She's always said that since we were kids and snow was fun. It still makes Gretchen laugh.

"Bzzzzzzz." Gretchen spreads her arms and flaps them, more like a bird than a bee.

I've looked at snowflakes and let Gretchen look too, and we've seen many shapes but nothing like a bee. As soon as I was old enough to use a microscope, Mom made me look and catalog what I saw to prove Gran wrong. I found hexagons, stars, branching stars—which mom called "stellar dendrites," and needles. Mom said it had to be about five below or colder to get needles.

Mom knew a lot about snow and climate change and comets but not enough about people to stay home when the looting and worse started.

I miss her.

I stare up at the sky through the window,

wondering what might be flying through those clouds other than snow.

Gretchen tracks my gaze and takes up watch beside me. "Looking for the queen?" Gran's told us that the snow bees have a queen—a queen bee, and the snow falls from the hem of her white, snow-spangled garments.

"Maybe. Yeah, sometimes I watch for her. Don't you?" I try to smile.

Let her think I'm chasing dreams. I'm looking for my mother, hoping she'll walk up the alley below in her bright red coat and long black hair and bang on the door, alive and well. And I'm looking for whatever rode in on the comet and shot down our ships. And for lights in the other buildings that might mean someone else is holding on. And for a break in the snow that might mean a change from . . . from *this*.

"Me too," Gretchen chimes in, and I see how wet her eyes are reflected in the window, and I think maybe she's watching for all the other stuff too.

***

That night, I'm stuck on that image of my mom coming up the alley and trying to get back in. What if she had somehow survived? Mr. Slim's guys don't open that door for anyone. Ever. Someone ought to be looking who still cares. I decide to stand watch. A vigil.

I slip out of our room as quiet as I can to not wake Gretchen, sleeping on the upper bunk. We have our pick of apartments now and move every couple of months just so something can be different.

Looking out over the tray of tomatoes along the living room window, I can see a few stars still visible through the pieces of Arizona in the sky. But I can't see out into the places beyond where my mom said a big comet like that had to have come from. My mom said that most long-period comets come from a place called the Oort Cloud, which is apparently a huge collection of comets, like if you dumped a million trays of ball-shaped, planet-sized ice cubes into space and they all just started rotating around each other in a big spherical mass.

When Gretchen and I play at being space invaders, we call ourselves the Oortic Army, which sounds a little like "arctic," and it feels that way since the impact winter. We play it exactly like hide and seek with the invader hiding. Since no one in our building has ever actually seen an alien, we assume they like to hide.

Mom knew the names of all the stars. She used to point out the patterns to me. I try to remember the name of the stars in the Big Dipper, as if reciting them perfectly was an incantation that could finally summon her. *Dubhe. Merak. Phecda. Megrez. Alioth. Mizar. Alkaid.*

I see nothing but snow falling and empty streets below.

I'm not going to cry even if it would water the tomatoes. She's dead. She's not coming back. I know it. Nothing's going to change. Nothing's going to get better.

I'm resigned to shuffle back to bed when a flicker of movement beyond the window catches my eye.

There's something moving down around the tenth floor. It keeps looking in windows, flying from one to another. I'm looking almost straight down at it, and it's dark, so all I can make out is the blur of wings. It should be too dark to see even that much, but there's something slightly phosphorescent about those rapidly beating wings.

I remember how Gran used to say the snow bees' breath against the window caused the film of frost we would find each morning, and I know this isn't Jack Frost or Bumble Frost or whatever happy airy-fairy she had in mind.

I think it's one of *them*.

It works its way across the bank of windows and then methodically rises and starts working its way back across the next floor, like the way I remember eating corn on the cob, one row at a time, back and forth.

I miss corn on the cob.

If I wait long enough, the creature will come by here. I don't want it to see me, but I want to see it.

I run and get Gran's hand mirror from the hall bathroom. If I stand flush against the wall beside the window and look in the mirror angling it just right, I might be able to get a glimpse of it without it seeing me.

Do I have the mirror positioned right? It's so hard to tell since it's mostly reflecting darkness. I risk a glimpse. Nothing yet. But I can see the creature is closer, only about two floors down, working its way down the row.

Eyes back to the mirror. Nothing. Still nothing.

And then I see it, and my empty stomach finds some scrap of lingering beet soup to turn to bile that rushes back up my throat.

It *is* like a bee, a human-sized white bee, but with the claws of a crab. It's got the fat, segmented body of a bee and two pairs of ribbed wings. But no bee in any book I've read has wings that glow in the dark or six pincer-like legs with saw-toothed claws, thick with white hair. In the space where a bee would have a head, a tangle of antennae writhe like tentacles.

One antenna lifts and turns a round, white eye at the tip of its length to face straight at the mirror.

The mirror explodes into a thousand shards—hexagons, stars, branched stars, and needles—like flakes of ice, some pieces as big as my thumb and others fine as dust. I pick up one of the bigger hexagonal pieces. The image of the creature is still reflecting, frozen into the mirror-glass, but each shard only shows a fragment, a tiny piece of the awful entirety.

I realize that my left eye is *burning*. I rub it, but it just hurts more, sharp as a knife. A cut so fine it didn't even hurt at first. Sharp as a needle. The pain doesn't fade. Did I get a shard of the mirror in my eye?

I grab the edge of the window-box to steady myself, catch sight of the tomatoes, and scream.

The tomatoes are wilting and decaying, shriveling and shrinking, graying from the inside out with patches of dark fungal growth seeping out their skins.

Did that *thing* fly window to window for the sole purpose of somehow spoiling our plants? No, no, no. We can't lose the food. We can't. We'll starve. Or more likely, Mr. Slim will calculate the losses and realize there'd be less mouths to feed and meat—actual meat—if they killed off the old women and children. Maybe that's been his plan all along, now that I think about it. Letting us live was an easy way to preserve our meat.

I hear footsteps behind me. I shouldn't have

screamed. I don't want Gran and Gretchen to see what's happened. Gran will know how bad it is. Gretchen probably understands more than I give her credit for.

I risk a glance at the window, and moving my eye makes it sting even worse. The creature's gone. And then I look back and realize they are too. The old woman lurching toward me has discolored skin and a bloated belly. Her nails have fallen off, and one eye's rotted to liquid, dripping down the side of her face. The blistered, capsizing skin of her remaining features has just enough structure that I recognize Gran.

The creature's somehow ruined her too, just like the tomatoes. The skeletal girl trailing beside Gran . . . I can't even look.

What did it do to them?

"Stay back!" I yell, brandishing a shard of the mirror at them. The little one tilts its head, and tendons open in its neck, seeping blood. "Ky . . . wuss wronn?" she mumbles. Her tongue is black.

"Everything's rotting." I yank a putrefying tomato off the vine, and it feels firmer and harder than I would have expected. I throw it at their feet, hoping they'll stop to eat it and I won't have to look at their ruined faces anymore.

"Ky . . . ky . . . ky . . . " the older one hisses, and the tone is angry. Kyle? Kill?

I have to get out of here.

They seem to be staring at the tomato. The little one kneels to scoop up the pieces of the one I threw. I push the entire window-box over. It lands with a crash and they shuffle towards it, clucking and moaning as it bleeds dirt, and I run for the door.

***

Whatever that creature did, it could have affected everyone in the lower floors. I run for the roof. I don't know where else to go. I don't know why it didn't affect me. I think I'm going to jump. I don't want to starve to death. I don't want to catch their rot. Without food, without company, there's nothing here but pain.

Would it be so bad to die? Maybe I'd jump, and hitting the ground would be like belly flopping into a pool, hurting a bit, but then you're through and swimming in some place wonderful and free, and your mom's there too, and it's heaven and summer, and . . .

I step out onto the roof, and the winter air whips into me, anchoring me back into this cold place. My eye is burning. I'm having trouble blinking in the wind, it hurts so much.

I rub my eye and realize there's a glistening white sled-like device, engines humming, over on the edge of the roof, facing out, like it's ready to sail off the building. Some kind of air-skimming sky-sled. There's a person sitting in it. A real person. No wings. No claws. All bundled up in thick white furs to stay warm. A woman, maybe. Dark black hair, black as the sky.

"Mom!" I yell and start clomping through the snow bank, straight for the sled. Somehow, she lived. And knew I was in trouble. And she came back for me.

She turns, and I see it's a stranger. A beautiful stranger. She's wrapped in a thick, fur-lined scarf covering her neck and mouth, but I can see her eyes and most of her nose. Her face is so pale, it's almost white. Her expression is almost rigid, and her stare is unblinking and glassy above her finely chiseled cheekbones. Like ice.

"What's wrong, child?" she asks, as if kids came running across this roof every day. Her voice is muffled under the scarf and by the wind, but her voice buzzes as if the whole sled is vibrating slightly from its hidden engines.

"I saw an alien," I choke out. My teeth are chattering. It's bitterly cold. I try to huddle into myself. "And everything's rotting—plants, people, my Gran, Gretchen. It infected us or something, right through the glass. Everyone but me. We've got to get out of here."

"You look cold. Come, huddle under these furs with me." Her ungloved hands, which rest in her lap, are white and delicate and do not move.

She doesn't have to ask me twice even though she sits there still as a statue and makes me do all the work of burrowing under. The furs have a slightly musky, feral smell that makes me think they are real and not just decorative. It's nice to be warm.

"Who are you? What are you doing here? Can you help them? The people left in the high rise? Are you fighting the aliens?"

"Why fight?" she asks quietly.

"Because." That's what you do, right? You fight. Even if it's stupid and hopeless. "Because it's our planet, and we need it. And we'll all die if we don't do something about these Oortic invaders who spoil everything."

"You'd have died if we hadn't come." If who hadn't come? Did she mean that she was an alien?

"Your nature is to be dying," she continues. "That's what makes you so delicious. You are little ammonia factories, designed for fertile putrefaction though I admit the most productive mining here isn't from your organics."

She leans down toward me, almost like she's sniffing the air around me. "You can see it, can't you, ice-eyed boy? How all organics rot?"

Ice-eyed boy? My eye does still hurt. What does she mean? I realize she's the first thing I've seen since the creature came to our window that isn't rotting. "Not you."

"No. Not me."

"You're one of them dressed up like a person." I flinch, picturing the bee-crab behind that stolen face. I should run.

I slide out of the blankets, and she doesn't stop me. But where? I have nowhere. Nothing. It's so cold, and I'm not ready to jump. Not really. I take a few steps away from the sled and turn back. "Why? What are you doing here?"

"We came from the Beyond-One, from the Hive of Spheres, to gather the methane from mineral deposits under your seas and in the deep Antarctic ice cores sealed in the frozen lattice of clathrate compounds. The ice that burns." Her voice buzzes, flat and toneless.

"You came from this . . . Hive of Spheres?" Was that the Oort cloud?

"To harvest ices—the stuff that comets are made of—like methane and ammonia?"

"Come with me, ice-eyed boy," she says. "A smart boy like you is wasted here. The Beyond-One, Yog-Sothoth, is a mass of spheres, the Hive of Spheres. Each comet is his eye. The ice giant planets, like Yuggoth and Neptune, are his eyes." She tilts her human mask of a head as if looking at the sky, but her frozen eyes remain glassy and unfocused.

"He is the Ice-Eyed All-in-One. Ice is perfect. Ice is eternity. We have ways to preserve the thinking part of you separate from the putrefying part. Eternity could be yours. Can you see it?"

She's obsessed with eyes and ice. But it got me thinking. Did the creature in the window do something to my *eye*? Is that why it burns? Is something wrong with how I see?

Does that mean Gran and Gretchen might be okay? Furious with me for destroying healthy tomatoes but okay? Am I just kidding myself to wish it, wanting it so much?

"Some of your most rational fellow organics understand the advantages of it. We approach the ones we judge cold enough to join us as brains preserved in a bath of liquid ices in spherical containers, each a node in the One-in-All that is the Hive of Spheres."

She's talking about cutting my brain out of my head like it's no bigger deal than getting a haircut. I need to get away from her. Gran and Gretchen are probably fine. I should run for our apartment. I look over at the door. Not that far. Would she try to stop me?

"Your mother joined us."

What?

"What an exquisitely rigid mind she has. I thought you might take after her and be worth collecting. I saw you in her memories."

"My mom? She's alive?" But she's joined the aliens? No, that's crazy. Impossible. What could this monster know about my mother?

I realize the alien is telling me I could be with my mom again. It's not the swimming pool heaven I'd imagined, but if my mom's stuck in a jar in this alien hive-mind thing, then she's probably not waiting for me in any heaven I could reach by any other means.

"You're a smart boy. Don't you want to live forever? You'd never be hungry again."

I am so very hungry. And I'm cold. Really cold. But am I the kind of cold she's talking about? Cold like Mom, much as I don't like to think about her that way? Would my mom just give up and join them, offered the chance to just be a brain and live forever? Maybe. Probably. Did she forget about me and not even try to fight or come back for me? Or is this her coming back for me now, best as she can manage, by sending a messenger? Why was the alien looking in our windows? Was it looking for me? Does she regret leaving me behind?

Then I think of Gretchen and Gran and how much I'm hoping that they are okay and not rotting from the inside out. They need me. I'm not going to leave them behind. Even if they don't need me, I need them. Even if they're dying and disgusting, I love them. What I know about love, I learned from Gran and Gretchen.

My eyes water thinking about them. I imagine Gretchen circling a scuffed baseball around my head, tracing a halo, whispering, "Can Kyle-earth be saved?"

Tears roll down my eyes, hot and wet.

The ice queen recoils from the heat and emotion. "I was wrong. You're just a blubbering boy. Ugly and foolish."

I run for the door of the roof. The queen doesn't chase me. My eye isn't hurting anymore. Did my tears melt the shard of mirror-ice?

I'm eager to get back inside no matter what I see

there. I'm not giving up on Gran, Gretchen, or those upended tomatoes. Even if the fruit's bruised or crushed, the seeds can still be saved. Sprouts will emerge. Summer will come. It has to.

ONCE UPON A DREAM

MATTHEW BAUGH

Based on Sleeping Beauty by the Brothers Grimm

A LONG TIME AGO—which is to say tens of millions of years—lived a King and Queen of the great island nation of Rley'h. They were not human, for this was long before the emergence of the race of man. Like their people, they were gargantuan creatures who were neither humanoid nor octopoid nor dragon-like in form but some blasphemous combination of all three. The king and queen were models of virtue among their kind—which is to say they were bloodthirsty, capricious, and harsh—and this endeared them to their subjects. They were also fanatical worshippers of Azathoth, the idiot god who blasphemes and bubbles at the center of infinity. But for all this, the royal couple was very sad, for they had no little one to love.

The King and Queen prayed and offered thousands of their subjects on their bloody altars for years but to no avail. Finally, the Queen said if she had a child, she would devote the child to the idiot god's service. Azathoth heard her prayers and took pity, and soon, she felt the stirrings of abominable life in her womb. The child grew quickly, and the Queen sealed herself away in a tower whose impossible angles and planes would have made the brains of human architects bleed. After several months, the blessed day arrived, and the Queen's little daughter burst through her belly in a shower of gore.

"*Cthulhu fhtagn!*" Which means, "my precious little one," the King whispered as he cradled his daughter. After the two feasted on the Queen's carcass, the King took little Cthulhu to the balcony of the tower and presented her to the people. The masses were delighted and celebrated for three days in a blood-drenched orgy. At the end of this, the King ordered a great feast and invited seven of the greatest Outer Gods.

"Ah, she is so lovely," said Shub-Niggurath as she lurched close to the cradle. "To her, I give the gift of beauty, which will be so great as to shatter the minds of mortals who dare to look upon her."

"I also have a gift," burbled Abhoth, oozing up next. "I give her the grace to slip through the barriers of space and time so no place will be safe from her coming."

"My gift is that she be a great dreamer," said Yidhra, who had assumed the shape of one of the King's people. "Her dreams shall be so vivid that they will seep into the consciousness of lesser beings."

Yog-Sothoth drifted closer in the form of a great cloud of incandescent spheres. "I give her the gift of artistry," he said. "With this, she may reshape the world to her liking."

"Then I will give her the gift of genetic

manipulation," said Glaaki as he slithered to the cradle, leaving a trail of luminescent slime as he went. "This will allow her to make servants for herself of the lesser races in the worlds she reshapes."

All the people of Rley'h cheered, but their cries of delight were cut off when a putrid yellow smoke filled the room. When the smoke cleared, they saw the cause. The bloated and tentacled form of Hastur had entered the chamber. He stood there, wrapped in his regal robes of saffron, glaring at the king with his six eyes.

"So you did not see fit to invite me, did you?" he demanded.

"I meant no disrespect," the King stammered. "It was an oversight, nothing more."

"I take no offense," Hastur replied. "In fact, I also bring a gift for your little Princess Cthulhu. She shall live and be as beautiful and gifted as all my brethren have said, but as she enters her twelfth millennium of life and comes of age, she will touch the Elder Sign and die!"

The King cried out in horror, but before anyone could act, Hastur departed as he had come.

"Cursed be Hastur," the King said. "Let his name never be spoken again on penalty of death."

Then, the last of the Outer Gods shambled forward; it was Nyarlathotep, the Crawling Chaos who had assumed the form of a faceless, tentacled bat.

"Your Majesty, I still have my gift to offer," he said.

"Can you undo this terrible curse?" the King asked.

"Alas, I cannot, for Hastur's power is greater than mine. However, I can alter his gift. When Cthulhu comes of age and touches the Elder Sign, she shall not die but shall fall into a deep sleep and shall remain thus until the stars are right and a prince comes to awaken her with true love's kiss."

The King thanked Nyarlathotep, but when the Outer Gods had gone, he sent out a command to all of Rley'h.

"Let the word go forth that all Elder Signs are to be gathered and crushed to dust," he said. "We shall spend a fortnight on this task, after which time, anyone possessing one shall be put to death!"

This was a blow to the people, for the Elder Signs, which were traditionally carved on five-pointed fragments of greenish soapstone, were very popular throughout the realm. Nevertheless, the people complied both out of love for the princess and fear of their monarch's wrath. Before the fortnight was out, there was nary an Elder Sign in all the world.

To take things a step further, the King had Cthulhu sequestered in the Temple of Azathoth, where the giant and amorphous shoggoths were her guardians and only playmates. Thus, Hastur's plan seemed to have been thwarted. But as Cthulhu reached her twelfth millennium, a wandering priest of Azathoth came to the temple. The shoggoths would have turned him away, but as fate would have it, they had spent the previous night feasting on the captives taken from a recently conquered land far to the south and were napping. It was little Cthulhu, in her innocence, who let the stranger into the sanctuary.

"My, what a lovely thing you are," the old priest said. "May I show you something that will be the perfect adornment?"

Cthulhu nodded her bulbous head eagerly, and the

priest produced a five-pointed piece of soapstone with the Elder Sign exquisitely carved into its surface. Cthulhu gasped with delight, having never seen such a thing before.

"What is it?" she cried. "Can I hold it?"

"Of course, my dear." The priest handed her the Elder Sign, and as soon as Cthulhu touched it, she fell into a death-like sleep.

The shoggoths woke when they heard the priest's terrible laughter and oozed into the sanctuary to see what had happened. They moved to engulf the priest in their gelatinous bulk, but he threw off his disguise, revealing himself as Hastur, and vanished in a cloud of yellow smoke.

The King was heartbroken when he heard the news. He had Cthulhu placed in her chambers and ordered a three-day orgy of violent mourning. As the people of Rley'h grieved, their cries reached Nyarlathotep, who took pity on them. He caused sleep to fall over all the inhabitants of the city so that they would not waken until their princess did, then he caused Rley'h to sink beneath the waves of the sea.

***

A thousand times a thousand centuries and more came and went while Cthulhu lay dreaming. During this great sleep, a new race of beings emerged on the Earth. They were humans and in the course of a very short time went from being hunter-gatherers, to settled agrarians, to city-builders, to industrial producers.

All the while, Cthulhu's dreams went out, touching and shaping the minds of the more sensitive of the humans. Finally, they came to Roderick Prince.

He was a gifted inventor and a romantic dreamer.

Needless to say, with such qualities, he was also a hopeless nerd with no social skills whatsoever. It didn't matter though, for Roderick Prince dreamed of something wonderful. Somewhere, beneath the sea, he dreamed, there was a woman, beautiful and voluptuous beyond the dreams of Hollywood, who waited for him. More than that, this woman whispered to Roderick as he slept. These secrets helped him to write software for a new generation of AI programming to be used in personal computers and made him fabulously wealthy.

Now that Roderick was rich beyond the dreams of avarice, he could have had his pick of comely companions, but he remained true to the one who was the girl of and in his dreams. She was the one who loved him when he was a greasy nobody; she was the one who had helped him, and the green-skinned princesses of lost cities had something no women of his world could match.

So it was that Roderick Prince bought a decommissioned submarine, outfitted it with state-of-the-art electronics, and sailed to the South Seas, where the island of Ponape was all that remained of the once proud city of Rley'h.

Roderick ordered the submarine to dive and explore the ocean floor. Before long, the crew reported buildings made of cyclopean blocks of stone and a tower so bizarrely constructed as to cause the sonar to return untranslatable signals.

This pleased Roderick greatly. Donning a deep submersion suit, he left the sub and strode to the base of the tower. The door opened at his touch, and he ascended a nightmarish progression of stairs until he reached a room from which issued a gentle glow. As he stepped in, the door shut, and the water drained away.

This puzzled Roderick but did not surprise him. In his dreams, such things often happened, and he knew what to do. He struggled out of the suit and stumbled into the next chamber, where his true love lay on her bower, her beauty imperfectly hidden by the most gossamer of gowns. He hurried to her side and bent to touch his mouth to the coral lips of his princess.

***

When Cthulhu felt true love's first kiss, she awakened instantly. Filled with a tender affection such as she had never known, she opened her mouth wider, sucked her prince's head in, and bit down hard. Blood spurted, and bones crunched as Roderick's body began to squirm and kick furiously. Cthulhu let the dream-illusion of her human form drop away as she used her tentacles to cram the rest of Roderick's squirming body into her mouth then rose and stretched.

Around her, she could sense the shoggoths and the inhabitants of the city awakening, while the island itself rose, displacing enough water to swamp the coastlines of the world's new continents. Of course, this didn't matter; once the city had risen, she would shape the world to her liking and repopulate it as well. The Old Ones were waking, and the world must be purged of other life.

Though, she thought, *perhaps not all the humans need perish.* Her stomach rumbled, and a wave of sentiment washed over her. Roderick Prince had loved her truly. Not only had he wakened her to fulfill her destiny, but he had nourished her as well. Such devotion should be rewarded.

***

In the days that followed, even the mightiest of human weapons proved futile against Cthulhu and her people. They destroyed the world's armies with frightening ease, and their servitors quickly depopulated the world of humans and other undesirable species.

But not all humans perished because Cthulhu's heart had been warmed by Roderick Prince's love and thoughtfulness.

And so Cthulhu preserved a last remnant of humanity and allowed them to live in Rley'h with her. Of course, she had to alter their bodies to allow them to survive in the radically transformed earth, and she had to alter their minds to instill in them the same loving devotion that her true love had felt.

And they all lived happily ever after.

CINDERELLA AND HER OUTER GODFATHER

C.T. PHIPPS

Based on Cinderella by Charles Perrault

A LONG TIME AGO in an accursed land far, far away, there lived a wealthy landowner named Marcus and his young daughter, Anna.

Marcus was the descendant of a powerful line of warlocks. Once his family commanded the spirits of the Dreamland, they regularly conversed with Nyarlathotep himself and were routinely invited to dine with the spirit of Abdul Alhazred in Azathoth's court. Unfortunately, Marcus was not the equal of his ancestors and quickly spent his vast fortune on frivolous entertainments. Anna, who possessed an uncommon intelligence, confronted her father one night after he came home from another drunken binge.

"Oh Father, what are you going to do?" Anna asked. "Our house is built upon the great underground cities of our ancestors where the intelligent rats gnaw and play! If you continue to waste our fortune, who will take care of them?"

Marcus cuffed her across the face before replying, "Silly girl, I have already come up with a solution to my problems. The Deep Ones from distant R'lyeh offer gifts of gold and great caches of fish to whoever will marry into their accursed bloodline. I attempted to offer you to one of their men, but they said you were too young. More's a pity, but I suppose I shall simply have to lie down with one of them myself and think of the fortune."

Anna, of course, was horrified by his words because her ancestors had long ago promised their descendants to Yog-Sothoth. The Deep Ones, with their degenerate rites and unnatural appearance, were uniformly pledged to Great Cthulhu. It was a blasphemy of the highest order to switch their family's allegiance.

Unfortunately, Anna's pleas fell on deaf ears, and her father married one of the Deep Ones a week later. This particular Deep One, a haggish woman named Salyssa, had more human blood than most and was able to pass herself off as a mortal woman with the right combination of veils. Her daughters, Annis and Carnyl, were more human-looking but still possessed tell-tale signs of their inhuman parentage.

Perhaps Anna might have won them over had she been a respectful, obedient child who joined in the depraved rites of Father Dagon and Mother Hydra. However, Anna was the descendant of warlocks.

Every night, she snuck out into the forest in the back of her home to carry out the fell rituals devoted to Yog-Sothoth's glory while praying to the Key and the Gate for deliverance. Even Anna's dog, Muffin, was sacrificed to the Outer God, showing the young daughter's piety.

Such disrespect did not go unpunished, however. At first, Marcus made a halfhearted attempt at defending his child, but the stresses of his unnatural marriage got to him, and he hung himself.

It was then Annis said, "We should sacrifice her to Great Cthulhu, Mother. Toss her in the ocean where she can join the ranks of all those who refuse to venerate He-Who-Is-Dead-But-Sleeping."

"No," Salyssa said, staring at her children. "As much as I would like to, Anna is a daughter of an ancient bloodline. Were we to kill her, we would bring down the wrath of Yog-Sothoth upon us, for he is in all places at all times. No, instead, we shall punish her for her misbehavior. We shall inflict such indignities upon her that she will come to worship Great Cthulhu voluntarily and take a Deep One as husband."

"She doesn't deserve such an honor," Carnyl said. "However, I like the plan of hurting her. What shall be the first thing we do to her?"

"We shall take away her name because it is the first thing her father gave her," Salyssa replied. "From this day forth, we shall refer to her only as Cinderella. She shall sleep in the fireplace amongst the ashes and with the rats."

Both daughters thought this an extremely good plan and had a hearty laugh over it. They took away all of Cinderella's dolls, burned her dresses, and forced her to work as a servant. In time, they came to deny she had ever been the daughter of their stepfather. The neighbors, fearing retaliation from the cult of Cthulhu, ignored the young daughter's plight and allowed the Deep Ones to treat her as a slave.

Cinderella, however, found the life less taxing than

it could have been. Her stepmother and stepsisters could not have known the rats in the walls were her friends, frequently bringing her news of the outside world and whispering all manner of dreadful secrets. As the years went on, she heard of the prince who was leading their country in the place of his hopelessly mad father.

The prince, a handsome, blond-haired warlock named Benedict, was a believer in the old ways and followed them fervently. Benedict had put himself in disfavor with the rest of the court by sacrificing his young bride to Azathoth on the night of their wedding. The resulting civil war had devastated the noble houses of the land, Benedict calling forth an army of flying polyps to devour them and their forces.

While his magnificent victory was a sign to the whole world of how the Outer Gods favored the prince, the gruesome destruction all of the rebelling noble families had left the kingdom without an eligible bride for its heir. Rather than marry outside the kingdom to one of the families who worshiped the strange idol-less god from Arabia, it was said Benedict had begun searching the ranks of commoners for a potential spouse.

"Oh," Cinderella sighed one day, sitting in her fireplace. "If only I could marry into the royal household. Then, I could practice my ancestors' religion in peace and keep Yog-Sothoth's altar filled with the hearts of men as opposed to the animals I trap in the woods."

"You can," one of her rat friends replied. "You are the descendant of Eibon, greatest of all ancient magicians, and inheritor of his sorcery. Were you properly trained, you could summon forth one of Shub-Niggurath's young to make Prince Benedict your willing slave and breed with him many fresh offerings."

Cinderella smiled at her friend, stroking his furry human-shaped head. "You are sweet to say, friend rat, but I am not properly trained. My father cared more for drink than dread supplications. Why, I do not think he ever waylaid a traveler so the hungry ones entombed below could have a meal!"

Cinderella was a child of good morals despite her faithless father. The fact the dead-but-alive remains of her ancestors were not fed by her step-family caused her no end of sleepless nights.

"Feh!" the rat replied, surprising Cinderella. "I am surprised at you, child, ignoring the power of the Outer Gods. They are there to be seized, not given. The secrets of ages past lay sleeping in the tomes of your forefathers. One merely has to seek these books out and possess the will necessary to perform the rituals within."

Cinderella blinked, considering the rat's words. "You mean to say that I should seek my grandfather's books and use them to summon a messenger of Yog-Sothoth?"

"Indeed I do," the rat replied. "The Deep Ones, craven fish-men that they are, have locked away your ancestors' libraries in the attic rather than destroy them. You must sneak the key from one of your stepsisters and study them in secret. In time, you will master the black arts, and the world will be yours to command."

Cinderella felt embarrassed that a rat had been

required to tell her such things. "I will do this. I will study the magic of my ancestors and wreak a mighty vengeance on my stepsiblings."

Stealing the key to the attic proved to be simplicity, for the Deep Ones had long since abandoned active torment of Cinderella. She had become just another short-lived mortal, destined to be devoured or driven mad by the imminent rising of the Old Ones. Cinderella scoffed at such arrogance, knowing well that what was imminent to the Old Ones could last longer than the duration of humanity's reign on Earth.

*Studying the Book of Eibon, Pnakotic Manuscripts, De Vermis Myst*eriis, and other works, Cinderella became well-versed in all areas of the occult. Choosing a particularly auspicious moment in the solar calendar, Cinderella lured a hot-blooded traveler to the heart of the forest. There, she sacrificed him on Yog-Sothoth's altar before repeating mantras not meant for human mouths to perform.

Hours passed before a nightmarish black centaur stepped from a gateway to the primordial abyss. The creature had a body akin to a horse but covered in a thick alien exoskeleton. Its head was long and whip-like with only a yawning chasm in place of face. Instantly, Cinderella fell to her knees and bowed before one of the many faces of Nyarlathotep, messenger of the Outer Gods.

"Milord," Cinderella cried, falling to her knees. "I am not worthy."

"Be at peace, daughter of Eibon, for I appear only to those who have caught my interest. Your ancestor long ago predicted your situation and ventured to distant Kadath, where he passed by the puny gods of the Earth to speak with me. I am to grant you your fondest wish and see it is brought to fruition."

Cinderella clapped her hands with joy, never imagining such an august personage would be her patron. "Then, if the choice be mine, I would marry Prince Benedict and destroy my stepsiblings as well as their hateful mother. I wish to be queen of all the realm and dwell with my beloved at the court of Azathoth for all time, listening to the otherworldly pipers who serenade the blind idiot god."

"Easily done," Nyarlathotep said, giving a courtly bow. "First, we must replace the rags you wear with silks from the plateau of Leng. We shall give you jewelry made by the finest artisans of Ulthar. Your rats shall be made into coachmen, the skull of your father buried nearby turned into your coach. Your features will be changed as well, for you are beautiful but only by human standards. I shall spare for you an entourage from the warlock courts of a place unpronounceable to your tongue. Finally, you shall wear a pair of glass slippers given to me as a present by a fallen priest of Hypnos."

"Glass slippers?" Cinderella asked, surprised such a thing existed.

"They carry upon them a dreadful curse of the Elder Gods to punish those who seek to pry too deeply into mysteries not meant for frail mortal minds," Nyarlathotep said, conjuring the slippers between his right hand's eight fingers. "You, Cinderella, are touched by the Outer Gods and shall suffer no ill-effects for wearing them. Lesser minds, however, will be driven mad from the glimpses of the Dreamlands they provide. Even your stepsiblings are too human to endure such secrets."

"Oh my lord, this is a princely gift," Cinderella said, stunned by the Outer God's generosity.

"As befits a princess," Nyarlathotep replied. "I must warn you, though, the stars were not quite right for my summoning. You must return before midnight, or all of my gifts will be undone."

Coincidentally or perhaps because of fate, the prince was presently hosting a ball in hopes of finding an eligible mate. The ball was not going well; the young women Prince Benedict encountered were either too frightened of his dreadful religion or too mired in local superstitions to change their ways to match his. There were cultists to the King in Yellow, Cthulhu, Ithaqua, and Tsathoggua but not a single follower of the Outer Gods.

"Oh, why must I be surrounded by such churlish savages?" Prince Benedict lamented. "Am I to be forced to marry a ghoul bride in hopes of having someone who does not quake in terror of the proper way of living?"

As if answering the prince's audible plea, Cinderella arrived with all the pomp and ceremony befitting a daughter of primordial warlock-kings. Tongue-less slaves from distant realms rolled out carpets of human hair while painted, faceless dancers enthralled the prince until the arrival of their mistress. The prince's heart skipped a beat upon seeing Cinderella, enraptured by the asymmetrical beauty Nyarlathotep had given her features.

While later versions of this tale would have you believe they danced all night, in truth, it was Cinderella's love of the arcane which won Prince Benedict over. From the cyclopean architecture of

Elder Thing temples to the distant world of Yuggoth, the two discussed all manner of things not meant for human ears.

So enjoyable was the time had by the pair that Cinderella nearly missed the deadline given to her by Nyarlathotep. Hearing the chiming of Yithian-made clock, however, she immediately rushed out the door to escape in her skull-carriage. Along the way, she dropped one of her glass slippers, playing along to destiny's plan.

The next days passed miserably for Cinderella and Prince Benedict. Cinderella's stepsisters were furious the prince had not chosen them, taking out their rage on their normally unnoticed sibling. Prince Benedict, by contrast, was enamored with the mysterious girl and brought all the soothsayers of the land to find her.

Each of them failed, often perishing in ways which could only be described as the wrath of the Other Gods. Prince Benedict, desperate to find Cinderella, decided to test the slipper on the young women of the land. The consequences of doing so mattered little to him because he could sense it was the will of the Outer Gods they marry. Despite the hundreds of young women driven mad in the process, the prince could tell he was getting closer to finding the mysterious girl who captured his heart.

Eventually, Prince Benedict reached Cinderella's house, where she was locked away in the basement in hopes the family's pet shoggoth would devour her. Salyssa had grown tired of her continued defiance and possibly sensed the growing power within her. Fortunately, Cinderella had learned the spells for mastering a shoggoth to her will.

CINDERELLA AND HER OUTER GODFATHER

No sooner had Annis tried on the glass slipper and gone mad, stabbing Carnyl to death with a knife, did Cinderella burst from the basement with her newfound pet and ordered it to feast upon her stepmother. Salyssa's last words were a plea to Dread Cthulhu to rescue her, but of course, that god lies dead but sleeping.

"Who are you that commands the rebellious servants of the Elder Things?" Prince Benedict asked, impressed by her dramatic entrance.

"I am the woman you seek, blessed by Nyarlathotep and the Outer Gods, destined wife to you and mother of a great kingdom," Cinderella proclaimed, curtsying in her rags because she was addressing royalty.

Though she did not possess the non-Euclidean features which had so attracted him before, Prince Benedict tested the glass slipper upon her. Cinderella, having seen many more terrible things than the sights they showed her, remained completely sane. Well, as she and the prince measured sanity.

"At last!" Prince Benedict said. "My bride!"

"At last!" Cinderella said. "My husband!"

The two were married in an obscene ceremony soon after, ordering debased celebrations to all the Outer Gods and Old Ones throughout the land. That very year, twins were born possessing all the attributes associated with Yog-Sothoth's unnatural children. For you see, both the prince and Cinderella had the Outer God's blood in their veins, and Nyarlathotep had arranged for their bloodlines joining in aeons past. The royal family summoned their godly ancestor on the twins' eighteenth birthday, destroying the kingdom utterly and flattening most of Europe in the process.

In reward for their actions, they were all raised up to dwell in Azathoth's court in wonder and glory forever.

Living happily ever after.

DONKEYSKIN

K.H. VAUGHAN

Based on Donkeyskin by Charles Perrault

THE GOVERNOR'S WIFE was very beautiful, and I can still remember the look on his face when he staggered from the infirmary covered in her blood the day she died in childbirth. The Governor wailed and moaned as soldiers rushed him off to his chambers to get him out of sight. It was not the grief broken across his face but what that open display of raw despair meant for us that frightened me. Even as a child, I understood we needed our leaders to be strong even if I could not have explained why. He swore he would not remarry unless he found another so beautiful and perfect.

Even now, there are many who don't blame the Governor for what he did to his daughter, Ashley. They said he was old enough to see R'lyeh rise on the old high-death screens, the black, oblong altars filled with the Old Gods' light before the grid collapsed. But no one alive then or since is untouched by the Return, so that does not matter. It does not matter what gifts he gave her or what promises he made. It does not matter whether he was kind or beat her. She may have been the spitting image of her mother, but you can't replace what was after it is gone. And there are things that are right and things that are wrong even if the degrees of a triangle no longer always add to 180 anymore.

***

"Nina, I'm so scared," Ashley said, and I'm sure she was since she was about to turn fourteen and of marrying age. Her own father declaring his intentions. I could see it on her face. I paused at hoeing the potato bed by the razor wire fence along the cracked airstrip and watched a bird-insect-rodent-zombie mash-up Byakhee flapping horribly against the bile-green summer sky. It came from the west, but since they traveled on other geometries, it was impossible to say where it had really come from. It landed somewhere near base HQ. All my life, I've seen those things, and I still get dizzy when my mind tries to understand what I'm looking at.

"I know," I said. I was nineteen and already long married to a soldier. Keith wasn't so bad, but then he courted me proper and wasn't any kind of relative. We had three children who survived so far.

"There's got to be something I can do," she said.

"Don't go killing yourself," I said. "It ain't right what he's doing, but I don't want you doing that."

"Well, what then?"

"I wish I knew. No woman's got a lot of choices around here."

I walked over to an old vinyl car seat dragged out by the fence and sat down. It was cracked and shot through with mold inside, but it brushed off okay for sitting. Across the cracked and pitted airstrip were rows of shanties and then the old buildings of Hanscom Airforce Base, nominal capital of the Commonwealth of Massachusetts. Beyond the wire, I could see the fires of farmhouses where the Hartwell forest used to be. It was cleared now. Farmers worked their plows behind mules and oxen. Ashley sat next to me, and we shared a drink of water.

"Have you talked to Gramma Kate yet?" I said.

"Daddy doesn't like me talking to her," she said.

"Well, then maybe that's a sign you should."

The Byakhee, or maybe it was a different one, launched straight up and vanished into the languid slick of oily green clouds, shot through with streaks of red like blood. I felt nauseated watching it.

"You'll go with me?" she said.

I nodded.

***

The Day of the Rise was coming, and there were celebrations every night. We decided to sneak away to see Gramma Kate during a priest burning. There were no real priests left, only holdouts who would not give up their old ways despite the evidence around them. They say in some places, it went the other way with Christian flagellants roaming the streets and everyone else crucified and dumped in mass graves.

A condemned man, old and gray, was tied up in a costume made to look like a cassock with a white collar. I didn't know him; he must have been captured in the outlying territories or been some kind of prisoner or spy from out of state. He babbled and prayed to his fantasy of a merciful god. The people looked around mocking, waiting for divine intervention, but there was none.

"How is Great Cthulhu different from your Jesus, old man? Ain't they both dead and risen?" the leader sneered, raising his voice high so the crowd could hear. "Here's how: Cthulhu exists."

He set the torch to the man, and the motor oil poured over him caught fire. The man screamed as the orange flames engulfed him and the crowd chanted, *Iä! Iä! He has died! Iä! Iä! He has Risen!*

By the time he stopped kicking, we had worked our way to the back of the crowd and were cutting across the base to the corrugated hut where Gramma Kate lived.

***

Gramma Kate wasn't anyone's real grandmother, just an old woman who was already grown in the before times, before the Return. Back then, she had degrees and knew about computers or something that mattered in that life. Now, she knew about other things, like which plants would still grow and which no longer would. What strange species falling through the cracks from alien worlds were edible. Protective spells and summonings, but she usually refused to use them.

She sat in a recliner in a shade of green she called "avocado," but it looked like the hide of a Deep One to me, mottled and scaled with age. It was worn and broken down, like her. Ashley and I sat on chairs next to her and waited while she talked. Once she started talking, you just had to let her finish.

"I still wonder if things would have been better if we hadn't nuked R'lyeh. So much energy released, space and time twisted. I still don't know what happened there. No one does. Quantum mechanics wasn't my field, and the physics all changed that day anyway," Kate said, winding down after a long walk through places and people from the dead times.

"Now," she said, turning her head toward Ashley a little bit. "I've heard all about this idea your father has. Has he done anything to you yet?"

Ashley shook her head before remembering that Gramma was blind and then said, "No."

"It's a shame. We were getting so close on rights and protections when I was your age. One bad day and we're back to fang and claw," she said, chewing on one of her dead fingers. "The way it is now, you have three choices. You can swallow your pride and honor and accept it for what it's going to be. Try and make the best of it and hope he dies soon. You can kill him. You do that, and they'll torture you to death, so you best make it a twofer if you go that route. Last, you can run away."

"Where would she go?" I said.

"It would have to be somewhere outside the surrounding farms the Governor controls. Any place close by and someone will recognize her and hold her for ransom. Twenty miles or more. I don't have to tell you what's out there waiting if you try that. I'm sorry I don't have better answers for you."

"Isn't there some kind of spell I could put on him?" Ashley said. "Make him fall in love with someone else?"

"This ain't Wicca. You could kill him or drive him crazier, but anything like that you try will take a piece of you with it. That's the only kind of magic the Old Gods brought with them. Besides, this isn't really about love."

"I have to go then. I'll have to take my chances."

"Alright then. There's a way to get out past the guards, but it won't be pleasant. And if it's the worst thing that happens because of this, you'll be lucky."

***

The donkey hung by its hind legs in the slaughterhouse. It was the Governor's favorite, given as tribute from the Worcester Barony when they swore fealty. The Innsmouth folk dressed it for the wedding banquet, transferring the guts and organs to a plastic tub with wet, sucking slaps.

"Do we eat that stuff?" Ashley gasped.

"No," I said. "But if it gets bad enough, we'll eat that or worse."

Innsmouthers, with their pallid complexions and strange features, were shunned. Everyone knew how they came to look the way they did. They were only allowed on base to work the unclean trades: knackermen, fellmongers, and offal pickers. It turned out their gods were the real ones after all.

I didn't like the way the old man with the flensing knife looked at Ashley, but we handed him Gramma Kate's amulet like she told us. I liked his smile even less.

***

We walked with the Innsmouthers and their carts of hides, bones, and offal in the dark, Ashley wrapped in the donkey skin. The skin was foul, barely scraped clean on the meat side, and blood oozed down in a clotting trail behind her. The beast's face, warm and wet, hung over her own, the eyeholes pulled roughly over hers like a mask still clinging to life. Flies buzzed and harassed us. I hoped that whatever the amulet was, it was worth enough that they wouldn't just take Ashley and sell her once she got on the other side of the wire.

The main gate stood ahead, guards with spears and rifles checking the line coming and going. Arriving dignitaries on horseback. Shabby laborers on foot. A tiny gap in the razor wire surrounded by shadows and torchlight.

"I'm so scared," Ashley gasped. "You have to walk with me to the gate. I don't think I can do this."

"They'll see me walking with you. They'll ask questions." But it looked like she was going to collapse, that bloody skin weighing her down, black blood dripping down her legs.

I squinted into the dark ahead, and my heart froze. Keith was working the gate. I knew he was on duty, but I didn't know where he'd be; he never told me those things. He was a sergeant and rated the remains of an old army shirt and an M-16. He might have had some bullets for it. He wore the symbol of the Key and Guardian of the Gate, a cluster of orbs symbolizing the Opener of Ways. Ashley grabbed my arm with her sticky hand as if afraid I would run. We walked together until the Innsmouth group reached the checkpoint. Keith saw me and frowned.

"Hey babe," he said. "What are you doing out?"

"I was, uh, walking the offal pickers out. This young girl heard I had children, and she was asking me some questions."

He looked at her, scrunching up his face the way he did when he was trying to figure something out. Suddenly, his face lit up in shock, and he glared at me.

"Nina, what the hell are you doing?" he whispered.

"Keith, you know what the Governor is doing is wrong."

"Dammit, that's not our problem. You think that's the worst thing happening in this world? You're gonna get us killed."

Ashley emitted a strained sound like she was trying not to cry more than she had tried to do anything in her life. The guards at the gate were watching.

"Keith, I'm asking you to decide what kind of man you are, and I hope it's still the kind I married."

He looked at Ashley and back at me. She was shaking. He bit his lip.

"Well, if momma ain't happy, ain't no one happy, right?" he said.

He waved her ahead toward the guards at the gate.

"You can search her if you want, but she's a garbage picker," he called. "She's unclean."

"Gods, she's dripping everywhere," one of them complained.

"Some of that's the skin, but it might be her time also," Keith continued. "I want her off the base quick on account of the wedding guests."

"Yeah, get her the hell away from me," another guard said, batting at flies.

They waved her through, and she joined the Innsmouthers on the other side. Keith pulled me close.

"I love you, baby," he said.

"Me too," I said.

"I gotta get back to work," he said. "May the gods be with you."

"And also with you."

The last I saw of Ashley, she was loaded into a cart train heading up to route 128 toward Innsmouther country. It would be a long way to the coast along miles of broken asphalt lined with empty rusting shells filled with bones.

***

I did not see her again for four years. I only know what happened secondhand, and she doesn't talk much about how she came to get her husband, the Prince. She went toward Boston, that sunken pit of filth collapsed into the harbor forty years ago, overrun with the Deep Ones and their Innsmouther kin. They say she was taken in by some minor official and that the Prince spied her at her work and fell in love like in a fairy tale.

She returned aboard her husband's war wagon pulled by teams of oxen, covered in bones and skulls. People screamed as they approached, but I recognized her right away. She still wore the remains of the donkey skin, now sewn with the skins of many others, a rotting tattercloak of flayed, oozing tissue. I could see human faces patched within by the glittering fire when they stood over the Governor, who begged on his hands and knees before them and mumbled about his baby girl. She laughed when her husband tore him to pieces with his claws and fangs, deep fish eyes glittering like black blood. He presented her with her father's face, and she draped it over her own and screamed. Her eyes, just like her mother's, gleamed through the holes.

They used to say that the ocean-brothers were evil and they were killed on sight by land-walkers. Now, we serve them. Keith is a lieutenant, and we march our armies across Connecticut toward New York against the mongrel ghoul kingdoms and their horrible cannibal god.

Iä! Iä! Cthulhu Fhtagn!

SWEET DREAMS IN THE WITCH-HOUSE

SEAN LOGAN

Based on Hansel and Gretel by the Brothers Grimm

HANSEL LIVED WITH his father and his younger sister, Grethel. Jacob came once a week to bring food in exchange for a cart full of chopped wood.

The first time he spoke of it, Jacob said there was talk of an illness sweeping across Europe. Fever, pustules, bleeding from the eyes and ears. Some thought it may have started with the bite of a diseased shrew brought by ship from a remote island off the Barbary Coast, but no one knew for sure. "Those poor Europeans," he'd said, "they're dying by the thousands."

The following week, he said it reached the Orient and he'd heard of folks falling ill in New York. The week after, it had already ravaged most of the eastern and southern states, and there were outbreaks as close as Arkham, but it had not yet reached Lothrop.

The next week, Jacob didn't come.

Not long after, the family was nearly out of food.

Hansel's father kept chopping wood, but without Jacob, it was of no use, and they went to bed with growling stomachs as their meals became smaller and smaller.

One morning, Hansel was awakened by the clattering of the front door. With his sister asleep, he ran outside to see his father walking the long dirt road toward Lothrop.

"Papa!" Hansel said. "Where are you going?"

"I'm going to town," he said with his head hung low, "to try and get us a bite to eat."

"But the illness! Jacob said the sick were everywhere. And when you get sick, no one ever gets better."

"I know, son. If we weren't so far out here in the woods, we'd probably have caught it ourselves by now. But it will have done us no good if we don't get some food on our plates. I can't hunt anymore. My eyes aren't sharp enough. I have to do what I can. But I promise I'll be careful."

"What if you don't come back?"

Hansel's father was silent for a moment. "I don't know, son. I wish I had an answer for you, but I don't."

Hansel felt a burning in his eyes as tears formed. His father held him tightly then gave him a pat on the back. "You be good, now. Take care of your sister. I'll return soon."

But he didn't. Days passed, and their meager supply of food dwindled further. When they were down to their last morsel of bread, Hansel decided they had to look for food.

"Do we take the road like Papa?" Grethel said, already looking frightened.

"We can't," Hansel said. "Anyone we meet could give us the illness. We'll have to go through the woods."

"But the witches."

"I know. But there could be other folks like us, so far away from the towns the illness hasn't reached them."

"But the witches!" Grethel demanded.

"I know," he said, "but it's our only chance."

Grethel acquiesced. Solemnly, she put their last piece of bread and a handful of berries under her apron. Hansel grabbed a flint and steel and a wineskin of water, and they set out into the dark and endless wood.

Hansel himself was not so convinced of the tales of witches in the surrounding forest, for these were stories their mother told them as she was beginning to go mad.

Their lives were much different when their mother was with them. Their father had not been a poor woodcutter but had attended the university in Arkham, as had their mother, each taking a turn caring for the children while the other focused on the lessons. They both studied mathematics, though their mother far surpassed the achievements of their father. Her professors were so impressed with her theories in quantum physics and interdimensional travel they gave her access to the otherwise locked vault in the Miskatonic library to aid more advanced studies.

It was here that things went badly. She stumbled across hidden texts, the *Book of Eibon*, the *Necronomicon,* and other books with strange, foreign names. She would later tell her husband these old, moldering tomes and their secret glimpses into the world of elder magic had uncanny connections with her studies in mathematics. In her pursuit of these connections, she'd uncovered a local tale of Keziah Mason, reported to be a witch who'd signed a pact with the devil and disappeared into the surrounding woods in the seventeenth century. Hansel's mother became obsessed with the story, terrified with the idea of this witch pursuing her black arts somewhere beyond the edge of the forest surrounding them.

This obsession gave way to madness, and as she withered in her torments, her family did its best to care for her—including Hansel and Grethel, who were very young at the time.

Finally, she succumbed to her insanity. Their father, in his grief, moved the children far away from the town, where he could toil in isolation, earning his daily bread as a woodcutter. Ironically, it was to the very woods his wife feared that he brought them. Though they lived there without incident for several years, there was always the lingering, oppressive fear of the world beyond the clearing in which their house sat. And it was there they must venture.

***

Hansel and Grethel walked all through the day, and at dusk, Hansel built a fire to keep them warm. They ate the berries and divided the bread into two small, equal portions but decided go the night without eating it so they would have something for the morrow.

The next day, they continued their journey with no greater luck. At midday, they ate their bread. Grethel finished her portion quickly and looked so famished Hansel handed over his portion.

"I couldn't eat your bread," she said. "You must be so hungry."

"Not at all," he said. "Those berries we got from the bramble bush earlier filled me right up. I couldn't eat another bite."

"Are you sure?" she said.

"Sure as sure can be." His stomach grumbled audibly with hunger pangs. "See," he said, "listen to all those berries rolling around."

Grethel ate the bread, and they continued on until nightfall. The next day, there was no food for either of the children. Hansel felt light and achy in the head and thinking their circumstance was without hope, though he didn't speak it aloud. As twilight neared and his knees were about to buckle, he saw something strangely pink on the forest floor. He picked it up. It was the size of a peanut and perfectly smooth. "What's this?"

"It's a jelly candy!" Grethel said.

"But how would a jelly candy get all the way out here in the middle of the forest?"

Grethel grabbed it and bit it in half. She smiled up at her brother. "It is! It really is a jelly candy!"

She gave Hansel the other half, and his sister was right. They scoured the area, turning aside pine needles and leaves. They found another in baby blue. Another in orange, and yellow. They followed the candy trail into a sunlit clearing, and there, they discovered the most extraordinary house. The walls seemed to be made of gingerbread, with a frosted cake roof and eaves of dark chocolate.

Hansel thought this must be a mirage, the delusion of a starved and weary mind. But when they approached the house and he broke off a chocolate chunk and tasted it, he found it was what it appeared to be.

Grethel did likewise, and her eyes brightened. "Oh Hansel, it's so good!" she said with creamy chocolate dribbling down her chin.

As they broke off more and ate as fast as they could chew, there was a rustling sound inside. They ran back behind the trees and heard a light, thin voice speak:

> *Nibbling, nibbling, like a rat.*
> *Do you hear it, pussy cat?*
> *Along the forest's edge they hide.*
> *Be they afraid to come inside?*
> *Be not afraid, see Nahab smile.*
> *Won't you come and stay awhile?*

Hansel held his sister, too frightened to come out from cover, sure the voice inside was that of the witch Keziah Mason. The candied door opened, and he prepared to see her twisted, centuried frame emerge onto the porch step. But the figure that appeared was a beautiful maiden with hair of radiant gold. She was young and beautiful as their mother had been before the madness.

"Hello, dear children. Don't be frightened. I mean you no harm."

Grethel broke from her brother's grasp and stepped out into the open. Hansel followed behind.

"Oh, there you are, my dears," said the maiden. A cat as white and fluffy as pure cotton weaved between her feet. "Please don't be afraid. I have plenty of food, and I'd love for you to join me."

The children crept forward, stopping a few feet away. "It's so lovely to have visitors. And what are your names?"

"I'm Hansel, and this is my sister Grethel."

"Such lovely names for such lovely children. My name is Nahab, and this is Brown Jenkins," she said of the cat.

"But he's not brown at all," said Grethel.

"That's very true. His color is snow white, but his name is Brown Jenkins. And he'd be as pleased as carrots and peas to have you for supper tonight. You will join us, won't you? Please say you will. We've been such a long time without guests."

Hansel looked at his sister, and she looked back at him. It was clear the choice she would have him make, so he did. "We'd be happy to join you for supper," he said.

"Very, very happy!" Grethel added, clapping her hands with excitement.

"The pleasure will be all mine. Please come in, and make yourselves at home."

They followed Nahab into her clean and brightly colored house, furnished in red, white, and gold with cushioned couches and soft rugs, and everywhere were bowls of fruits and nuts and sweets.

"Well, seeing as it is now supper time," said Nahab, "let's not waste a minute. What would you to like to eat?"

"Oh, anything would be lovely," said Hansel.

"Anything at all," Grethel added.

"Yes, but what would you like to eat more than anything else in the whole wide world?"

"Pancakes?" Grethel offered timidly.

"Pancakes it is!" Nahab said.

"With syrup?"

"And butter?"

"And cinnamon apples?"

"And candied nuts," the children said in turn.

"With all of that and more!" Nahab went to the kitchen and returned mere moments later with a tray filled with the very meal the children had requested.

"It is done already?" Hansel said. "But how is it possible?"

"How did you know what we'd want for supper?" said Grethel.

"I couldn't have known, of course," said Nahab. "Tonight is always pancake night. You must have smelled them cooking, and your nose told your stomach, and your stomach told your mouth, and your mouth told me that this is what you wanted more than anything else in the whole wide world."

Neither child was inclined to argue. They joined their host at the dining table, and she must have been as hungry as they. She started into the buttery, succulent cakes without saying grace. Hansel filled his belly with the biggest and best meal he'd had in as far back as his memory would take him. As he watched his sister do the same and saw the smile of their warm and beautiful host, he felt for a moment that tears might spring to his eyes. But he held them back, knowing that he was the big brother and his weeping days were behind him.

After supper, when the sun was down, they had warm cocoa with marshmallows and became very sleepy. Nahab led them to a bedroom at the back of the house, where two soft and puffy white beds were waiting for them. They slid into the sheets, and Nahab said, "Sweet dreams, children. It has been a blessing having you here tonight. And when the night is through and a new day dawns, there's no reason you should have to leave should you not want to."

Just before she blew out the candles, Hansel noticed the strange shape of the room, the way the ceiling above them canted downward and one of the walls angled inward. But it mattered not. The bed was warm and their bellies full. He could already tell that his sister had drifted off into sleep, and he was not far behind.

***

As Hansel slept, he dreamed. And in his dream, he saw the events of the evening replayed, but this time, the details were stark and hideous. He saw the house from the edge of the forest, but it was not gingerbread that made the walls nor frosted cake that composed the roof. It was old and weathered wood draped with the fetid meat of rats and field mice. He saw his sister tear off a piece of the eave and chew, but it was not creamy chocolate that dribbled down her chin but the brown blood of a rodent carcass.

In his dream, when the door opened, it was not the lovely Nahab that stepped out onto the porch; it was a stooped and withered old woman. It was the witch Keziah Mason. Worst of all was the creature that weaved between her feet. Brown Jenkins was not a fluffy white kitten at all. He was something like a rat, but rather than paws, he had hands like those of a human. And the face was like a bearded human face, with a mouth full of sharp canine teeth.

The dream continued into the dark and decaying

interior of the witch's house, revealing the dish of spoiled meat that was their real supper and the filthy cots on which they slept.

But this dream did not end with the present. It continued on to show what will, or what may, be. In this future vision, the children slept, but when the hour struck midnight, a black door opened in the corner of the room where the slanted ceiling met the angled wall. This door gave Hansel's sleeping self a withering sense of dread and the knowledge that it was a gateway to a terrible world beyond his own. And for a moment, this vision took him past the threshold to see the deranged vista, where massive, illogical structures loomed like monuments to insanity, and a tangled labyrinth teemed with insectoid and cephalopodic creatures that defied clear description. Hansel's dreaming eye turned to one of these heinous entities. It was not squid or centipede but a morbid cousin of both and of other creatures heretofore unknown. Above all of this chaos was a throne where a dark and demented figure ruled over all. It was Azathoth, whose dreaded name was inscribed in the *Necronomicon*.

Even as he dreamed, Hansel wondered how he could know this name. He had not read that secret text; his mother had.

And there was the answer. From some far off land, Hansel's mother was guiding him, whispering in a voice too quiet to hear but loud enough to comprehend. She was showing him the terrible fate that awaited him.

Dreaming Hansel left the mad world beyond the black door and returned to the room in the witch-house where he and his sister slumbered. In this future vision, the malignant old crone and her familiar entered the room. Brown Jenkins climbed into Grethel's bed, curled around her shoulders, and sunk his sharp, yellow teeth into her neck. Her eyes opened, and as if obeying a distant call, she climbed out of bed, walked somnolently to the black door, and stepped through the gateway and into a violent alien world where no human should venture.

Brown Jenkins came back through the door, and dreaming Hansel understood that the creature was Keziah Mason's emissary, that not even she could pass safely across the threshold. Azathoth demanded a sacrifice, and a vile old witch would do as well as any.

Just as Brown Jenkins climbed into bed with Hansel and was about to bite into the flesh of his neck and repeat the process, the dream ended. Hansel's eyes snapped open, and he found himself in the bedroom with his sister, inside the fluffy white sheets. He heard a clock strike twelve, and just as in his dream, a shimmering black door appeared in the corner of the room. A moment later, the bedroom door opened, and the witch, now in the form of the beautiful Nahab, entered with the cute, white version of Brown Jenkins purring at her feet.

Upon seeing that one of her intended victims was awake, the witch started. "Oh my!" she said. "I didn't mean to wake you. Brown Jenkins was hoping to cuddle while you slept."

"I'm so sorry," Hansel said, speaking quietly so he didn't wake his sister. "I'm afraid the mere touch of a cat's fur will cause my eyes to swell and my throat to close."

Even in her beguiling form, the witch's expression

betrayed a sinister coldness. "Well, we wouldn't want that. But seeing as you're awake, I have a surprise for you."

"Really? A surprise?" he said. "Perhaps we can wait until morning. I really am very tired."

"I'm afraid tomorrow will be too late. It is such a wonderful surprise. I promise you'll be absolutely delighted."

"Okay, then," he said, not seeing a way to refuse. He got out of bed and joined her at the front of the room.

"Look!" she said and pointed to the black door. "Your surprise is just through there."

An idea struck Hansel like a splash of cold water. "Through the wall?" he said. "I'm afraid I don't understand."

The witch's brow furrowed. "No, through the door." She jabbed her finger insistently at the dark gateway. "Through that door there."

"I'm sorry," he said, "but I'm afraid I don't see a door. I only see a corner where two walls meet."

"Are you blind?" said the witch. "There is a door right there in front of you. Just go through it already."

"Okay," Hansel said, "but you'll have to show me where it is. I don't want to walk into the wall."

The witch scurried to the door. "It is right here, right in front of you. Now stop delaying, and walk through it!"

"Why's everyone yelling?" said Grethel, sitting up in bed and rubbing her eyes.

"Hush!" hissed the witch. "It's not your turn yet."

With the witch's attention diverted, Hansel lunged forward and shoved her through the black door. She screamed with both shock and mortal terror, and it was not the wailing of a young woman but of the evil old crone. This tortured shriek quickly faded into the distance, as if she was falling from a great height. Brown Jenkins jumped in after her, and the door snapped shut, disappearing from the room. At the same instant, the witch's spell broke, and the house was revealed for the rotting shanty it was.

Grethel was startled and confused. She looked at her grim surroundings and wept. Hansel climbed into bed with her and held her until she calmed and was once again able to sleep.

***

With the sunrise, the pair searched the squalid house and took what few unspoiled morsels of food they could find. Once more, they headed out and walked all through the day. As the sun fell low in the sky, they came at last to the town of Lothrop. Hansel was but a few years old when last he'd seen the town, but he recognized it instantly.

The only difference was that now, the streets were empty. He and his sister walked from one end of the village to the other without seeing another living soul.

When at last they were sure that not one person yet remained, they went to the strawberry field at the north end of town. They ate until they were full then sat and plotted what they would do from here. They decided that later, perhaps, they would venture on toward Arkham and see if that city was likewise deserted. But they would not travel on just yet. For now, they would stay in Lothrop. Since they were the only ones in town, Hansel decided they would make the biggest house in town their home. He would call himself the King of Lothrop, and she would be the Queen. It would be a lonely existence, but this was how they had lived most of their years. They no longer had their father, but they still had each other.

As they looked for the house that would be their castle, Hansel spied a patch of wildflowers. He thought that before the sun went down, he might pick enough to sew into a circlet to give to Grethel, for every queen needed a crown.

FEE FI OLD ONE

THOM BRANNAN

Based on Jack the Giant Killer by Joseph Jacobs

ONCE UPON A TIME, there was a land of desolation and danger. The Kingdom of Man was reduced to rubble and ash by monsters and their followers. But in that time, there were an intrepid few who took the fight to the minions of evil. One of them was Jack, the Giant Killer. This is one of his tales.

***

Jack looked at the house, disbelieving. He leaned back, gazing to the eaves of the impossibly-slanted roof, and his eyes watered as he fought to keep them from crossing. A gargantuan door hung open with a darkness beyond darkness inside the house, but it was the only shelter he could find in this valley . . . and there were *things* that prowled at night.

It had been this way for years. Hungry creatures came from the sea, monsters that looked like men to the unwary. Or death from above, bat-like creatures that blotted out the moon and fell from the sky to snatch up unsuspecting pilgrims. Ever since the institutions of Man toppled to make way for the return of the Great Old Ones and all of their ilk.

"The stars were right," was all the wise men said.

Gathering himself, Jack shook that off, sent a silent prayer to the new King of Men. "The stars have changed," he said. Jack took a step over the threshold, clearing his throat.

"Hello? Is anyone home?"

In answer, a spark flashed deep in the monstrous house, growing to a soft light, and before long, Jack could see it was thrown by a bizarre metal lamp. That was all he had eyes for. The lamp was a soft brass color, etched all over in glyphs that writhed when he was not focused on them. His breath caught in his chest as he saw the dark green and clawed finger that held the ring of the lantern.

The giant Deep One came into view, its steps awkward and inhuman. It wore no clothing, and Jack's stomach wrenched at the sight of the thing's backwards knees. He tore his eyes from the lurching locomotion and froze as he met the gaze of the Deep One.

An improbably wide mouth curved slightly upward at the ends in a froggy smile. The Deep One licked its chops, its slug-pale tongue rolling over thin lips and receding chin.

"Welcome to my house, humble as it is," the Deep One said in a croaking, gurgling voice, which seemed to stumble over the jagged teeth on the way out, teeth that shone in the wan light.

Jack, who found himself in an inadvertent crouch, lowered his hands and looked up. "You're not going to eat me?"

Noxious breath washed over him as the Deep One laughed, a waterlogged sound. "Oh, no, my young Englishman. I am not so rude or . . . carnivorous as my cousins to the north."

Bowing, Jack put his hands out. "My apologies then. You're much more polite than they are."

The gargantuan Deep One rose up. "Of course I am. They know nothing of hospitality. Would that you were to travel north when your stay here is complete and tell them how much better I am than they are in my capacities as host."

"I entered your abode for shelter from the dark," Jack said, eyes narrowed, "and from all the dark contains. And—"

"The dark," the Deep One scoffed. "You know little of the dark. I care not what you've seen. I could tell you tales that would leave you ready to die rather than step outside."

Jack blinked, and the corners of his mouth twitched.

As if on cue, the Deep One yawned, and a twinkle lit his eyes.

"Welcome, young man. Welcome to the home of Father Dagon. Who do I have the pleasure of hosting this evening?"

"My name is Jack."

The Deep One chortled, as if the name was familiar to him.

"Come then, Jack. Let us see the superior hospitality Father Dagon has for you."

***

Lying awake in the dark room, Jack kept the blanket up to his chin. He fought back another wave of nausea.

The room, the bed, the pillow, and the blanket all had the stink of the deep ocean, the smell of barnacles long dead and rotting.

Hours had passed since Father Dagon had shown him to the room, and he wondered if the hook he'd seen earlier was the right one. The Deep One, the grandest of them, had to show how much better he was at *everything*, not only as a host.

Jack's mind raced. How would the creature react to being *bad* at something? And it was bad . . . the duplicity shown at the mention of the hospitality of the Deep Ones to the north, where there was none. They were vile and cunning creatures who were both vicious and sneaky.

Ah, Jack thought. *There it is.*

He *was* tired. He had just come from another job in the south of England. Three more freed maidens for the Kingdom and possibly a better future. The man-to-woman ratio was disheartening. From the words of one of the creatures, they made "better eating."

"It hardly matters," he whispered, tired of waiting for Father Dagon's betrayal. Jack closed his eyes to sleep.

He rolled over, and there was a slithering noise in the dark. He did not move, but there was an itching in his mind, the feeling of something slimy and wet writhing in his skull.

Though here you lodge with me this night
You shall not see the morning light
My tail shall dash your brains outright!

Sighing, Jack rolled out of bed and retrieved his sack. From it, he pulled a set of his clothes. He put them on the bed and tip-toed to the closet. There, he found a set of extra pillows, which he grabbed and stuffed into his clothes. Rolling his sack into a small ball, he slapped his hat onto it and put the ensemble on the bed, drawing the blanket to its "chin."

Knowing what was to come, Jack went into the closet and closed the door behind him. He put his back to the wall and sunk down, laying his forehead on his crossed arms, resting them on his knees. Within moments, he was asleep.

Several hours later, while the night was still and dead, the air in the room stirred as the door opened. Jack woke and peeked through the crack in the door.

Father Dagon stood in the room, looming over the bed and shaking with silent laughter. Spinning in place, he brought his tail down on the form beneath the blankets with a mighty thud, one that shook the house.

Then another.

And another.

And another.

Grunting with satisfaction, Father Dagon left the room, and Jack went back to sleep.

Yawning and stretching, Jack wandered into the Deep One's kitchen. Father Dagon sat up at the table and peered at Jack, who smiled at him. "Thank you so much for the lodging this evening. I know not how I would have fared in the dark."

Father Dagon's first reply was lost in a watery sputter. He got himself under command and bowed his head to Jack. "How have you rested? Did you not feel anything in the night?"

Scoffing, Jack put his bag down. "Oh, nay. Nothing but a rat, perhaps, which gave me two or three slaps with her tail." He stretched again. "Mayhap I should be on my way before I get caught again in the night."

"No!" Father Dagon near-shouted. "I mean, I would be a poor host indeed if I did not feed you before you were back on your travels."

Jack nodded, considering. He did not want to eat anything the Deep One had to offer; he had no wish to grow gills in the future. "I would be much obliged," he said.

As Father Dagon rose to full height and turned away to his larders, Jack picked up his pack and emptied it into the next room. He slid the bag under his shirt and, with much effort, climbed up into one of the oversized chairs.

"Ah, what an intrepid traveler you are," Father Dagon said on his return. "And here I was, worried you would not be able to make it on your own." Smiling with his knife-slash lips, he set down a large bowl in front of Jack. In it was at least four gallons of green and brown liquid, still bubbling and hot. Fumes rose up to greet Jack, and it was only with great control that he was able to keep from passing out.

He looked up into Father Dagon's green eyes. "Have you any hossenfeffer with which to garnish this?"

Father Dagon's eyes narrowed to slits, and a hissing sound came out of his throat. Then the mask was back in place, all amphibian charm. "I'm not sure. Allow me to take a look."

He lurched out of the room, and Jack set about lifting the bowl. He set the end of it on his chin and fought back a retch. Carefully, he reached under his shirt and opened the bag then began to pour. The awful, hot slime poured over his face and down his front, most of it making it into his bag. He threw up then, the vomit mixing with the soup, which was sure to have transformed him had he eaten any.

As he was setting the bowl down, Father Dagon returned. "Alas, Jack, I have no—why, you finished the entire bowl!"

Weak and near delirium from the fumes, Jack sat back in his chair and smiled up at Father Dagon. "That I have. And so rude of me not to offer any to you, my host."

Laughing, Father Dagon, picked up a bowl from the counter and set it on the table. "I had more ready." He sat and put his face to the liquid, breathing in deeply. "Have you ever smelled such a thing?"

Burping to stifle another retch, Jack shook his head. "I have not."

Grunting, Father Dagon picked up the bowl and slurped down all its contents. "Ah, that hit the spot! I bet you did not eat it as quickly!"

Jack nodded. "That it did. And now, as a token of my appreciation for both the use of your comfortable bed and such a filling breakfast, allow me to show you a trick."

Standing, Jack reached under his overshirt and produced a long knife. "Observe!" He slashed at his belly, and all the green and brown soup came splashing down, covering his legs and boots and the kitchen floor.

"By the deep!" Father Dagon yelled, jumping to his feet. "I can do that myself!"

Snatching the blade from Jack, Father Dagon ran it across his own belly with all his monstrous strength.

All the soup came out as well as his entrails. As Jack watched, the greatest of the Deep Ones fell down dead in his own kitchen.

Looking down at the corpse, Jack nodded. "For my King." He rustled through the pockets of the ruined bag and checked a sopping-wet list. "Right. Dagon . . . check. Who's next?"

Whistling, Jack peeled out of his ruined clothes and left the kitchen to change into a fresh set. And then he would be ready.

Onward to Arkham.

THE KING OF THE GOLDEN MOUNTAIN

MORGAN SYLVIA

Based on the King of the Golden Mountain by the Brothers Grimm

ONCE UPON A TIME in Kingsport, there lived a merchant widower. He had lost his young wife under strange and mysterious circumstances, but she had borne him a son before she died, and the child, named Heinel, helped the merchant ease the anguish of the loss. After the chilling events preceding and surrounding his wife's death, the widower found himself possessed by a burning need to keep active. He strove to stay busy and thus keep his thoughts from the unholy shadows and inexplicable happenings that plagued the barren hills nearby. He poured all of his time and effort into his shipping business and managed to fill both his pockets and his hours.

The months passed, the seasons changed, and the merchant's fortune grew along with his son. For a time, he managed to find, if not peace, a sort of equilibrium. He managed not to think about the dark times and terrifying circumstances that had claimed his wife. He managed to ignore the sounds in the forest, the heavy, electric chill that often hung thick in the air, and the irregular tracks he found in the muddy yard behind the old barn. He fought his nightmares back with the help of a local apothecary and played with his son.

For a time, things were well enough.

For a time.

One night, there was an unusual storm. The sea churned and crashed violently against the cliffs; though the inland sky was clear, offshore eerie flashes of greenish light could be seen, seeming, oddly, to originate from somewhere beneath the waves. The merchant looked out the window at the restless ocean, and his skin prickled with the sense of something *off*, of some malevolent being watching through a thin veil of reality. He would have chalked his fears up to nerves or foolishness, but his dog's incessant, frenzied barking and the way his cat arched its back and hissed at something unseen did not allow him that comfort.

That night, he dreamt of the water god, the foul, tentacled thing that ruled the icy depths. The following morning, he found his son's bedroom floor wet with the watery tracks of some unidentifiable being. It was not the first time the merchant had been subject to such phenomena. He made himself a strong drink and sat trembling while he pored over his ledgers, forcing himself not to think about anything but the numbers.

He had shaken the worst of his fear when his doorbell rang. Opening the door, he found standing on his porch the lighthouse keeper, a gruff, bearded old man who did not often come to shore.

"I've bad news," the man said without further greeting. "Your ships were taken. Both of 'em."

"Taken?"

The man's gaze seemed to hold the essence of the sea, as though his eyes and soul had taken on the very nature of the mysterious, unholy fathoms. "Claimed," he said. "*He* took them."

The merchant opened his mouth to ask a question, but the lighthouse keeper turned away and shuffled off without another word. His meaning became clear later that day when the first bits of his ships' wreckage were found strewn across the beach, along with the remains of a creature some said was a whale and some insisted was not.

Thus, the merchant lost his fortunes and fell from wealth into poverty within the space of a few short hours.

Seeking to ease his nerves, the merchant walked along the shoreline. Though the ocean was little comfort, he preferred it to the hills. In time, he discovered an old, abandoned boat and, pausing to study it, noticed a path he had never seen before, which he followed into the woods. He found himself in an eerie glade, where a black stone obelisk stood, marked with eldritch runes. An odd, heavy air hung about the place as though an unseen presence held court. No birds sang. Not even a cricket broke the silence. So the merchant was doubly startled when he turned and found he was not alone. A small, dark man stood there, a few steps away, though he had approached without making a sound.

The little man had a peculiar appearance; his skin was almost leathery in texture, his eyes as dark and deep as midnight. "You are sorrowed," he said in an accent the merchant could not place. "What is your sorrow?"

The merchant thought he should just keep walking, but something in the man's eyes did not—would not—let him move. "No use telling," he mumbled. "You cannot help me. No one can help me."

"Who knows? I have helped many. I may help you as well." The dark man stepped closer. "Tell me what ails you. I may be of some use."

The merchant explained how his wealth had been lost, gone to the bottom of the sea in the frightful storm. The stranger nodded and made sympathetic noises. It was only later that the merchant realized he did not seem the least bit surprised.

"Do not worry," the man said. "I can solve your worries. All you need to do is promise to come back to this place in precisely twelve years and bring me whatever meets you first when you go home. Do this, and you will have everything you want."

The merchant thought in one part of his mind that it was nonsense and in another part that he should run away immediately. But the third part, which was ruled by greed, held that it would be only the dog or cat he sacrificed, which was a small price to pay should the offer prove true.

"Twelve years," the foreigner said, holding out a form. "That is when the gate will open."

And so the merchant cut his finger, signed his name in blood, and walked home, an unpleasant ringing in his ears.

As he entered his yard, his young son, Heinel, ran out happily, so thrilled at the sight of his father that he wrapped his arms around the merchant's legs and looked up at him, smiling, his laughter like bits of sunshine.

The merchant went cold, realizing what he had done. And as his son giggled and bounced, the merchant shivered in terror. He looked back the way he had come, wondering if he could undo the pact. But it was too late. The deal had been struck. Sealed in blood.

His terror faded as days passed and nothing out of the ordinary happened, and he convinced himself, despite his muddy shoes and cut finger, that it had been just one more vivid dream. Another nightmare, nothing more.

A few weeks later, he went into the barn to look for bits of metal that he could sell, for he was destitute by then. He noticed abnormal footprints leading into an old tack room he had not set foot in for years. Slowly, the merchant opened the door and looked inside.

A huge pile of gold gleamed amidst shadows and dust. The gold was stacked up on the floor to nearly the man's height, and it was worth far more than what he had lost.

***

Days passed, became weeks, became months. Became years.

And the merchant's fortune grew . . . as did his son.

As the twelfth year drew closer and then loomed, the merchant's nightmares returned, grotesque, horrible dreams recalling his lost wife and the terrifying circumstances of her demise. Again, he began to notice odd, unexplainable things happening around the house and barn. As the merchant became more morose, Heinel noticed and then questioned his father's depression.

The boy smiled when he was given the truth.

"Don't worry, Papa," he said. "That little man will not be able to harm me."

When the time came, the merchant and his son walked down the shore, found the ruined boat and the path, and made their way to the stone obelisk.

The son drew a circle of salt on the ground and then carefully drew runes. "Get inside the circle," he said to his father. "We'll be safe inside."

The air shimmered above the odd symbols.

The merchant looked at his son. Several thoughts crossed his mind; the boy knew things he should not; he wondered how Heinel had gained such knowledge, for he had burned those dreadful books his mother kept; and, lastly, that it was his mother's blood, acting in him, though he had not spoken to her family since her death. But he had no time to voice any of those thoughts, for at that moment, the last of the light fell from the sky, and a terrible sound came from the hills.

When the sound faded, the small, dark man was there. He had not aged a day. He said nothing but approached father and son.

He could not cross the circle.

He walked around, toed the line, but could not cross. As the unholy sounds in the hills grew louder, the boy spoke. "Have you nothing to say?"

The stranger looked at the merchant. His eyes were blacker than midnight, and his voice held an odd tone. "Did you bring what you promised?"

The merchant said nothing. He could not speak, so great was his fear.

"What do you want here?' Heinel asked.

"I wish to speak to your father," the foreigner said. "Not to you."

There was the sound of a scream from somewhere in the village.

"You have cheated him," Heinel said. "Release the bond."

"Fair and softly," whispered the man. "Right is right. I have paid my money, and your father has had it and spent it. So be so good as to let me have what I paid for."

The boy said nothing.

"Fair and softly," the stranger said once more. "Right is right."

"I never consented." Again, Heinel smiled. "Step into the circle."

And so the battle line was drawn. The night drew on. The horrible sounds continued, and from time to time, they could see a tree shake. Again and again, the man tried to claim his due but could never cross the circle. Eventually, it came down to bartering. It was decided that Heinel would get into the boat at the end of the path, and the merchant would set him adrift with his own hand. The boy's fate would lie with the gods, be they fair or hideous.

The boy and his father left the circle and went down to the shore. "Mother told me in a dream that I would be fine if I followed my own path," Heinel said. Then, he bid his startled father farewell and stepped into the old boat.

The merchant and the old man watched as the boat moved into the current. Offshore, the greenish lights began to flicker again, and a hot wind blew. The waves churned.

And then, with a splash of water, the boat was gone.

"It has happened," the little man said. "They did it. The others have done it. They have opened the gates at last, at last! *They come.* They come. Nyarlathotep, Oh, Nyarlathotep!"

The merchant wept for the loss of his son.

The foreigner, satisfied, smiled. "It has begun," he said. "*They* come. *They* come."

He was gone before the merchant could reply.

The sea became quiet once more.

Far out over the ocean, where the boat had vanished, a claw ripped through the fabric of time and space.

The Old Ones came at last to Earth, pouring through that breach. *They* came from the realm of chaos they ruled down to Earth. *They* walked the Earth and made it *Theirs*, took souls and flesh and life to feed *Their* terrible appetites. *They* broke cities and ripped holes in the Earth, and *They* and *Their* servants brought countless horrors to the masses of humanity.

***

The boat, however, did not sink. Instead, Heinel found himself run ashore in a strange land. He had little knowledge of his journey, only horrible dreams—or were they memories?—involving cosmic forces. The glimpses he recalled terrified and fascinated him, yet faced with an unknown land, he put those things to the back of his mind and focused on what was before him.

A beautiful and terrible city rose into a sky that held a preternatural tint, colors human eyes were never meant to see. The stars above were unfamiliar, and the wind carried a foul charnel stench. The terrain rose and fell with bizarre shapes, as though molded by some calamity he could not fathom. A mountain behind the city held a faintly gold tinge.

Welcome home, something whispered.

The boy pulled the boat ashore. He surveyed the alien landscape before him, noticing that directly in front of him was what appeared to be a castle. It held a dreadful magnificence that place, and though it seemed desolate, something of its air, of its nature, said it was not quite as empty as it seemed.

Heinel remembered something his mother had said to him in one of the dreams she had visited him in. *The prize awaits you in the castle.*

And so he entered the great gates, on which were carved occult symbols that might have frightened him, but he was already familiar with such sigils. Inside, he marveled at the intricate architecture of the place, of the whorls and patterns that drew his mind so he had to force himself to walk away. He moved through room after room, but he saw no one until at last he found a white snake coiled up on a cushion. As he watched, the snake changed, growing and mutating until it took the form of a woman.

"You've come to sssset me free," she said.

When she spoke, her voice was colored in tones that could drive men mad. Had Heinel been fully human, he would have gone insane at the sound, but his mother's blood was mingled with that of other races.

Instead, he fell in love.

"I've waited twelve years," the snake said. "Waited for you to come and save me and set me free. Lisssten to me. Tonight, a dozen men will come. They will be wearing armor, but you will see only blackness in their helms. They will ask you questions. Do not speak to them. Do not reply. Do not answer. They will strike at you, but do not fight them. Let them beat you." She stepped closer. He could see that, even in human form, she had a forked tongue. "Let them burn you. Let them whip you. Let them do what they will. They will leave at midnight. They must go away at midnight."

She walked a slow circle around him. "They will come again tomorrow, doubled in number. On the third night, there will be forty. And they will sssstrike . . . off . . . your . . . head, but then their power will fade, for I will be free. And I can revive you. I *will* revive you."

It came to pass; she spoke truth.

Twelve men came that night, and some seemed human and some not, though, as she predicted, he could not see their faces. They wreaked havoc on his flesh, yet through the horrible torments, Heinel bit his tongue. He bore all and spoke not a word. On the third night, the princess came to his lifeless, headless corpse, kissed him, and with unholy magicks made him whole again, both more and less than he had been.

The bizarre folk of Ilek-Vad came to celebrate their wedding, and Heinel found himself King of the Golden Mountain.

Time passed in strange cycles in the city of Ilek-Vad, but it passed nonetheless. After the queen bore him a son, Heinel found himself missing his human father and wanting to visit him. He began to argue with the queen, who did not want him to leave the city.

"The world you left behind no longer exists," the queen said. "Do not go back there. The Old Ones rule there now. It is not what it was. It is not safe."

But he persisted, and eventually, she agreed, giving him a ring, which shone with an unearthly light. "Take this," she said. "It is a gate of its own accord. But you must promise to never, ever use it to summon me there. Do not speak my name. Do not speak the name of our son."

"I promise," Heinel replied.

"Go then," she whispered.

Heinel returned to the world of man. He found it a changed place indeed. Where once forests had grown, there were vast swaths of dead trees. Many had been snapped in half as though by some vast hand. What had once been farmland was barren. Kingsport stood in ruins, and those that still lived there had received no word from outside in all the years Heinel had been gone. Cars did not come through anymore, the roads were cracked and overgrown, and there were no longer any stores they could go to for supplies. The citizens of Kingsport lived on fish and what they could scratch from the soil.

The townspeople remembered Heinel. They gave him clothing so he would not stand out in his unusual garb and took him to the merchant. The old man did not believe it was his son until Heinel showed him the peculiar birthmark on his arm, which his father remembered.

Heinel told his father about the land and the world he ruled. His father grew agitated, remembering things he wished to forget, and refused to believe him. "Madness," he said. "That madness was your mother's curse. Speak not such blasphemy. They will hear you. Oh, *They* will hear you."

As the merchant began to ramble on, Heinel,

forgetting his promise, summoned his queen and his own son merely to prove he spoke truth.

His queen hid her anger at his betrayal, but that night, when Heinel was sleeping, she took the ring from his finger and left with the child.

Heinel spent years searching for a way to reclaim his throne and have his revenge on his queen. The world he had grown up in no longer existed; it was a ruined, dead world, but the Old Ones knew him for one of their own and let him be, and in their other servants, he found some aid. In time, through years of study, he found the means to return to the realm he had lost. Horrible screams were heard emanating from the merchant's house the night after Heinel left for good, but no one dared enter.

The last that was seen of Heinel was of his twisted form disappearing through the gates of the great castle. The head of the queen hung fresh on the wall, dripping blood.

The merchant was never seen again.

The gate between realms closed in time.

But it was too late.

THE LEGEND OF CREEPY HOLLOW

DON D'AMMASSA

*Based on The Legend of Sleepy Hollow by
Washington Irving*

ARTHUR ABRAMS WAS a relentlessly rational person, living proof that even a good thing can be carried too far. He didn't believe in luck, women's intuition, flying saucers, alien abductions, life after death or any other unproven religious tenet, and certainly not the supernatural. His insistence upon empirical evidence was a way of life. If you told him the sun was shining, he labeled the information as provisional until he had an opportunity to look out a window for himself.

In his late twenties, Arthur was an assistant professor of physics at Miskatonic University who recognized there were social and political components in his quest for tenure. This is how he first met Martin Ichabod. Ichabod was both a trustee and an alumnus, and he had become one of the richest men in New England by the time he was thirty. He had started with equipment rentals as the Ichabod Crane Company and expanded into construction, real estate, and apartment house management within two years. Although his business empire was headquartered in Boston, he had built an impressive mansion not far from the university in a wooded area known as the Hollow. During the week, the house was generally abandoned to the servants—Ichabod had never married—but the master of the house came back almost every weekend.

Ichabod had hosted a dinner party designed to raise funds for the university library's proposed expansion, and Arthur was among the academics whose job included cajoling wealthy invitees into opening their wallets. He was introduced to Ichabod by Professor Van Tassel, and the two men shook hands warmly while sizing each other up.

"Call me Martin. I have little patience for formalities."

Arthur glanced around at the crowd, which had broken up into small groups. "Then you must find all of this rather tedious."

"If you think of it as a game, it isn't that bad. From the proper perspective, all human activities are pretty insignificant after all."

"Except the quest for knowledge. I consider that the supreme purpose of the human race. If ever we should discover there is nothing new to learn, the shock would undoubtedly result in our extinction."

"Then you don't believe there are some things man wasn't meant to know?"

Arthur's face wrinkled unpleasantly. "I find that sentiment both foolish and insulting. It implies there is a greater intelligence which has decided to place limits on human accomplishment. I reject that categorically."

"Then you dismiss the stories of monsters appearing out of nowhere in Northern China?"

"Without reliable evidence, I certainly can't offer it as a viable hypothesis. I don't believe in one god, let alone an entire pantheon of them."

"Perhaps they are mortal after all but infinitely superior to us, godlike even."

"The same argument applies."

They parted a moment later, and Arthur didn't see him again for an hour, when Ichabod offered to conduct a tour of the mansion. He joined a handful of the curious and was subsequently impressed by the size of the library, although a disappointingly large proportion of the books were devoted to the occult arts, which Arthur considered mere fantasy. Ichabod had filled his house with paintings and sculpture, but they had a dark and twisted aspect which Arthur found vaguely disturbing.

One of the other guests pointed to the bronze double doors at the end of one corridor. "And what does this formidable barrier conceal?"

Ichabod smiled. "My inner sanctum, whose secrets I will maintain if you don't mind. Everyone has someplace they wish to call their own, where they can indulge whatever fantasies might occur to them without fear of ridicule. My own are somewhat prosaic, but they are nonetheless priceless to me."

And nothing else of interest occurred on this occasion.

***

Further interactions between the two men might have been equally innocuous had it not been for the advent of Katrina Bergen. Katrina was a graduate student in the mathematics department whose long, blond hair attracted Arthur's attention even before he engaged in a conversation with her and sensed a kindred spirit. His perception was not entirely accurate. Although she spoke approvingly of rigid proofs, deduction and induction, and the great role of science, she was also something of a suppressed romantic. In public, she invariably carried reference books and scientific studies but had a secret cache of romance novels in her bedroom closet and occasionally drew the shades on her windows, turned down the volume on the television, and watched romantic comedies clandestinely ordered from Netflix.

Arthur met Katrina at an interdepartmental event and was smitten. He became firmly convinced that his infatuation was reciprocated despite the absence of encouragement on her part. Katrina wanted someone bold and dashing to sweep her off her feet and ravish her.

Arthur's approach was too ethereal. The university threw a party to celebrate the groundbreaking for the library extension. Arthur threaded his way through the crowd, searching for Katrina, and when he finally spotted her, she was deep in conversation with Ichabod. It was not until that moment that Arthur realized how physically impressive the magnate was: tall, with a full head of wavy dark hair, a strong chin, good complexion, broad shoulders, a handsome man by any standard. But it was his presence that made him so formidable. He dominated conversation even when he was silent. Arthur realized he had a rival for Katrina's affections.

When he joined them, Ichabod's eyes flashed with irritation, but Katrina gave him a welcoming smile.

"Arthur, you're just in time. I need an ally, or I'm going to lose this argument. Martin contends that given the vastness of the universe, the probability that there are intelligences superior to our own lurking out there somewhere approaches certainty."

"To say nothing of the possibility of other universes unknown to us," Ichabod added confidently.

"I think we have to discount the results of idle speculation." Arthur's voice had drifted into lecture mode. "We simply don't have enough information to theorize in a meaningful way. Reason requires we discard conjecture and form our opinions solely on the basis of established fact."

"That seems too limiting to me," said Ichabod. "You underestimate the value of imagination and intuition."

"Unless we base our actions on reason, we risk wandering into superstition."

Reluctantly it seemed, Ichabod's eyes left Katrina and fastened on Arthur. "One man's superstition is sometimes another's secret knowledge."

"Nonsense. Knowledge held in secret has no utility. When someone tells me he has learned some truth that transcends what we know of the physical universe, I can safely assume he is either lying, delusional, or a fool."

Ichabod's smile never changed, but his eyes flickered with something dark and hidden. "Into which of those categories do I fall then?"

Arthur felt a twinge of alarm. Ichabod was an important man. To risk his displeasure over such a trivial issue, even in quest of Katrina's approval, was not a rational choice. "I have no reason to believe you guilty of any of them," he answered diplomatically.

"Then I risk disappointing you by insisting there are things in this world that do not lend themselves to the kind of rational analysis you so admire. There are forces which are not only beyond our science but perhaps beyond any system of logic we poor mortals might contrive. The news out of central Africa suggests we may be on the brink of discovering just how inadequate we are."

"The wild stories are no doubt exaggerations of the usual atrocities, possibly complicated by some exotic new disease."

"I wish that I believed you were right."

Both men recognized that battle lines had been drawn. It was not clear to either of them whether their intellectual differences were simply a reflection of their mutual admiration for Katrina or whether she was in fact simply the excuse for their philosophical rivalry. It was a muted battle rarely fought at close quarters, but their mutual antagonism was soon a matter of public knowledge.

Katrina was alternately embarrassed and pleased by the attention both men paid but confessed privately that while both had their good points, neither was precisely what she was looking for. The two men generally managed to stay out of each other's way, but their parallel campaigns inevitably intersected. On the rare occasions when they met, both men were cool if not actively unfriendly. Arthur wrote an opinion piece opposing one of Ichabod's administrative initiatives. Ichabod suggested that a project championed by Arthur might be a waste of university resources.

Their decorum finally slipped at another fundraiser at the Hollow. Arthur was in a surly mood.

The spread of unrest throughout the world had depressed the economy, and his research budget had been gutted. He suspected Ichabod was behind the decision.

The crowd was relatively small, and he located Katrina with no difficulty. She was sitting on the verandah that ran along the east wall of the mansion. Ichabod sat across a small wicker table from her. They greeted Arthur when he approached though with noticeably different sentiments. Katrina invited him to sit down, which he had planned to do anyway. "Martin has just been telling me there has been a bizarre report from Antarctica. Apparently, an ancient city has emerged from the ice."

"Arthur has a low tolerance level for such things." Ichabod raised a glass to his lips and pretended to drink.

"I have better things to do than entertain fairy tales." He knew he sounded miffed and childish, but he didn't care.

"So you don't believe the world has been undergoing unprecedented changes in recent months?"

"These stories are products of uneducated minds, like abominable snowmen, flying saucers, and headless horsemen. If such things existed, science would have plumbed their secrets long since."

"I thought men of science were taught to keep an open mind."

"Within limits. Show me one of these phantasms, and let me measure and weigh it and investigate it rationally. Only then will I consider accepting it as truth."

"They say faith moves mountains."

"I would rather have a battalion of bulldozers."

Ichabod leaned back, and the seat creaked. "You're very sure of yourself, Arthur."

"Actually, I recognize my shortcomings, and they are many. There are vast fields of knowledge I can recognize but never fully understand. But I insist that all knowledge derives from reason." He glanced at Katrina. "Two and two always equals four, and no uneasy spirit or alien intelligence can alter that fact."

"I wonder what would happen if you were confronted with evidence that contradicted your rigid world view. Would you be able to remain the same person if you encountered an alien intelligence of whom we are unaware but who are all too aware of us?"

"That question can only be rhetorical. Unless you can offer some such proof, I can only conclude you are indulging in whimsy."

"It would be a kindness if I were to withhold such evidence. I'm not sure you could withstand the shock."

Arthur felt his temper slipping. "Please don't try to patronize me. It only reflects on your own character."

Ichabod stiffened. "You should be careful what you wish for. I might devise some means to satisfy your demands and shatter your convictions."

"Go right ahead. A truly rational mind can assimilate new knowledge readily enough, and though I have my faults, irrationality is not among them."

"Then perhaps you will dine with me three nights from now. If you have the courage to do so, of course."

"It would be my pleasure," said Arthur, meaning something else entirely.

At the appointed time, Ichabod greeted him heartily, and Arthur found himself warming to the man despite his inclination to do otherwise. They ate alone at an enormous table in the dining room. Arthur fought the impulse to relax, reminding himself that he was in the camp of the enemy. "It feels rather wasteful using this room for just the two of us."

"It would be an even greater waste to let it stand unused. Under different circumstances, I might have invited others to join us, but what I wish to show you tonight is something I have never allowed another human being to witness. I am, I confess, somewhat in awe of your intellect, but before you accuse me of flattery, I should add that I believe you have wasted your potential just as a party of two wastes the capacity of this room."

Arthur's hackles rose. "I don't consider the adoption of standards of credibility as being wasteful."

"Please don't take offense. I believe the demonstration I have prepared for you will cure you of your skepticism. Will you have coffee?"

The servants cleared the table as the two men sipped a rich blend of coffee, which Ichabod said was his own concoction. "And now, perhaps, we should attend to tonight's business."

"By all means."

Ichabod led the way silently through the house to the corridor, which terminated at the bronze doors. He took an oversized key from his pocket and undid the lock then pulled the right hand side open. It moved smoothly and quietly, but Arthur could see it was much thicker than an ordinary door and appeared to be solid metal. "I hope you don't keep some kind of dangerous animal in there."

Ichabod sniffed. "I admit that there is some danger involved but only if you fail to obey my instructions. There are safeguards to ensure your physical wellbeing. You must tend to your mental health yourself."

They stepped into a kind of anteroom whose walls were lined with paintings even darker and more disturbing than those in the main part of the house. Arthur glanced at an abstract and tried to follow the lines of color and detect a pattern, but for some reason, he kept losing his place. Irritated, he wrenched his eyes away. There were a dozen or more pedestals placed throughout the room, each bearing a bit of sculpture, most of them studies of animals. Or rather, he told himself, studies of mythical animals. He saw an elaborate dragon cast in pewter, a squat, bloated figure in bronze that he decided was either a goblin or a troll, and several others he didn't recognize at all. The most striking was in the center of the room, and he initially took it to be a centaur. As he came closer, however, he realized it was something else entirely. It had massively muscled legs, and the body somewhat resembled that of a horse, but where the neck and head should have been was a rather featureless column that contained two eyes and an oversized mouth but no distinct head.

"That's a shuggoth," explained Ichabod.

"And what, pray tell, is a shuggoth?"

"A servant, sometimes a soldier."

"It looks unfinished, like a child's experiment with clay, a headless horseman or something of that nature."

Ichabod nodded. "My talents are limited, and my

subject very specific. I could hardly add wings or feathers or a long, spiked tail."

"This is your work?"

"It's a poor effort, I admit, but I couldn't lead the model to a studio on a leash."

Arthur assumed this was a joke. "Is this what you brought me here to see?"

"No, I hope to show you the original or another of its race. Follow me."

Beyond the anteroom was a more conventional door that opened into what at first appeared to be a home theater. Arthur blinked when Ichabod turned on the lights. He saw a kind of projector although there was no film reel, and its contours seemed wrong, the metal twisting in directions that seemed to defy physical examination, reminding him of the paintings. The screen was oval, its horizontal axis much longer than the vertical one, and backlit. There was almost invisible movement, as though dirty clouds rubbed against one another just beneath the surface. Set against the near wall was a table upon which two large piles of photocopied pages of some ancient book sat side by side. Arthur glanced at them but didn't recognize the characters, but then again, archaeology was not his field.

"If you'll just have a seat over there," Ichabod pointed toward a red plush chair on the far side of the room, "I'll get things started."

As soon as Arthur had complied, Ichabod turned over several pages of the photocopy, as though looking for his place. Satisfied after a moment, he turned to his guest.

"Whatever happens, whatever you see, you must not

leave your chair. It is positioned so you can only observe the portal from an acute angle. This is for your safety. Nothing on the other side will be able to see us as long as we remain at the periphery of the viewing area."

"Are you afraid I'll frighten your ghosties away?"

"Scoff if you like, but humor me in this. You do not want to be noticed by any creature who might appear when I open the portal. I said you were in no physical danger, but that only holds true if you obey me implicitly."

Arthur might have argued, but he didn't want to offer his adversary an escape route. Let him carry out the charade according to his own rules. Arthur was confident he could disentangle chicanery from reality. "All right. What do I do?"

"Simply sit quietly. Sound doesn't pass through the portal, but if you speak and distract me, I might make an error in the invocation."

Arthur sat back, crossed his arms, and wondered briefly if this was an elaborate joke or if Ichabod was actually insane. His doubts continued when the other man powered up the odd machine, which emitted no visible beam, and began to read, his voice rising, a half chant, half shout that contained no intelligible words. He could identify certain recurring sounds like "yog-sothoth" and "rillia" but nothing more.

It seemed to go on forever. Arthur grew increasingly irritable and shifted in his seat. At times, his body felt odd, as though the proportions of his limbs were changing. He decided there must be some hypnotic quality to Ichabod's speech and shook himself both physically and mentally. The screen, or portal as Ichabod called it, remained unchanged.

Or did it? The faint suggestions of shapes Arthur had seen earlier were now more distinct, and the sense of movement increased. There were occasional flashes of color, and once or twice, he thought he glimpsed something more substantial. He was aware of a growing tension in the room, and the air felt charged as though before a thunderstorm. It grew increasingly difficult to stay seated and silent, and he turned to Ichabod, intending to ask just how much longer this farce was to last, when the screen suddenly cleared, and a distinct image formed.

It was a landscape of shattered rocks and tortured plants, none of which he could recognize. Siberia, he theorized, or some remote part of Australia. But it was not the landscape that caught his attention; it was the figure that stood within it. There was nothing to provide a clue to its actual size, but the creature was clearly the model upon which Ichabod had based his sculpture. He had captured only a hint of its likeness. The animate reality—if this was reality—was far more menacing. Arthur sensed power and malevolence like heat from a radiator. The creature stood half facing the portal, its eyes open and unblinking, but it gave no sign it was aware of being observed.

It couldn't be real. Arthur knew Ichabod could afford an elaborate CGI projection, and that was surely what this was, designed to fool him into faltering in his commitment to reason and science. It was more than a joke; it was an unforgivable insult.

He surged to his feet and started across the room toward his host. His heart was beating rapidly—it couldn't be fear, could it? Arthur decided it was anger. Ichabod saw him move and immediately stopped reciting.

After one look of incredulity, he shouted, "Stop where you are! Don't move a muscle!" It was spoken with such force that Arthur complied instantly. But it was too late.

The massive head of the shuggoth turned, and the eyes fastened on Arthur. He felt sweat break out all over his body, and his temple began to throb. But it was a trick! It had to be. "Very clever. Motion sensors or microswitches under the floor? It's quite sophisticated, I grant you, but it takes more than Disneyland tricks to intimidate me."

Ichabod's arm flashed out and slapped the side of the projector, which hummed softly for a second before falling silent. The image on the screen faded out gradually, and the last thing visible was the shuggoth's eyes, which were still staring directly at Arthur. Despite his conviction that it was an elaborate prank, he felt nauseated.

"I told you not to leave your chair, you idiot! It saw you! I never meant for that to happen."

Arthur forced a laugh that sounded distinctly insincere. "Drop the act. Show's over. I rate it five stars for special effects but only one for verisimilitude."

Ichabod looked shaken, but Arthur was regaining his composure. "If this was supposed to shake my beliefs to the foundation, it failed, I'm afraid. Good use of technology though."

Ichabod shook his head. "It doesn't matter now. Once you've been seen, you become a portal yourself. With luck, it might not come for you soon. Time runs differently on the other side. But it will come for you eventually, Arthur. I'm very sorry, but I did warn you."

Arthur's self-confidence had returned, and he felt

nothing but the urge to leave. "No hard feelings, Martin. It was actually rather amusing. But I must go. Don't bother to see me out. I know the way."

The two men never met again. Ichabod dropped his courting of Katrina Bergen the same day San Francisco was swallowed by an earthquake. This did not, however, help Arthur's situation since Katrina was regularly seen in the company of an aspiring poet. Arthur decided he must have been mistaken in his estimation of her intelligence and never shed a tear.

He had bought himself a small cottage on the outskirts of Arkham where he tended a meticulously organized flower garden. None of his neighbors complained about him, and none of them were among his intimates, so he'd been missing for three full days when the university requested that the Arkham police investigate his absence from the classes he was supposed to be teaching.

The house was empty and silent. A teapot had boiled dry on his stove, but there was no indication of violence and no hint of where he might have gone. The only remarkable aspect of the situation was Arthur's garden. The ground there had been stamped flat, crushing every living thing to pulp, as though a herd of elephants had run back and forth for several days. The authorities sent workers in to excavate the area, and on the third day, they found the little finger of Arthur's right hand, pressed flat like a butterfly between panes of glass. They never found the rest of him, but after Shub-Niggurath appeared in Providence, they were far too busy.

THE END?

Not quite . . .

Dive into more of our anthologies:

Gutted: Beautiful Horror Stories—An anthology of dark fiction that explores the beauty at the very heart of darkness. Featuring horror's most celebrated voices: Clive Barker, Neil Gaiman, Ramsey Campbell, Paul Tremblay, John F.D. Taff, Lisa Mannetti, Damien Angelica Walters, Josh Malerman, Christopher Coake, Mercedes M. Yardley, Brian Kirk, Stephanie M. Wytovich, Amanda Gowin, Richard Thomas, Maria Alexander, and Kevin Lucia.

Tales from The Lake Vol.3—Dive into the deep end of the lake with 19 tales of terror, selected by Monique Snyman. Including short stories by Mark Allan Gunnells, Kate Jonez, Kenneth W. Cain, and many more.

Tales from The Lake Vol.2—Beneath this lake you'll find nothing but mystery and suspense, horror and dread. Not to mention death and misery—tales to share around the campfire or living room floor from the likes of Ramsey Campbell, Jack Ketchum, and Edward Lee.

Children of the Grave—Choose your own demise in this interactive shared-world zombie anthology.

Welcome to Purgatory, an arid plain of existence where zombies are the least of your problems. It's a post-mortem Hunger Games, and Blaze, a newcomer to Purgatory, needs your help to learn the rules of this world and choose the best course of action.

The Outsiders Lovecraftian shared-world anthology—They'll do anything to protect their way of life. Anything. Welcome to Priory, a small gated community in the UK, where the only thing worse than an ancient monster is the group worshipping it. Is that which slithers below true evil, or does evil reside in the people of Priory? Includes stories by Stephen Bacon, James Everington, Rosanne Rabinowitz, V.H. Leslie, and Gary Fry.

Tales from The Lake Vol.1—Remember those dark and scary nights spent telling ghost stories and other campfire stories? With the *Tales from The Lake* horror anthologies, you can relive some of those memories by reading the best Dark Fiction stories around. Includes Dark Fiction stories and poems by horror greats such as Graham Masterton, Bev Vincent, Tim Curran, Tim Waggoner, Elizabeth Massie, and many more. Be sure to check out our website for future *Tales from The Lake* volumes.

Fear the Reaper—Did you know Death was a girl? Ever wondered if it was possible to cheat death? To kill Death? Or that it's possible to escape and even become death? Includes Grim Reapers stories by legends like Rick Hautala, Gary A. Braunbeck, Joe McKinney, Richard Thomas, Jeremy C Shipp, Jeff Strand, and many more.

For the Night is Dark—Darkness, our most primitive fear since shadows first moved. Includes stories by Crystal Lake Publishing alumni like Gary McMahon, William Meikle, Jasper Bark, Tonia Brown, Blaze McRob, Daniel I Russell, Kevin Lucia, Armand Rosamilia, Ray Cluley, and many more.

If you enjoyed this book, I'm sure you'll also like the following Crystal Lake titles:

The Third Twin—A Dark Psychological Thriller by Darren Speegle—Some things should never be bred . . . Amid tribulation, death, madness, and institutionalization, a father fights against a scientist's bloody bid to breed a theoretical third twin.

Embers: A Collection of Dark Fiction by Kenneth W. Cain—These short speculative stories are the smoldering remains of a fire, the fiery bits meant to ignite the mind with slow-burning imagery and haunting details. These are the slow burning embers of Cain's soul.

Aletheia: A Supernatural Thriller by J.S. Breukelaar—A tale of that most human of monsters—memory—Aletheia is part ghost story, part love story, a novel about the damage done, and the damage yet to come. About terror itself. Not only for what lies ahead, but also for what we think we have left behind.

Beatrice Beecham's Cryptic Crypt by Dave Jeffery—The fate of the world rests in the hands of four dysfunctional teenagers and a bunch of oddball adults. What could possibly go wrong?

Visions of the Mutant Rain Forest—The solo and collaborative stories and poems of Robert Frazier and Bruce Boston's exploration of the Mutant Rain Forest.

The Final Reconciliation by Todd Keisling—Thirty years ago, a progressive rock band called The Yellow Kings began recording what would become their first and final album. Titled "The Final Reconciliation," the album was expected to usher in a new renaissance of heavy metal, but it was shelved following a tragic concert that left all but one dead. It's the survivor shares the shocking truth.

Where the Dead Go to Die by Mark Allan Gunnells and Aaron Dries—Post-infection Chicago. Christmas. There are monsters in this world. And they used to be us. Now it's time to euthanize to survive in a hospice where Emily, a woman haunted by her past, only wants to do her job and be the best mother possible. But it won't be long before that snow-speckled ground will be salted by blood.

Run to Ground by Jasper Bark—Jim Mcleod is running from his responsibilities as a father, hiding out from his pregnant girlfriend and working as a groundskeeper in a rural graveyard. Throw in some ancient monsters and folklore, and you'll have Jim running for his life through this folk horror graveyard.

Blackwater Val by William Gorman—a Supernatural Suspense Thriller/Horror/Coming of age novel: A widower traveling with his dead wife's ashes and his six-year-old psychic daughter Katie in tow returns to his haunted birthplace to execute his dead wife's final wish. But something isn't quite right in the Val.

Tribulations by Richard Thomas—In the third short story collection by Richard Thomas, *Tribulations*, these stories cover a wide range of dark fiction from fantasy, science fiction and horror, to magical realism, neo-noir, and transgressive fiction. The common thread that weaves these tragic tales together is suffering and sorrow and the ways we emerge from such heartbreak stronger, more appreciative of what we have left—a spark of hope enough to guide us though the valley of death.

Devourer of Souls by Kevin Lucia—In Kevin Lucia's latest installment of his growing Clifton Heights mythos, Sheriff Chris Baker and Father Ward meet for a Saturday morning breakfast at The Skylark Dinner to once again commiserate over the weird and terrifying secrets surrounding their town.

Wind Chill by Patrick Rutigliano—What if you were held captive by your own family? Emma Rawlins has spent the last year a prisoner. The months following her mother's death dragged her father into a paranoid spiral of conspiracy theories and doomsday premonitions. But there is a force far colder than the freezing drifts. Ancient, ravenous, it knows no mercy. And it's already had a taste . . .

The Dark at the End of the Tunnel by Taylor Grant—
Offered for the first time in a collected format, this
selection features ten gripping and darkly
imaginative stories by Taylor Grant, a Bram Stoker
Award® nominated author and rising star in the
suspense and horror genres. Grant exposes the
terrors that hide beneath the surface of our ordinary
world, behind people's masks of normalcy, and
lurking in the shadows at the farthest reaches of the
universe.

Little Dead Red by Mercedes M. Yardley—The Wolf
is roaming the city, and he must be stopped. In this
modern day retelling of Little Red Riding Hood, the
wolf takes to the city streets to capture his prey, but
the hunter is close behind him. With Grim Marie on
the prowl, the hunter becomes the hunted.

**If you've ever thought of becoming an
author, I'd also like to recommend these
non-fiction titles:**

Horror 101: The Way Forward—A comprehensive
overview of the Horror fiction genre and career
opportunities available to established and aspiring
authors. Including Jack Ketchum, Graham
Masterton, Edward Lee, Lisa Morton, Ellen Datlow,
Ramsey Campbell, and many more.

Horror 201: The Silver Scream Vol.1 and *Vol.2*—A
must read for anyone interested in the horror film
industry. Includes interviews and essays by Wes
Craven, John Carpenter, George A. Romero, Mick
Garris, and dozens more. Now available in
paperback, as well.

Modern Mythmakers: 35 interviews with Horror and Science Fiction Writers and Filmmakers by Michael McCarty—Ever wanted to hang out with legends like Ray Bradbury, Richard Matheson, and Dean Koontz? *Modern Mythmakers* is your chance to hear fun anecdotes and career advice from authors and filmmakers like Forrest J. Ackerman, Ray Bradbury, Ramsey Campbell, John Carpenter, Dan Curtis, Elvira, Neil Gaiman, Mick Garris, Laurell K. Hamilton, Jack Ketchum, Dean Koontz, Graham Masterton, Richard Matheson, John Russo, William F. Nolan, John Saul, Peter Straub, and many more.

Writers On Writing: An Author's Guide—Your favorite authors share their secrets in the ultimate guide to becoming and being an author. *Writers On Writing* is an ongoing eBook series with original 'On Writing' essays by writing professionals. A new edition will be launched every few months, featuring four or five essays per edition, so be sure to check out the webpage regularly for updates.

Or check out other Crystal Lake Publishing books for your Dark Fiction, Horror, Suspense, and Thriller needs.

BIOGRAPHIES

Inanna Arthen (Vyrdolak) is an artist, voice actor, freelance book designer, and author of The Vampires of New England Series: Mortal Touch (2007), The Longer the Fall (2010), and All the Shadows of the Rainbow (2013). Book 4 is currently in progress. Inanna is a lifelong scholar of vampire folklore, fiction, and fact. She runs By Light Unseen Media (http://bylightunseenmedia.com), an independent press dedicated to publishing vampire fiction and nonfiction. She is a member of Broad Universe, New England Horror Writers, Independent Book Publishers Association (IBPA), and Independent Publishers of New England (IPNE), and an occasional contributor to Blogcritics.org.

Matthew Baugh is an ordained minister who writes stories about robots, monsters, pulp heroes, and eldrich horrors from the dawn of time on the side. For more about him and his stories, please visit his blog "Fantastic Frontiers" at http://mysteriousdavemather.blogspot.com/

David Bernard is a native New Englander who now lives (albeit under protest) in South Florida, where the locals break out snow parkas when the temperature drops below 60°. His most recent works include stories in Rymfire Books' *State Of Horror: Florida* in which he destroys a railroad, the Pill Hill Press anthology *BUGS!* in which he destroys a subway, and the Harrow Press anthology *Mortis Operandi* in which he destroys Al Capone. Being an overachiever, he is currently working on a new story in which he destroys the entire planet.

Thom Brannan (est.1976) has been a submariner, a nuclear operator, an electrician, and now works on an offshore drilling platform. He's a freelance editor for Permuted Press and anyone else paying. He has been published in several anthologies, in several genres. Thom finds his inspiration equally from Robert B. Parker and H.P. Lovecraft. He is the author of *Lords of Night* as well as the co-author of *Pavlov's Dogs* (with D.L. Snell) and *Survivors* (with Z.A. Recht). Thom lives in or around Austin, Texas with his lovely wife, Kitty, a boy, a girl, and a pair of dogs.

Winifred Burniston is the pseudonym for a perfectly mundane woman who lives on Cape Cod. Her secret identity is as an educator, warping the minds of future generations. During the school year, she tries to fit in as much writing as she can and often pesters her husband into reading her deranged short stories. And in the summer, she tries to catch up on her reading, starts preparing for the coming school year, and works on not wiping out the tourists clogging up the traffic and taking forever ordering coffee in the morning.

Don D'Ammassa is the author of 12 books, including science fiction, horror, murder mysteries, and non-fiction. His most recent is the collection *Translation Station*. Don lives in Rhode Island with his wife Sheila, two cats, and over 60,000 books.

Peter N. Dudar is the author of the Bram Stoker Award® nominated novel, *A Requiem for Dead Flies*.

A graduate of the University at Albany, Dudar has been publishing fiction for over a decade, with his works appearing in numerous anthologies and online fiction sites. When not writing fiction, Dudar is a contributor at Cinema Knife Fight (his monthly column, "Me and Lil' Stevie" examines film adaptations of the works of Stephen King) and hosts a blog called "Dead By Friday" at Wordpress.com. His first story collection *Dolly and Other Stories* will be published this summer by Evil Jester Press.

Mae Empson's stories and poems often reference fairy tales, folklore, or Lovecraftian mythos. Her fairy tale-inspired publications have appeared in *The Pedestal Magazine, Cabinet des Fees, Enchanted Conversation*, and *Crossed Genres*. Her Lovecraftian publications have appeared in anthologies from Prime Books, Innsmouth Free Press, and others, including *Future Lovecraft, Historical Lovecraft, Cthulhurotica*, and *Techno Goth Cthulhu*. Mae is a member of the Horror Writers Association and of HorrorPNW—the Pacific Northwest chapter of HWA. Mae Empson has a Master's degree in English literature. She lives in Seattle, Washington. Follow Mae on twitter at www.twitter.com/maeempson. Read Mae's blog at http://maeempson.wordpress.com.

Scott T. Goudsward lives and writes in the wilds of New England. He has a novel, an anthology, and two co-authored non-fiction books under his belt. He grew up on King, Koontz, Zelazny, and Saberhagen. *Twice Upon An Apocalypse* is his first co-edited project with Crystal Lake. Upcoming stories can be found in Dark Regions "Return of the Old Ones." His recent fiction can be found in *Atomic Age Cthulhu* and *Anthology*

Year 3 and *Snowbound with Zombies*. Scott's latest non-fiction books, co-written with brother, David, *Horror Guide to Massachusetts* and *Horror Guide to Florida* and *Horror Guide to Northern New England* are now out from Post Mortem Press. Scott's latest novel *Fountain of the Dead* is now out, also from Post Mortem Press. Scott is one of the Coordinators of the New England Horror Writers and co-edited their latest anthology, *Wicked Witches*.

J. P. Hutsell was born and raised in moss-encrusted and humidity-drenched southeast Tennessee. He continues to live there with his wife and son. He grew up on a steady diet of King, Koontz, Lansdale, and McCammon. Later on, he discovered the so-called "pulp" authors with Lovecraft standing tall amongst a forest of giants. "In the Shade of the Juniper Tree" is J. P. Hutsell's first published story.

Michael Kamp was born on a cold night in February in the frozen wasteland of Denmark. After wrestling a polar bear in the traditional Danish coming-of-age ritual (true story—well, true-ish) he chose the path of the storyteller. Several novels and a fair amount of awards in his native tongue later, the time has come to go beyond and take a shot at the English markets. He works the nightshift, writes out his nightmares, and hopes to someday create a story so frightening readers won't dare to finish it. He lives with his wife, kids, and a pet troll. www.fromthefrozennorth.com

Rachel Kenley has edited nine anthologies, four with retold fairy tales, including *Once Upon an Apocalypse* with Scott Goudsward. A Jersey Girl currently trapped without good diners or boardwalks in New England, Rachel is a novelist, speaker, workshop leader, and co-founder of the Writers Business School (www.writersbusinessschool.com). When she is not writing, she is homeschooling her sons, trying unsuccessfully to keep up with laundry, and laughing as much as possible. She loves reading, chocolate, her morning cup of coffee, and can also be found (perhaps a little too much) on Facebook (www.facebook.com/authorrachelkenley)

Sean Logan lives in northern California with his wife and a big scary Rottweiler that will run at the first sign of trouble. At night, he writes horror stories, and at his marketing day job, he writes about something really scary: banking software. His stories have appeared in about two dozen publications and can be seen in *Black Static, Vile Things, Pseudopod* and in volume one of *Once Upon an Apocalypse.*

Bracken MacLeod has worked as a martial arts teacher, a university philosophy instructor, for a children's non-profit, and as a criminal and civil trial attorney. His short fiction has appeared in several magazines and anthologies, including *Shotgun Honey, The Alchemy Press Book of Pulp Heroes, Shroud Magazine, Reloaded: Both Barrels Vol. 2, Locked and Loaded: Both Barrels Vol. 3, Shock Totem, Beat to a Pulp, Dread: A Head Full of Bad Dreams, Eulogies III, Protectors 2: Heroes, LampLight, ThugLit,* and *Splatterpunk.* He is the author of *Mountain Home, White Knight,* and most recently *Stranded,* available from TOR Books. His collection, *13 Views of the Suicide Woods,* is coming in 2017 from ChiZine Publications. He lives in New England with his wife and son, where he is at work on his next novel.

William Meikle is a Scottish writer now living in Canada with twenty novels published in the genre press and over 300 short story credits in thirteen countries. He has books available from a variety of publishers, including Dark Regions Press, DarkFuse, and Dark Renaissance, and his work has appeared in a number of professional anthologies and magazines. He lives in Newfoundland with whales, bald eagles, and icebergs for company. When he's not writing, he drinks beer, plays guitar, and dreams of fortune and glory.

C.T. Phipps is a science fiction and fantasy author from Ashland, KY. A lifetime fan of *Call of Cthulhu* and its various spin-offs, C.T. Phipps jumped at the chance to add his own spin to the mythos. He is the author of the best-selling *Supervillainy Saga*, *Esoterrorism*, *Straight Outta Fangton*, and *Cthulhu Armageddon*. His chief inspiration is his wonderful wife, Kat, and their adorable dogs.

Pete Rawlik used to be a celebrity book dealer but gave that lucrative career up to write weird fiction and make some serious money. He vehemently denies rumors that for the last twenty years, he has been gainfully employed in the field of environmental management, and if he was, he certainly was not properly compensated. His work on Lovecraftian fiction, drawing on resources contained within his personal collection, has garnered much interest from readers, editors, as well as representatives from certain organizations devoted to the elimination of corrupting moral influences. His work has been published by Miskatonic River Press, Black Coat Press, Innsmouth

Free Press, Prime Books, and Fedogan and Bremer. *Reanimators*, a Lovecraftian tale of life, death, and the undead is his first novel.

Armand Rosamilia is a New Jersey boy currently living in sunny Florida, where he writes when he's not sleeping. He's happily married to a woman who helps his career and is supportive, which is all he ever wanted in life . . . He's written over 150 stories that are currently available, including horror, zombies, contemporary fiction, thrillers, and more. His goal is to write a good story and not worry about genre labels. He runs a very successful podcast on Project iRadio too . . . Arm Cast: Dead Sexy Horror Podcast—interviewing fellow authors as well as filmmakers, musicians, etc. He also loves to talk in third person . . . because he's really that cool. You can find him at http://armandrosamilia.com for not only his latest releases but interviews and guest posts with other authors he likes! And e-mail him to talk about zombies, baseball, and Metal: armandrosamilia@gmail.com

Zach Shephard lives in a small western Washington town where he writes fantasy, science fiction, and horror stories. He spends much of his free time playing board games, which allows him to either battle Other-Worldly horrors or race robots around a factory, depending on his mood. Check him out at www.zachshephard.com, where you'll find links to all his stories and announcements of upcoming publications.

Morgan Sylvia is an Aquarius, a metalhead, a coffee addict, and a work in progress. She lives in Maine and is a full-time freelance writer. Her work has appeared in *Axes of Evil 1 and 2*, *Forgotten Places*, and *Wicked Witches*. In 2013, she released her first book, *Whispers From The Apocalypse*, a horror poetry collection. Her debut horror novel, *Abode*, will be released from Bloodshot Books in 2017.

K. H. Vaughan is a refugee from academia with a Ph.D. in clinical psychology. In his other life, he taught, published, and practiced in various settings with particular interest in decision theory, forensic psychology, psychopathology, and methodology. An avid fan of H. P. Lovecraft and gaming, he has played *Call of Cthulhu* since the early 80s. He lives with his wife and three children in New England. Information on upcoming releases can be found at www.khvaughan.com.

Simon Yee lives with his fabulous wife and non-euclidean son in the middle of San Diego. He has written nine scenarios for various Chaosium monographs, such as *Dead Leaves Fall* and *The Gods Hate Me*. When he is not writing, he works as a mental health professional with the homelesss and enjoys the wisdom that he finds with these people.

Hi, readers. It makes our day to know you reached the end of our book. Thank you so much. This is why we do what we do every single day.

Whether you found the book good or great, we'd love to hear what you thought. Please take a moment to leave a review on Amazon, Goodreads, or anywhere else readers visit. Reviews go a long way to helping a book sell, and will help us to continue publishing quality books.

Thank you again for taking the time to journey with Crystal Lake Publishing.

We are also on . . .

Website
http://www.crystallakepub.com/

Books
http://www.crystallakepub.com/book-table/

Blog
http://www.crystallakepub.com/blog-2/

Newsletter
http://eepurl.com/xfuKP

Instagram
https://www.instagram.com/crystal_lake_publishing/

Patreon
https://www.patreon.com/CLP

YouTube
https://www.youtube.com/c/CrystalLakePublishing

Twitter
https://twitter.com/crystallakepub

Facebook page
https://www.facebook.com/Crystallakepublishing/

Google+
https://plus.google.com/u/1/107478350897139952572

Pinterest
https://za.pinterest.com/crystallakepub/

Tumblr
https://www.tumblr.com/blog/crystal-lake-publishing

We'd love to hear from you.

With unmatched success since 2012, Crystal Lake Publishing has quickly become one of the world's leading indie publishers of Mystery, Thriller, and Suspense books with a Dark Fiction edge.

Crystal Lake Publishing puts integrity, honor, and respect at the forefront of our operations.

We strive for each book and outreach program that's launched to not only entertain and touch or comment on issues that affect our readers, but also to strengthen and support the Dark Fiction field and its authors.

Not only do we publish authors who are legends in the field and as hardworking as us, but we look for men and women who care about their readers and fellow human beings. We only publish the very best Dark Fiction, and look forward to launching many new careers.

We strive to know each and every one of our readers while building personal relationships with our authors, reviewers, bloggers, podcasters, bookstores, and libraries.

Crystal Lake Publishing is and will always be a beacon of what passion and dedication, combined with overwhelming teamwork and respect, can accomplish: unique fiction you can't find anywhere else.

We do not just publish books, we present you worlds within your world, doors within your mind from talented authors who sacrifice so much for a moment of your time.

This is what we believe in. What we stand for. This will be our legacy.

Welcome to Crystal Lake Publishing.

We hope you enjoyed this title. If so, we'd be grateful if you could leave a review on your blog or any of the other websites and outlets open to book reviews. Reviews are like gold to writers and publishers, since word-of-mouth is and will always be the best way to market a great book. And remember to keep an eye out for more of our books.

THANK YOU FOR PURCHASING THIS BOOK